The Unforeseen

Together, can they find the killer?

R.B. Carr

COPYRIGHT

Trient Press

3375 S Rainbow
Blvd

#81710, SMB
13135

Las Vegas,NV
89180

Ordering Information:

Quantity sales. Special discounts are available on
quantity purchases by corporations, associations,
and others. For details, contact the publisher at the
address above.

Orders by U.S. trade bookstores and wholesalers.
Please contact Trient Press: Tel: (775) 996-3844;
or visit www.trientpress.com.

Printed in the United States of America

Publisher's Cataloging-in-Publication data Roberson,
Sr.,Ernest

A title of a book :THE UNFORESEEN

ISBN HardCover: 978-1-953975-68-3

        Paperback: 978-1-953975-66-9

E-book: 978-1-953975-67-6

THE UNFORESEEN

R.B. Carr

PROLOGUE

Press Release, September 3

KANSAS CITY, Mo. – Richard Primovero, a resident of Kansas City, Missouri, has been indicted for his drug-trafficking conspiracy role. The arrest occurred during a law enforcement operation last week and resulted in the seizure of firearms and a large amount of cash.

The federal indictment was unsealed following a law enforcement operation on Wednesday, September 14, in which 20 defendants, in addition to Primovero, were arrested. All those arrested are suspected associates of the Civella Crime Family, whom Primovero is reputedly the head of. The indictment alleges that all 21 of the defendants participated in a conspiracy to distribute at least a kilogram of heroin, as well as cocaine, crack cocaine, oxycodone, codeine, and marijuana, from January 1, 2011, through October 15, 2019.

The charges contained in this indictment are simply accusations and not evidence of guilt. Evidence supporting the charges must be presented to a federal trial jury, whose duty is to determine guilt or innocence. Mr. Primovero is currently out on bail awaiting trial. This case is being prosecuted by Assistant US Attorneys Adam Brile, Ashley Paul, and Jason Norman.

Approximately 200 federal agents and local law enforcement officers were involved in the operation. It was investigated by the FBI, the Kansas City, Mo., Police Department, and IRS-Criminal Investigation, with support from the Bureau of Alcohol, Tobacco, Firearms and Explosives, the Kansas City, Kansas, Police Department, the Lee's Summit, Mo., Police Department, the Missouri State Highway Patrol, the US Marshals Service, the Jackson County Drug Task Force, and the Independence, Mo., Police Department.

This case is part of the Department of Justice's Organized Crime and Drug Enforcement Task Force (OCDETF) program. The OCDETF program is the centerpiece of the Department of Justice's drug supply reduction strategy. OCDETF was established in 1982 to conduct comprehensive, multilevel attacks on major drug trafficking and money laundering organizations. Today, OCDETF combines the resources and expertise of its member federal agencies in cooperation with state and local law enforcement. The principal mission of the OCDETF program is to identify, disrupt, and dismantle the most serious drug trafficking and money laundering organizations and those primarily responsible for the nation's illicit drug supply.

CHAPTER 1

September 4, 1:30 pm

Inside the Leavenworth Minimum Security Federal Prison, Joey Cabrini was in his cell laying on his bunk reading a Nelson DeMille novel. The book that had just become available in the Prison's library. Reading was one of the few pleasures Joey was allowed when not doing some mundane duty assigned by the guards or working out in the prison yard. He was really enthralled into the story when there was a knock on his cell's steel door. "Now what," he mumbled to himself. Because it was minimum security, the men were free to wander wherever they wanted during the day when not on a work detail, and thus his cell door was unlocked. Getting up, he stepped to the door and opening it, expecting to see one of the guards with some detail for him to do since he hadn't been chosen for any during the morning's headcount. However, instead of a guard, it was the Prison's official mail courier, a man everyone called Brooks because he looked like the character from Shawshank Redemption. Strange how popular prison movies were with prisoners Joey always thought.

In his hands, Brooks held a clipboard and a pen, which he pushed towards Joey. Taking the items from him, Joey asked, "What's this?"

"Official letter, you gotta sign for it," Brooks said curtly, not being a man who often spoke himself.

Official letter? Joey wondered as he signed the paper. During his eight years in the system, he had rarely gotten mail and didn't recall ever signing for an official letter before.

Handing the clipboard back, Brooks studied the signature momentarily. Seemingly satisfied, the man placed the clipboard back onto his cart and then opened a locked box with a key he removed from his pocket. Reaching inside the box, he removed a shamrock green envelope and handed it to Joey. "Congratulations," the man said as he began pushing the cart away down the hall.

Joey watched him go before returning to his bunk, letting the door slam closed behind him, a sound that he had once found disturbing but no longer thought about at all. Sitting down, he finally looked at the envelope. First, he insured it was actually for him. It was indeed addressed to Joseph Piero Cabrini III at the official prison address. He then looked at the return address. It was from the Depart of Justice, US Parole Commission.

Seeing it, he recalled applying for parole when he first became eligible at the behest his case officer, though he was confident it was a waste of time. Thereafter, he had attended a parole hearing with three stone-faced officials in the main Prison's conference room, a few miles up the road. The hearing lasted all of 35 minutes, but the trip had taken up a majority of the day as Joey's case had been but one of many cases on the docket that day. Returning to the minimum security facility, the transport driver had asked him how it went, and he remembered saying, "not well." having felt anything but good vibes from the panel. Nonetheless curious, he carefully opened the envelope, afraid to tear the papers inside with hands that were suddenly shaky. Inside was a 3-page letter. Reading it, he saw he was being granted an early release. "Well, I'll be damned."

Reading closer, the letter indicated that he would be released on parole on September 19 at 12 pm. Upon his release, he would have 24 hours to make contact with his Parole Officer, Jon Jackson, whose downtown Kansas City Missouri office address and phone number were included. The letter went on to give him some references for local charitable organizations who could help provide him with a place to temporarily stay and job services. That was it. Nothing about transportation or anything else, merely 24 hours to get in contact with a parole officer in Kansas City. Maybe 24 hours was how long they thought it would take him to walk the 35 miles or so from the Prison to downtown Kansas City?

By evening chow, Joey had read the letter so many times that he had memorized it word for word. He was still in shock by the whole thing, never imagining that he would be given an early release. Still, in a daze, he walked through the chow line. He allowed the servers to fill his tray without a thought towards what they placed on his metal dish. Tray in hand, he found an empty table and sat at the bench. Picking up his fork, he looked at the plate. "What the hell is this stuff? Spaghetti noodles, some kind of meat and peppers? I won't miss this," he thought to himself.

His thoughts were interrupted when he felt the table vibrate. Looking up, he saw that he had been joined by another prisoner named Maxwell. Joey knew Maxwell was doing time for insider trading and tax evasion.

"What are your thoughts about it?" Maxwell asked.

"Thoughts about what?" Joey responded, not wanting to reveal his thoughts about his parole to anyone. Especially not Maxwell, one of the foremost prison gossipers. Maxwell remained under the impression he still stood to profit from collecting information. One of the first things Joey learned inside the Prison's painted cinderblock walls was there was more gossip there than had been in his grandparent's home when his grandfather and his fellow Italian immigrants sat around the table drinking wine and playing Scopa.

"About what? Where've you been, man? About your old boss getting indicted last night?"

"What?" Joey asked, confused.

Maxwell pointed towards the television mounted high above the serving line where Joey saw a picture of his boss, or former boss, Richard Primovero, being led to the back of a car. Before being convicted of money laundering; and mail and wire fraud Joey had been Primovero's right-hand man and had been fingered by a couple turncoats in a federal investigation targeting Primovero. On the strength of very little evidence and the testimony of the two rats whom he was assured would be dealt with, Joey had been convicted. The Government had come down hard because of his suspected but unproven connections to organized crime in nearby Kansas City, for which he was sentenced to 15 years. Without sound, Joey was unable to hear what the television was saying. "What are the charges?" he asked Maxwell, who he was sure would know.

"The usual, drug trafficking and Rico violations. Did you really not know?"

"No. I've been in my cell all day reading."

"Well, whaddya think now? Maxwell asked eagerly.

"Sucks to be him," Joey said flatly, not wanting to engage the man.

Maxwell continued trying to get Joey to talk of his former boss, but Joey refused to engage the man. Instead, he forced himself to eat as much of what he assumed was supposed to be yakisoba as quickly as possible before getting up and returning his tray to the return line.

As Joey walked back to this cell, he was approached by two inmates and a guard asking about Primovero's recent arrest. The topinc had apparently been the main topic of conversation within the Prison since the report came across the common area's televisions and library's newspapers that morning. Because of the constant gossiping, everyone knew that Joey had previously worked closely with the man though he had never discussed it personally. Nonetheless, there were no secrets in Prison, and that evening his cell had more visitors than the Prison's sick call and chapel. By the time lights went out, Joey had been asked about it more times than he could count, oftentimes by men who never had so much as looked at him previously.

His head was still spinning from all of the day's events when he laid down to sleep. What are the odds of his being paroled the same day Primovero was indicted? He thought, smiling, his head sinking into the thin pillow. A moment later, however, he shot straight up in bed. What are the odds of his being paroled the same day Primovero was indicted! He didn't know, but he was sure he knew what Primovero would judge those odds to be!

The next morning after a night of fitful sleep, Joey tried to consider his position. Before he was sent to Prison, Joey had been a wizard with money. He knew markets, investment strategies, the power of money, and how to make that power grow in both legal and not so legitimate ventures. Operating with cold calculation based on the information from his own sources and the resources provided by Primovero, Joey had helped to build the foundation for the empire his former boss now sat upon. He did not begrudge the man his success nor his position a top the Family. Preferring to be in the background and out of the limelight, Joey was happy being unknown. Plus, even in the background, working with Primovero obviously had its advantages: money, prestige, women, and power.

On the other hand, being affiliated with Primovero also had placed a target on Joey's back. Not only from Primovero's enemies, of whom there were many but also from the police and feds who had been targeting Primovero since he came to prominence. Apparently, after nearly a dozen years, the Feds had finally gotten their man.

Since the gavel came down, Joey had repeatedly been approached by various government agents and agencies offering him deals. For providing testimony or evidence against his former associates, especially Richard Primovero, he had been offered everything from a suspended sentence, witness protection, and even life long care for his mother. Joey never even considered the offers and had been prepared to serve the entirety of his sentence, knowing that it was healthier to keep his mouth shut, even inside Prison than to rat on Primovero.

The first six years of his sentence were spent in the medium-security United States Penitentiary at Leavenworth. He kept his nose clean with both the guards and, more importantly, his fellow inmates. His former associates had told him he wouldn't have to worry about the inmates because he was protected. Regardless of the assurances, he kept mostly to himself. He performed whatever mundane work task he was assigned each day to the best of his ability, not because it was expected but because he had always been taught to take pride in his work. His free time, he spent reading whatever was available in the prison library and working out in the prison yard alone. Due to his good behavior and overcrowding, two years ago, he had been transferred to the minimum-security federal prison camp a few miles down the road, where he continued to stay out of trouble.

Then yesterday came the official letter granting his parole. While it was unsaid in the letter, Joey understood that it wasn't his actions as much as the overcrowded prison system, good behavior, and his conviction being for non-violent crimes combined that garnered the early parole. But the news of Primovero's indictment had put a dark cloud on his happy day. Joey began to wonder if the early parole wasn't the blessing he'd hoped for, worried what his former bosses might think about him getting out after serving only a little over half the initial sentence. Could Primovero believe he flipped after all this time? Knowing the man's paranoid nature, he knew he could, especially given the incredibly inconvenient timing of his parole and Primovero's indictment.

At 10:30 am, Joey was completing a set of weighted pull-ups in the exercise yard when he was surprised once again. While catching his breath after his last set's exertion, Joey was approached by a guard named Thompson. "You have a visitor," the guard stated plainly.

"A visitor, who is it?" Joey asked curiously, having not had a visitor in nearly four years since his mother had become too ill to make the trip to see him.

"I don't know," Thompson replied, "They just sent me to fetch you."

Taking off the chain and 25-pound plate that dangled from around his lean waist, Joey followed the guard inside. He expected to be directed to the visitor's room with its open space, multiple tables, and chairs where prisoners were allowed to have visitors for an hour, so long as the visit was scheduled ahead of time through the visitor's office. Instead, he was directed to a private room where prisoners were permitted to speak with their attorneys. It was the one room in the Prison the prisoner's conversations weren't supposed to be strictly monitored. However, he knew that both he and his fellow prisoners remained paranoid and were leery of the truthfulness of the privacy.

The cheaply paneled room had worn berber carpet on the floor and stained ceiling tiles on the ceiling wrapped around the fluorescent light fixture. The only furnishings were a chipboard folding table and four molded plastic chairs; two blue and two orange, all with chipped chrome legs. Beneath the orange chair closest to the door, he had just entered was a large iron ring bolted to the floor.

Having briefly been in the room on two other occasions in which he turned down offers from the Government to provide evidence against his former associates, Joey knew what was to follow. Without being told, he extended his arms, allowing Thompson to handcuff him. The guard then placed him in ankle chains that were attached to the handcuffs using a small chain. Satisfied the chains were secure, the guard directed Joey to sit in the orange chair nearest the ring. Allowing Joey a brief moment to find a comfortable position, Thompson chained his shackles to the ring. Giving the restraints one last shake to ensure they were locked, Thompson left, leaving him alone in the room staring at the uninspiring walls with their decades' old posters, advising visitors of what to do in case of an emergency.

As he waited, Joey anticipated another government official was about to enter the room in a final effort to see if he would be willing to turn evidence against his recently indicted boss. Figuring this would be another short meeting, he wondered if he could back into the exercise yard before lunch. Then the door opposite the one he had entered opened and in walked in a man he would have never in a million years guessed would be visiting him: Primovero's longtime attorney, Frank Nelson. The man had been the second chair during Joey's trial. Technically the man was supposed to be supporting his own defense attorney, Alan Wolff, during his trial, but in reality, the man was present to ensure Joey didn't share any family secrets. Obviously unsuccessful in his defense, it was the first time he had seen the man since his conviction. In the eight years since the man appeared much the same, short and frail-looking with a shaven pointy head and skin that was peculiarly pale as if it had never seen the sun. In fact, the only sign of aging on the man that Joey detected was some gray hair in the man's beard.

The two men exchanged a brief awkward hello as if neither wanted to be in the room. Joey for certain had nothing to say to the man and suggested that Nelson should have been worrying himself with a defense strategy given Primovero's recent indictment. Nelson assured him however, that wasn't a problem he need to worry about as Mr. Primovero "was coordinating his efforts at this moment to respond to the indictment."

Instead, in the short meeting, Nelson went on to tell Joey that Mr. Primovero had arranged a ride for him upon his release. The drivers would be instructed to "take care of him" as the boss wanted to "reward him" by taking him to lunch at his favorite old lunch spot "The Peanut." Having owned a luxury condominium nearby, Joey had undoubtedly enjoyed his share of meals at the restaurant because it was convenient, and Joey himself wasn't much of a cook. However, he couldn't recall having ever dined with his former boss there, as Primovero preferred to take him meals either at home or in one of the restaurants he owned. Joey supposed he shouldn't have been surprised that Promiser knew of his former eating habits, as the man always seemed to know more than anyone else about everything, and knew just how and when to exploit the information he held. Thus Primovero maintained an army of people on his payroll who provided him with information.

When he asked Nelson why The Peanut specifically, Nelson had simply stated that Mr. Primovero had not shared that information with him. Joey was not surprised by the admission. Despite his constant collecting of data, Primovero always one to play his cards close to the vest and rarely shared information with others. Thus, Joey determined it was logical Primovero wouldn't have shared his reasoning with the hired help, especially an attorney, a profession Primovero rated just above politicians and below the homeless in the hierarchy of society.

So why the Peanut of all places? Joey asked himself as Nelson continued to ramble on, apparently content to rack up more billable hours. If Primovero were going to reward him for his loyalty inside surely, he deserved something more than a basket of wings, as good as they might be. The only thing Joey could recall that made any kind of sense to him was that Primovero had once shared with him that he preferred to meet with people on their own turf. There were two reasons Primovero explained. First, there was a lot an observant person could learn from someone's surroundings: how they lived; what was important to them. Secondly, people are generally more comfortable in their own surroundings. The more comfortable someone is, the more likely they are to overshare because their guards are down. So was it Primovero's intent to take Joey somewhere nostalgic to interrogate him in hopes that the comfortable atmosphere would help loosen his tongue.

After 15 minutes, the guard knocked on the door, indicating that they had five minutes remaining. The signal prompted Joey to ask another question. "How did you know I had received my parole? I only found out yesterday?"

"As you are well aware, Joey, Mr. Primovero, has resources of information everywhere. He does not share the sources of his information with me, but I have found over the years that his information is rarely if ever wrong."

Following Nelson's visit, Joey returned to the exercise yard, determined to use his last 30 minutes before lunch to finish his workout, and to think. Replaying the meeting with Nelson in his mind, the more and more bothered he was by Nelson's refusal or inability to tell Joey how he or Primovero knew he had been granted the early parole. Joey certainly hadn't told them. It was unnerving for sure.

Then as he was in the middle of a set of single-arm dumbbell rows, he was suddenly struck by Nelson's words from the beginning of the meeting. Primovero wants to "take care of him" and "reward him" after he was released for prison!

CHAPTER 2

September 7, 8:45 am

Jim Winters sat at his desk with a cup of steaming black coffee looking out the window with its million-dollar ocean views from his high rise condominium with it's matching price tag in Jacksonville, Florida. At 68-years-old he was only semi-retired, unlike most of the building's other senior residents. Because he still dabbled in work, every morning, he made his way into the second bedroom of his 2 bedroom space, which was set up as an office to check his email and various web boards for any jobs that enticed him.

Jim Winters sat at his desk with a cup of steaming black coffee looking out the window with its million-dollar ocean views from his high rise condominium with it's matching price tag in Jacksonville, Florida. At 68-years-old he was only semi-retired, unlike most of the building's other senior residents. Because he still dabbled in work, every morning, he made his way into the second bedroom of his 2 bedroom space, which was set up as an office to check his email and various web boards for any jobs that enticed him.

Similarly, if you had a product that needed to move across the world, he could arrange that. No questions asked. He had contacts all over the world, men, and women who specialized in any number of things. But unquestionably, his most lucrative enterprise was his pool of contract killers, for those especially sticky problems as he liked to say.

At his age and with enough money put away to last him until he was 100, he no longer had to work and only took on the jobs that he felt were with his time and efforts. Always discerning in his work, he had become even more so in the last three years, only accepting jobs that met specific criteria. They had to be something interesting and had to pay well; very well, and they had to be working for people with whom he had worked before. He no longer needed the stress or vetting potential clients.

Opening his business email, he found four messages. Two he knew were rejections before he even opened them by looking at the sender. One from someone he didn't know. The second rejection was from someone he knew but didn't particularly like, who always wanted to argue cost after a job was finished, another stress he no longer needed.

Moving on to the other two messages, the first was from a woman in Montreal, who called herself Abigail. Winter and Abagail had done lots of business over the years. He found her both charming and reasonable, a rarity in his work. Typically, she asked him to find her mules willing to run Canadian Pharmaceuticals across the border, but she had something more interesting once in a while. Opening the message, he ensured the message contained all the coded identifiers that confirmed the sender was who she claimed to be and not just someone who had somehow procured her email account. Satisfied she was who she said she was, he read the coded message. She was looking to expand her operation again and requested his assistance in procuring distributors in the Pittsburgh area. She was offering a sizable finders fee. Neither exciting nor rich enough, he quickly determined. He nonetheless answered her email out of curtesy, something he did not often do for others.

The fourth email was from a man he knew to be from the Portland area, known as Duckworth. Duckworth was not charming, but he paid his bills on time and without argument. Duckworth was a man who dealt with antiquities. Generally, it was tedious quite dull work, but in need of something to occupy his mind, Winter opened the email. Repeating the verification process to ensure the man's identity was genuine, Winter was assured it was Portland's man. Then he read the message, Duckworth was looking for a buyer for a pair of authentic Japanese Samurai Swords, that his previous buyer had fallen through on. Duckworth was offering a 10% commission. Easy money, but again it was not a job that moved the needle. Thus he simply deleted it.

Taking a sip of his coffee, he was getting ready to navigate to a news website when his computer chimed, informing him another message had been received. The email was from an address that he did not recognize, but the subject line certainly caught his attention: The Chieftain. Winter hadn't heard the name, The Chieftain in a long time though the two had done regular business together for a period of 3 or 4 years, long ago before the man simply stopped requesting his services. Hell, he had thought maybe the person was dead or something, a real possibility in his business. Having not heard from The Chieftain in so long, Winter wondered how the man had gotten his new contact information and was hesitant to open the email, fearing a trap of some sort. The feds, he knew were undoubtedly getting better at such things. Yet he knew there were lots of people who knew how to get a hold of him if need be, and certainly, the Chieftain would be a person who had proven previously he was capable of getting that information. It was merely a necessary part of Winter's business model.

Taking a moment, he tried to recall what he could regarding The Chieftain. For obvious reasons, no one in his business operated with their real names, nor did they share many details. However, Winter was in a unique position that allowed him to ascertain a great deal of information about individuals. As insurance, he kept files on all those he did business with. A few clicks of his mouse and Winter opened his file on the man. Reviewing the information he had collected on the Chieftain, Winter was reminded he operated in the Midwest. Previously Winter has arranged a variety of services for the man in St. Louis, Kansas City, Wichita and Omaha. WInter had arranged money laundering for a sizable quantity of dirty cash at regular intervals, transportation services to move goods, and even fixed a few low-level fights. Their last transaction had been almost 12 years prior when he had provided some muscle for a turf war that never really came to fruition between factions of the Civella crime family, in Kansas City.

Seeing the tie to the Civella crime family, his hesitancy to open the email increased all the more, having seen the news that the FBI has just indicted Richard Primovero, the suspected current head of the Civella family. Not a man to believe in coincidence, Winter began fitting the puzzle pieces in his head, trying to determine if he was being targeted in a sting himself. Considering a moment, if The Chieftain were Primovero, why would the man turn against him of all people? Besides, if Primovero were telling secrets to the Feds, he had way bigger fish to turn in than Winter. But what about the alternative, he asked himself.

What if Primovero were the Chieftain and was reaching out all these years because he needed an assist? Unsure he studied the file more closely.

During the years he was assisting The Chieftain, the Civella family was in a bit of shambles. For a handful of years after the long time Capomandamento, don or godfather, Antonio "Tony" Civella and his underboss, Francesco "Frank" Carlucci had died unexpectedly in a helicopter crash there had been chaos within the family as factions developed and began fighting for control. At the time of his death, Tony's son, William, was considered too young to step into the role at age 23, and thus the job went to a man named John Bukaty, who was an unpopular choice, despite his being a made man inside Tony's inner circle. Not only was the man not of Italian heritage, but worse, he also proved to be completely inept. His inability to maintain control led to his eventual disappearance and presumed death. With Bukaty no longer in the picture, William made a play for the crown as did two other men: Jacopo "Jake" Moretti, the family's former enforcer, and Jason Simone whose family had been involved with the Civella since the beginning. In the next three years, Moratti managed to kill William and send Simone into hiding. During those three years, the organization continued collapsing from within.

It was during this time that the Chieftain had initially contacted Winter for help running some projects. Reviewing the file, Winter saw the man's assignment were all interconnected in a manner that was both cunning and fruitful for all those involved, including Winter. Then the Chieftain has inquired about some muscle for the upcoming turf war, which Winter provided at a premium cost. Two weeks later, Moretti himself was dead, and Simone had come out of hiding to endorse Richard Primovero for the job. Until that point in time, Richard Primovero had been a virtual unknown, at least to Winter, who had good sources. Since then, Winter hadn't heard from the Chieftain but knew the Civella family under Primovero's leadership had risen to prominence once again.

That brought him back to his original question. Could Primovero be the Chieftain? It certainly made some sense.

"Assuming Primovero is Chieftain, what do I really know about the man?" Winter asked himself aloud. Primovero was one of those few men on earth who seemed to truly possess the Midas touch. Winter knew that the police certainly knew of the man and had their suspicions about his activities, as they did most of the country's crime bosses. But suspecting someone was doing something illegal and proving it were two different things. The authorities had never been able to get any substantial evidence against the man until recently based on the indictment. For nearly a decade, it seemed Primovero and the Civella Family were playing chess while his rivals and the authorities were playing checkers: no matter the situation, he was always 2 and 3 steps ahead. He had even heard of other crime bosses asking the man for his advice, thinking he had some magic soothsayer abilities.

Finally, curiosity got the best of him. Opening the email, Winter carefully checked off all the encrypted verifiers he and the Chieftain had set up long ago to ensure they were there. They were, but he double-checked just to be sure. Identity confirmed, he read the body of the text.

The request nearly took his breath away. The Chieftain asked Winter to provide a team of hitters, a wheelman, an explosives expert, and two laborers who knew how to keep their mouths shut for a job that would take place in 12 days. The Chieftain was willing to pay 3 million, plus another million to cover expenses. Winter would be paid his customary 10 percent or $300,000, which would be paid separately from the 3 million intended for the team.

The numbers were staggering and almost seemed excessive, as life and death could be bought so much more cheaply, he thought. Then he began looking closer at the brief outline of the plan, the Chieftain had provided.

Though the Chieftain intentionally hadn't provided all the fine points, which would be reserved only for the men who accepted the job to do, there was enough detail in the outline for Winter to appreciate the plan's grandness. Winter didn't see any apparent holes in the brief overview, though he was in the people business, not the tactical business. He didn't have the stomach for that, Winter knew. Nonetheless, he understood the need for the number of requested men and the amount being offered. There was every likelihood that some would die even if the plan went off flawlessly. If it didn't, it was more likely they would all wind up in prison or dead, which was why Winter always insisted on his money upfront. Not doing so would be foolhardy in his business.

Nonetheless, the idea of being a part of the scheme provided him with a pang of excitement he hadn't felt in years. If the Chieftain and company succeeded, the story would become legendary. Hell, it could rival the Saint Valentine's Day Massacre of Chicago in 1929 as the pentacle for organized crime plots. Even if only a small role, the possibility of taking part in a scheme of such magnitude not to mention the $300,000 fee was undoubtedly enticing. He was in, he decided, all fear of a trap forgotten.

CHAPTER 3

September 7, 7:45 pm

Since his release on bail two days prior, Richard Primovero had felt almost a prisoner in his own home, despite having a full staff of household servants to make his life one of ease. The 56-year-old Primovero often wondered what his mother and father would think of the multimillion-dollar home he now owned in the affluent Mission Hills neighborhood on the Kansas side of the metropolitan area. His parents had been immigrants from the famed Italian Hill Country between Florence and Rome. They had migrated to the greater Kansas City area to pursue a better life than that of a day laborer on the local farms. His father heard there were good jobs at the Kansas City rail yards that sent western beef to the eastern packing houses from his cousin, who had come over years prior. For three years, his parents had scraped together all the money together that they could. Using their small savings, his parents made their way across the ocean, and halfway across the continent to Kansas City.

Speaking little English, his parents had first rented and then bought a two-bedroom, one-bathroom bungalow with a detached garage in the rear in a rough northeast Kansas City Missouri neighborhood called Columbus Park.

They had chosen the area for it's affordability and the neighborhood's sizeable Italian heritage population where they felt more comfortable. Despite his father working at the rail yard, loading and unloading the freight cars, his parents always seemed to be hustling just to ensure that he had food to eat, a roof over his head and clothes to wear.

Though his closets were now full of exclusively custom made, tailor-fitted clothing of the most exceptional vintages Primovero had never forgotten he had grown up wearing primarily hand me downs from the other neighborhood kids. To him, his home was a symbol of how far he had come in life, and being a prisoner inside was simply unacceptable.

Though his lawyers had managed to keep him out of jail, the federal government had successfully managed to make his life more difficult. The court had frozen all of his assets, that they knew about, as both sides awaited trial. This proved nothing more than a minor inconvenience as he maintained his day-to-day lifestyle using his other resources. More bothersome, since his indictment, he saw the police, the media, or both every time he looked outside. The presence of either interfered with his ability to conduct business in his customary face-to-face manner. Fearful of wire taps and other eavesdropping devices tied to technology,

Primovero refused to do business any other way.

On the one occasion, he had tried to leave his home, his car was trailed by a convoy of parties, including a federal agent. They brazenly followed him inside his tailor's store and the nearby restaurant as he tried to have a peaceful dinner. After that experience, he decided he would not again leave his home until it was absolutely necessary.

On the other hand, being primarily confined to his home had allowed him ample time to think. A chi vuole, non mancano modi, as his mother used to tell him. Loosely translated it meant where there's a will there's a way. In Richard Primovero's experience, given enough time to consider a problem, he could find a viable solution. This situation was no different; he had determined. Having already made his first move on the chessboard by sending Nelson to Leavenworth, tonight would be step two in his plan to fix the problem he was now faced with. No way did he trust his lawyers' ability to do so, especially when they dared to say he should consider a plea!

In the basement of his home, Primovero sat, his back to the wall facing the only door in or out of what he called his War Room, watching as his lieutenants arrived one by one. The room was without windows, paneled in a rich cherry wood that perfectly matched the hardwood floors below, and lit by soft light emanating from a simple chandelier and floor lamps. The walls, floor, and ceiling had all been soundproofed. In addition, there was the added protection of an electronics jammer that had been installed during the room's construction so that no prying ears could pick up anything discussed inside the room's four walls. Despite the protection the room provided against external eavesdropping threats, each man was required to give up their phones and weapons as they entered the space.

It was the first time since his indictment, arrest, and subsequent release on bail that Primovero would be speaking with his lieutenants. He knew the men understood he would contact them when he needed them. Thus it came as no surprise when all his men confirmed they would attend the meeting.

Primovero also knew his lieutenants understood the significance of the meeting being in his home. Even in regular times, he rarely invited any of his business associates into his house, preferring to keep his home as much his own personal sanctuary as possible. Even more infrequent was it that he would meet with all his men at once. A student of history, he preferred to compartmentalize his organization so that no one string could unravel all his work. Furthermore, the four men attending the meeting didn't really like one another, which didn't bother him as he always figured they were less likely to conspire against him if they couldn't get along.

In the room, they gathered around a round table that was intended to convey a sense of equality among the group, something he picked up from King Arthur's stories and his knights of the round table, stories he loved as a child. Similar to Arthur though, every man in the room knew who was in charge. Primovero had the respect of each man in the room for his ability to lead the organization, taking it to greater heights than it had been in its history. Never a micromanager, he delegated the authority to each of them to make run their respective day-to-day operations. Still, always with the understanding, he had the final say, and they never made any significant changes or attempted to undertake a new initiative without his say so. If he thought there was a correction to be given, he gave it. At the same time, if he thought they deserved praise, he gave that as well. And when the occasional hard decision arose, he made those too. More importantly, the man was unafraid to get his hands dirty himself, never asking for anyone in his employ to do something he hadn't or wouldn't do himself.

If the table were a clock and Primovero were sitting at 12:00, then the man to his left sitting at 2:00 was his most loyal and longest-tenured associate Tommy Cuppari. Cuppari was bigger than Primovero, at 6 feet tall and

220 pounds, with a silver horseshoe of hair around his head and dark eyes. As a youth, Cuppari had been a competitive power lifter and still hit the gym as much as he could, though having had both shoulders and a knee surgically repaired, he could no longer throw the heavy weights around like he used too. The pair had grown up together in the same neighborhood. In fact, Cuppari was the only person in the room, and likely the world, who still called Primovero "Primo", the nickname that he had been given in the old neighborhood. Primovero had always been the brains, while Cuppari was the muscle. Primovero knew that as Cuppari saw things together, the two had climbed to the top, and together they would stay there. He appreciated the man's undying loyalty and took comfort in the fact that as far as Cuppari was concerned, anyone threatening "Primo" was threatening Cuppari himself. Even as youngsters, Cuppari had protected the smaller man. In contrast, Primovero had always helped guide the man's life choices, including joining the family, where they had risen through the ranks together. As his muscles and strength had subsided over the last handful of years, his confidence waned too. However, Primovero ensured him he was still a key contributor to his team, reminding him that he held the title of capo bastion, or underboss, meaning he was the second in command for a reason. Despite the title and reassurances, Primovero knew his old associate was smart enough to see that he was slowly being

replaced and relegated to more of a bodyguard, driver and confidant role. Primovero also knew his friend's suspicions had been reinforced by his not telling him what the meeting was about. He knew if there was anyone in the room whom he should have confided in, it was his oldest friend. Yet he had chosen not to tell the man. To his credit, Cuppari sat in his customary chair, patiently waiting for the meeting to begin.

To Primovero's right at 10:00 sat Chad Lessons, his consigliere or third in command. He was tall and lean with sharp features and perfectly combed sandy blonde hair. At initial glance, most would have called him a very handsome man until they looked into Lessons' eyes, which were electric blue. Even the uneducated could see the danger that lurked in the pair of icy orbs. The man rarely spoke but was always observing what was going on around him, and he rarely, if ever, missed anything. The man had grown up in St. Louis and began as a simple courier for the family. At the age of 19, he was attempting to deliver a package to Primovero, who himself was only a lieutenant at the time when he was stopped by three men who were determined to intercept the package. When the smoke cleared, the three men laid dead, and Lessons handed over the bag unscathed. It made an impression on Primovero, who brought the young man into his inner circle and had grown to rely more and more upon the unflappable man since, especially the last handful of years, when

Cuppari was out of commission following his surgeries. Good with any kind of weapon as well as his hands, the man was simply death without the black robe and scythe. But more than that, the man was smart and reliable and unafraid to tell Primoveo, what he actually thought unlike most of the yes men who worked for him. Unbeknownst to anyone, including Lessons, himself, the man was also his chosen successor to lead the family upon his exit. If the man was curious as to what was to be discussed, he gave no outward indication.

At 7 o'clock sat Tony Wentz, a caporegime, or high ranking captain who was in charge of many of the family's soldiers. He was a distant cousin of Primovero. In fact, it was his grandfather who had told his own father about the rail yard jobs all those years ago. He had been brought into the inner circle after proving himself very adept at accomplishing many of Primovero's most unsavory tasks. Wentz was short, about 5'7" and nearly as thick as he was tall. Built like a bowling ball, the man was an avid weight lifter and obvious steroid user. He and Cuppari had often lifted together before the older man had started to break down physically. Due to the girth, the man had no neck, and his arms were as big as the average man's thighs. He had nearly shoulder-length black hair slicked straight back, emphasizing his large forehead and deep-set beady eyes. Unlike Lessons, Wentz was loud and boisterous, often speaking of himself in the third person. His self given nickname was the hammer, which he bragged he stole from some lawyer commercial he saw when he was in Vegas. He, too, was reputed to be well versed in weapons but preferred to use his hands and fists when called to action. The man had a short fuse and was easily provoked thus had to be managed accordingly but was as loyal as a bulldog, and if the man had an ounce of fear in him, Primovero had never seen it. Of all the men in the room, he seemed the most anxious, hoping for a chance at some action, something that hadn't happened recently.

In the 5 o'clock position at the table, the last man sat. Sam Caynor held no fancy title but was a family associate. He was of average height and had a bit of a spare tire around his midsection, resulting from his love of gourmet food, fine wines, and his sedentary lifestyle. At the table, he was clearly the physical misfit. Similarly, he had a completely different skill set than the other 3 men summoned to the meeting. Sam was the family's accountant and was the only man other than Primovero who knew where all the money and operations stood at any given time, with insights into the drug trafficking, the casinos, protection rackets, and every other enterprise Primovero was involved in. The man was incredibly intelligent and was unembarrassed by his intelligence, often giving off an heir of superiority to others that rubbed many the wrong way, especially Wentz. Moreover, because of his position, he was very flippant to the men around him feeling protected under the umbrella of Primovero's influence, something that had saved him from a beating on at least two occasions from both Wentz and Cuppari. Flanked on either side by the two men, he looked straight ahead, awaiting the boss to speak.

After Jenni, his household manager served the last of the drinks, water, coffee, or tea for all, she left, closing the large doors behind her. Primovero waited a moment longer, giving the woman a chance to ascend the stairs, while he savored a sip of the coffee had brought him, appreciating her perfect ratio of coffee to creme to sugar.

Standing, he said, "I am sure you have all been concerned about recent developments, particularly my indictment. I appreciate the patience you have all shown during these past few days, but I needed a moment to get my thoughts together and develop a strategy to handle this unfortunate situation. As you are all aware, I have two of the best attorneys in the country on retainer in Gretchen Francis and Frank Nelson. They have assured me that the case against me is weak at best. In fact, Gretchen says that the case itself really comes down to one item and one item only: the ledger that the cops confiscated when they invaded my office."

"But the ledger is written in code," Sam interrupted. "Unless the police can decipher it, it is just a bunch of meaningless letters and numbers."

"Interesting you should mention that Sam. You are correct. The ledger is written in code. How many people are there who can decipher that code?" Primovero asked the man.

"Just you and I," Sam responded proudly, looking at the other three men in the room with a haughty look upon his face.

"Just you and I," Primovero repeated, letting the words hang in the air causing the other three men to look from Primovero to Sam.

It took a moment for their collective gazes to affect the man, whose look changed from one of over importance to one of concern. Taking his eyes off Primovero, he looked to the other three men in the room. Their expressions did little to settle his fear. When his eyes returned to Primovero, there was suddenly a gun in his hand. He opened his mouth to protest but could not get the words out before the silence room was filled with two loud thunderous explosions made that much louder in the enclosed space. Explosions Sam never heard.

The other three men at the table looked from the body lying on the floor to their boss holding the gun. Cuppari's face revealed a look of surprise. He had not seen his boss hold a gun since before he became the head of the family, and he had rarely done so before then.

On the other hand, Wentz simply smiled an evil smile, obviously happy at the man's demise. "Serves you right, asshole." He said, bending over the corpse to inspect the two holes in the man's face: one just above the right eyebrow, the other just below the right eye. "Nice shootin boss", he added.

However, Lessons remained unreadable as if the suddenness of the gun's appearance and subsequent death hadn't affected him at all.

Sitting the weapon down on the table, Primovero calmly sat. "Once again, our friend Sam was mistaken. We were not the only two who know how to decipher the ledger, there is another."

"Who?" Wentz asked, eagerly hoping to be set free.

"Joey Cabrini," Lessons answered, speaking for the first time since arriving to the house.

"That's right," added Cuppari. "Sam took his place after Joey went to Leavenworth."

"Indeed, you are both correct," stated Primovero. "And our friend Joey is about to be released."

"Released? He's been gone that long?" Wentz asked.

"It appears Joey has been issued early parole." Primovero answered.

"And you want us to take care of him?" Cuppari asked.

"He will be taken care of, but first, I need to talk to our old friend about a few things," Primovero said. He then laid out the pertinent detail of his plan to the three men. By the time he was finished, all three were smiling broadly.

"It's genius," Wentz exclaimed.

"I love it," added Cuppari.

Looking to Lessons, the man remained silent, though even he seemed impressed by the plan. Satisfied, the three men were on board with what he had shared, Primovero said, "Now let's dispose of poor Sam there."

CHAPTER 4

September 7, 9:45 pm

Winter was incredibly aware his success was built upon his ability to provide the right person for the right job without exception, and this time was no different. Winter knew he would need to assemble the best team he had ever put together in order to successfully accomplish the Chieftain's scheme. Adding to the challenge was the condensed timeline, though Winter found himself strangely invigorated by the need to work fast. Full of renewed vigor, he had spent a significant part of the day putting names together of men who could be used, what roles they could potentially fill, and who was and wasn't available on short notice. While he was able to accumulate a pretty impressive list of prospective names, he could not find many willing to commit to working on a team without knowing whom they would be working for.

The job required a man who could not only plan a mission but also one who could command the respect of the rest of the team, otherwise, it was doomed to fail from the beginning. In the past, he would have immediately contacted a man named Tripler, who was a proven veteran who had succeeded on these kinds of missions previously and a man Winter had worked with many times before. Unfortunately, Tripler was no longer available. Two months prior, Winter had contracted him to kill a man named Galvan in New Mexico. Less than a week after he had accepted the job, Tripler's head had been found in a box on the man's doorstep who had placed the contract on Galvan.

With Tripler no longer an option, Winter put together a list of five other candidates.

Winter's preference would be for a man known only as Logan. While Logan was relatively new to the business, having only come to prominence in the last handful of years, he had pulled off some of the cleanest jobs Winter had ever heard of under some of the least desirable circumstances. Yet he had never failed to get the job done, leaving nary a trace of his existence beyond that of the target's body. There were two problems, however, one he had never heard of Logan working with a team, though there was a lot about the man he didn't know. Secondly, the only way to contact the man was through Paige, a rival of Winter. Winter knew she did not like him personally and never had. The sentiment was mutual.

Scratching Logan off the list, he next attempted to contact a man named Remington. The man was rumored to have been a former soldier of the Mossad, Israel's equivalent to the CIA, who had managed to leave their employ and start working independently. Winter knew the man primarily operated in Europe but had done jobs in the United States. In fact, Remington had done a job in Detroit, which Winter had arranged less than two years prior. His inquiry to the man received a quick response declining the invitation as he was already employed.

Similarly, he was turned down by the third and fourth men on his list: a man named Soap and a woman who called herself Shay. Both were considered first-rate operators whose names would have carried a lot of weight with some of the operators he had contacted to fill the team. Soap provided no explanation for his declination. On the other hand, Shay had stated initially she was available, but after seeing the Cheiftain's outline, she declined the mission, calling it a suicide mission that she wanted no part of.

The last possibility was a man who called himself Napier. The man was experienced in the business for well over a decade, and Winter had previously worked with him. There was a time when he was one of the most sought after hitters in the business for his ability to get results. Though recently, some people in the industry, he knew had begun to shy away from the man because, unlike Logan, the man often left a trail of pure carnage in his wake unconcerned with any collateral damage that occurred. The man was completely without scruples, valued human life, not at all, and was only loyal to money.

That being said, when you hired Napier to kill someone, they ended up dead. Just as importantly, Winter knew if Napier was put in charge of a team, the other men and women would follow his orders. Whether they followed out of respect or fear of the man made no difference. However, Winter was under no illusions, knowing that the Napier's selection as leader would likely cause some candidates from his other list to decline the opportunity as well. Regardless, out of viable options, he sent the man an email outlining the job.

*****

September 8, 7:00 am

The man who called himself Napier was on standing on the deck of his home on a large secluded piece of property he had acquired years before staring at the river and low mountains pondering the proposition he had received the night before from Winter. He had done work for the man previously but had no particular like or dislike for the man. His money was as good as anyone else's in his mind. He had nonetheless hesitated to accept the job.

The plan was certainly bold and challenging based on the brief preview provided, two things he enjoyed in his work. However, it was also fraught with obvious danger and pitfalls simply due to its mechanics. Without a doubt, the man paying the bill was either desperate or downright crazy to have cooked up such a scheme, though admittedly, there was a beauty to it. Or at least there could be.

Still, he hesitated. He was too old and too wise to throw his life away, and one screw up here and death was almost inevitable, and to survive meant prison. Given a choice, he was pretty sure he preferred death. Unlike other jobs, once the ball got rolling on this, there would be no way to abort, not that he had ever done so, but the option to do so was a comforting safety net.

Having thought it through, all night, he finally decided to respond to the man. He framed his response carefully, expressing his concerns but without flatly turning the job; though he expected that would be enough to end the conversation.

Yet shortly after hitting send, Winter replied: "If you are unwilling, I can always see if Logan is available..."

Logan! Napier had never met him, but he had grown to despise the man. Seemingly out of nowhere, Logan had appeared. Quickly he had earned the reputation as the man with the Midas touch within the industry. Since Logan's emergence, Napier knew for a fact, he had gotten fewer work opportunities, at least for the premium jobs. He had no issues admitting his jealousy of the man's notoriety. Napier didn't like to consider himself to be second best at anything, least of all his profession. He was better than Remington, Shay, Soap, and any others he told himself. And he was certainly better than this upstart calling himself Logan!

The email continued: "Of course you know if you successfully complete this job, you will be the king of the mountain once more."

Napier understood Winter was manipulating him, but he didn't care. The man's words had the desired effect, and he tentatively accepted the appointment, albeit with a few conditions of his own.

*****

September 8, 12:30 pm

Winter did not feel bad about having to manipulate Napier by playing to his sizable ego to take the job leading the team of mercenaries. It was part of the game as Winter saw it. It was not a complete victory, however, as Napier had a few stipulations of his own. Usually, that would have been a nonstarter for Winter. Still, given the short notice and lack of other viable options, he played along despite his own reservations regarding the man's conditions.

First, Napier said he required more money than the $300,000 Winter had offered. Instead, he wanted a full half million! Winter had expected the man would ask for a bump, but $500,000 was well beyond what he had imagined. Nonetheless, he reminded himself of the same thing he often told clients: "You get what you pay for" or his other favorite to clients, "Skilled labor ain't cheap and cheap labor ain't skilled."

Unfortunately, the demand for such a large sum for Napier, also meant that Winter would be limited in the amounts he could offer to pay other members of the team. This, too, Winter knew would likely impact his ability to put the best team together. However, he was still confident in his ability to assemble a solid group of trigger pullers. Somewhat ironically, Napier's second stipulation helped Winter out in that regard as he insisted upon the inclusion of four other men on the job. They were men that Winter would never have chosen himself, but it wasn't his neck on the line.

The first pair Napier had insisted upon was the Brockton twins: Cain and Able. Winter was well informed about the brothers as he had hired the duo for a pair of jobs previously. Born and raised in southern California, the two red-headed Irish lineage twins grew up in a poor, primarily Hispanic neighborhood in San Diego. The pair learned quickly survival depended on their ability to watch out for one another and a willingness to fight back. By age 15, they were both members of the local gang, and by age 22 were hardcore murderers for hire. A decade later, the pair were mercenaries plain and simple. The pair of brothers had been all over the world doing jobs for the cartels, warlords, politicians, and anyone else with a dollar. Both men were reportedly excellent snipers, proficient with any weapons, and were virtually fearless in a fight. They had a reputation as men who pulled the trigger and asked no questions, which was all well and good for this job.

However, the pair were tough to work with, and one of the reasons Winter would never hire them again and did not want them on this particular job. Three years prior, Winter had been asked by one of his most loyal South American clients to provide a few experienced shooters for a bank job in Caracas. The solicitor was one of the leaders to one of the many anti-government factions within Venezuela and was going to use the money from the job to pay for future services in his ongoing war with the country's sitting dictator.

The customer had advised that he anticipated that the entire job would take 4 to 6 weeks. Winter had told the brothers to anticipate being in the country for a month while the specifics were ironed out. Until the night of the heist, their employer needed them to maintain a low profile and help him plan the mission. The two brothers had been gone less than 10 days when Winter received a message from the customer that he needed his money back as the twins had been sent home. According to the man, they had gotten drunk in the village bar every night since they had arrived. Making matters worse, the pair had picked fights with the local men during their drinking binges at night and the other team members during the day as they nursed their hangovers. If that weren't bad enough, the two bragged to the women they encountered what they were doing in the county. Because of their actions, the customer had to abort his plans for the robbery. He was also forced into hiding after the government had been tipped off due to the pair's loose lips. The twins had just managed to get out of the country themselves ahead of arrest, which wouldn't have been possible but for the customer's help. Despite their actions, the two insisted that Winter pay them for their time. Not only had he refused to pay them for the job, but he also swore to never hire the pair again. Since the incident, Winter had not been contacted about contract work from the Anti-Venezuelan group again, which had a significant impact on Winter's bottom line.

The next man Napier had explicitly requested was a man known only as "Fish." Fish had never done any work for Winter, but he had looked into contracting him previously. Fish was an explosives expert who evidently had been trained to work with munitions in the coal mines of southern West Virginia when he was young. However, when the previous President's administration adopted new environmental regulations, many of the Appalachian coal mines had to close because of the coal's sulfur content. Fish, along with thousands of others, were left without a job. However, the man discovered he could freelance his skills in any number of ways and make substantially more money, especially if he wasn't concerned about the legality of his work. Blaming the government for his unemployment, he had no objections to the work and had successfully blasted everything from safes in banks to tunnels under prisons.

The man was undoubtedly talented. It was that talent that had led Winter to seek out the man for a significant contract he had lined up for a job in Alaska involving the sabotage of the pipeline. The man's response to his inquiry was enough to confirm the rest of the man's reputation. The man was unquestionably incredibly intelligent but was the type who liked to remind everyone how smart he was as well. After Winter had sent the Fich the job details, Fish had responded with a complete critique of the plan. The response completely alienated the client. In addition to the ill-advised critique, Fish had demanded more money than the job was paying. The extra cost he explained was because of "the need for his expertise." If that weren't enough, his reply had indicated the supplies he would need to do the job "correctly" were far more expensive and challenging to acquire than what the person hiring wanted to pay. Unwilling to relent on either demand, Winter had not been able to hire him for the job. After not being hired, Fish had called Winter, "a cheap bastard." Winter hadn't approached the man about work since.

Finally, Napier asked for a man called the Butcher on the team. Winter had never heard of the man until Napier had named him for the team and had found little since other than the man was supposedly a wizard with knives and enjoyed up-close work. Winter appreciated the man's willingness to get close to people, but in this job, if the targets got up close, something had gone incredibly wrong. Further, Winter did not think this was the type of job to send an inexperienced soldier on, the pressure was going to be intense.

Nonetheless, Winter knew his reputation was also at stake as the team's organizer and he wasn't a man who liked the unknown. Thus, Winter filled out the team's remainder with people he knew and had worked with previously. All competent men who had proven capable individually. His biggest concern remained their ability to work together to pull this job off as there was no denying that there were no guarantees it could be successfully pulled off. Winter didn't want his reputation besmirched by a failure in his last days.

CHAPTER 5

September 10, 9:30 am

Three days after sending his message to Winter, the man calling himself Chieftain received confirmation that everything was arranged and ready to go, once Winter received the money. Hitting the button to transfer the money, he was immediately depressed, reminded the cost of freedom would leave him with less available cash than he was accustomed to having in his account or liked. Taking a breath, he told himself it was a necessary expense. Once he was free of his predicament, he would be able to rebuild his nest egg; already having explored ideas for a few new business ventures and some old debts to collect upon.

Within the hour, he received confirmation that the funds were in the escrow account and the specifics related to the assembled team his $4,300,000 had purchased. Unsurprisingly, he did not recognize any of the assembled team's names though that didn't mean he wasn't curious about them. Of particular interest was his point of contact and the team's leader, a man known as Napier, to whom he would send his full plan.

Unfamiliar with the name, he quietly checked with some people he knew who would know about the man before forwarding the full plan. The information he had been given about the man was consistent from all he had questioned. The man was smart, he had balls, and he was a cold-blooded killer. Not a lot was known about Napier's background, but those he spoke with all informed him that Napier got the job done once he signed on. Although those same sources had unanimously warned that the man could lose his temper, which lead to fits of recklessness, causing unnecessary damage to people and property.

Interestingly, during his inquiries, another came up unsolicited by the people he had inquired: a man named Logan. Logan, they said, was just as deadly, though was much more precise. As one man told him, Napier was like using a hand grenade to kill someone while Logan was like a sniper rifle. Either would kill, one was just way less sloppy and more precise. The Chieftain reasoned there were times a man needed the grenade over the sniper rifle, and his plan could be just such a scenario. Besides, he wasn't in a position to question Winter's choice of Napier over the Logan. At this point, he was committed; no need for buyer's remorse.

Satisfied Napier was legitimate. The Chieftain made arrangements to contact the man in a manner that made the correspondence untraceable from his end. He was confident the man did the same from his end otherwise, Winter would have never hired him. By design, it was the last contact he and the man would have before they met in person. Thus, after sending Napier the full detailed plan so he and his team could begin gathering all the items and intel required to carry out the mission to secure his freedom, he reminded himself it was out of his hands now. The bed was made, it was time to sleep in it.

The following morning, lying in his bed wide awake, the sun coming through the window shining upon his lean frame, he remained still, enjoying the warmth, trapped in deep thought. He hadn't used the name Chieftain in years and had hesitated to do so, but despite his best efforts, he could see no other way, unable to ignore that his way of life was definitely about to change. The damn indictment had wholly altered the equation. He knew the indictment itself didn't mean much of anything, especially if his plan went the way he expected it too, but it put a spotlight on things that undoubtedly complicated matters.

Despite efforts to distract himself, the Chieftain continued ruminating over his plan again and again, for the next week. Looking for any small detail he could have missed, any contingency that needed to be covered. There were none, not that he could have done anything about it if there had been. Thus he reassured himself by continuously reminding himself that he had quietly been planning the whole thing over the last few years. He knew he had looked at it from every angle imaginable. He knew where all the danger points were, and he had worked out contingencies for them all.

Still, he remained nervous knowing the scheme's success was the only way he would ever indeed be free of the DA, the cops, and the family. Thirteen men: eight shooters, two laborers, an explosives expert, a driver, and a competent man to lead them, Napier. Was there really anything else he needed? Obviously, a few more men could make it easier on the front end, but they would just make it messier in the end when he had to get rid of them all. Witnesses just wouldn't do for a man intent on disappearing.

The plan itself was a pretty straight forward sleight of hand proposition. On September 19, he was going to enter the Peanut's downtown location as if were any other Thursday afternoon. He would sit down, have a drink, and talk with the man who had betrayed him. He would engage the man in conversation until exactly 2:00 pm when the eight shooters and Napier were going to storm the restaurant. Coming in, they were likely to face resistance from family members, requiring they shoot a few of the men. That was ok as they were all potential witnesses against him, which meant they were all marked for death regardless. The shooting would also show the patrons the men with the guns were serious, hopefully ensuring the survivors' obedience. The shooters would then take the entirety of the place hostage, barricade themselves in, and await the police and FBI's arrival. Once secure inside, Napier would bide his time to draw out the negotiations until dusk while the other men worked to secure their escape.

The downtown Peanut was situated ideally for the plan. Located near the corner of Ninth and Banker streets, the restaurant was located on the opposite corner of the same block as Eighth and Washington Streets. A few years prior, engineers had unexpectedly come upon an unknown door to the defunct Eight Street Tunnels when they broke ground for a bank, and its accompanying parking garage was now located there. The Eighth Street Tunnel had been built in the 1880s in less than a year. Its purpose was to allow the City's streetcars to bypass the bluffs. Instead of going over the hillside, the 810-foot tunnel was built through the hillside. The project however, proved a failure. The tunnel itself was strong as could be standing 18 ft tall at the center of its arch, made of brick, steel, and concrete, however, the designers failed to account for the stress the steep grade would have on the cables that powered the streetcars. They had designed the tunnel, so that is dropped 8 1/2 feet over every 100 feet. The combination of the steep grade and the loaded cars' weight constantly pulling against the huge cables wore the cables out at an alarming rate and made maintenance costs prohibitive. So costly that in 1903 a new tunnel was built.

The new tunnel was built roughly parallel to the original tunnel. The steep grade was greatly reduced, alleviating the cable stress problem. Because of the lesser grade, the new 8th street tunnel was nearly 4 times as long as the original at 3100 feet. Upon completion of the new tunnel, the original Eighth Street Tunnel was sealed off for public use, becoming nothing more than a maintenance bay for the new tunnel. The original was essentially forgotten as the City continued to grow around it. As the City grew, buildings were eventually erected upon its domed structure over the years. The new tunnel remained in use until 1956 when it too was closed. Then over time, the entire system, both the original and new structures were forgotten.

Then in the mid-1990s, a developer bought the large tract of land atop the forgotten subterranean structures, planning to revitalize the area. In the process of construction, they stumbled upon the tunnel system once again. The city and historical foundation quickly moved to preserve the structure. Yet, because the tunnels themselves have never been open to the public because of water seepage and mold problems, their existence remains relatively unknown even to this day. Even of those who are aware of its existence, few could tell you where the tunnel was located, and even fewer yet who could tell you where it was accessible from.

If his calculations were correct, and he was sure they were, the explosives expert and the two laborers would enter the original tunnel through the door located on the lower level of parking garage at the corner of 8th and Washington. The entrance was reportedly fairly easy to find, sitting behind the two large HAVC systems for the bank and protected by two massive chain link gates chained and padlocked. The three men would simply cut the lock, gain access, close and lock the gate behind them. New lock in place the area should appear normal to any passerby.

Inside the tunnel, the trio would have two tasks. First, they would ensure they could travel freely from the original eight street tunnel into its replacement, clearing the entirety of three quarters of a mile length from the garage their exit point at the opposite end under the Delaware Street overpass. Once the tunnels were clear, ensuring The Chieftain and the surviving members of the assault team could make a fast getaway when the time came, the three men would return nearer the access point at 8th and Washington to locate the original tunnel's service tunnel.

The service tunnel had allowed workers to access the tunnel from Ninth Street, thus saving them time from walking the steep line's entirety. Like the Eight Street Tunnel itself, the old service tunnel had been sealed off with bricks but ran directly below the Peanut. The explosives expert and the laborers would knock a hole through the brick wall to the service tunnel, follow the tunnel to beneath the restaurant, and then simply blast a hole through the restaurant floor to be opened when he was ready to leave. Upon establishing access to the restaurant from below, the explosives expert would rig the building and a few hostages with explosives. The hostages would then be released to run to the cops while he, Napier, and the assassins' team escaped to the tunnel. Once safely below the ground, they would simply blow the building. They would make their way to an awaiting car parked near the Delaware Street overpass behind the chaos of the scene. The wheelman would then drive him to a nearby airport where a private plane awaited to take him to the old country. There a luxurious villa awaited along the shores of the Mediterranean. He would remain there till the end of his days.

Satisfied with the plan he got up and stretched when he was hit by a wayward thought, When this is all over, I'm going to miss the bed and not have to cook or do laundry for myself.

CHAPTER 6

September 10, 1:30 pm

Napier sat in his chair, staring at the complete plan from the man called The Chieftain. The project in it's entirety was even more grandiose than he could have imagined from the original outline. Yet in reading it, Napier couldn't help but appreciate the beauty of it all, it was indeed a challenge worth his full efforts. Still, there were a few small tweaks here and there needed to make it closer to full proof; though he knew perhaps more than anyone, the best-laid battle plans were for shit once the first bullet was fired and there would be many fired in the execution of this plan. That being said, there was no doubt in Napier's mind that he and his quickly assembled team would need as much time as they could get to prepare and rehearse. He and his mish moshed team would need to be ready for any foreseeable contingencies to pull it off.

To prepare, Napier and the entire team were to gather at a farm about 45 minutes north of Kansas City near the town of St. Joseph, Missouri, on September 12. The farm belonged to the Deen family, whose son John, Napier had done some work for previously through Winter a few years prior. However, John had died a few months earlier when the US Marshals had stormed the farm looking for him. John was killed by a sniper in the early hours of the morning as he tried to shoot it out with the assault team that had placed his family in cuffs while serving a warrant for him. Less than two weeks later, the family patriarch had also died from a heart attack while he awaited trial for knowingly harboring his fugitive son. Now the family had sold off many of the farm's assets but remained desperate for money. Thus they were more than willing to allow Napier and his crew to rent the space for a week to train.

*****

September 12, 8:20 am

Napier had traveled with the Brockton twins and had been the first to arrive at the farm. After exchanging greetings with the family and paying half of their week's rent, he and the twins were shown the old barn and the fields beyond where they would be permitted to train for the week. Inside the barn, they discovered the large space that Napier intended to build their mock-up site for training was full of old boxes, rusty parts, and a massive hunk of metal that Napier recognized as an old motor of some sort. He decided that the team's first opportunity to work together would be removing the debris and cleaning the space allowing them room for their practice space. The loft, however, was mostly clear of junk and would be their quarters for their stay. Napier had the two brothers get the cots from their car and set them up. That complete, the three went to the field to set up a weapons range. One by one, they were joined by the other members of the team.

The first man to arrive was a man who simply introduced himself as Joe. A man of average height and the trim build of a runner, Winter had said the man was one of the world's best shooters and had done a few jobs where he had successfully put his skill to work. Hearing the man's reputation, the twins immediately insisted he show them he could shoot. It didn't take long for Joe to prove Winter correct as the man's ability with a rifle was as good as any Napier had ever seen. Despite a fairly significant wind, the man consistently hit a four-inch circle at 500 yards with the precision weapon he carried. His shooting prowess quickly endeared the man to the twins, though Napier found the man odd. Nonetheless, his ability to get along with the cantankerous duo combined with his skill with a rifle made Joe the perfect choice to join the brothers for their role in the mission.

According to the Chieftain's description, the Peanut was on the west end of a long two-story structure that was separated into thirds allowing space for two other businesses. Because the building was built at the top of the hill, the second floor appeared optimal for an observation and firing platform for the team. Situated on the end of the building, there were only three sides to defend: the south side, which was the front of the building that overlooked Ninth Street, and the west and north sides looked over the alley that separated the building a parking garage. The large parking garage was only two stories tall itself, but because it was built along the steep hill's natural contour, the structure's roof was level with Ninth Street while its basement level was level with Eighth street. Three skilled gunmen placed there with its supposedly wide-open views and clear fire fields to the streets and across the roof of the garage would make holding off any assaults easier during the daylight hours. The only problem was the west side wall had no windows, and thus they would have to knock a hole in the wall to allow for a gun port.

When Napier had first seen the plan, he thought of the brothers for the firepower they brought to the table, and their willingness to use it. Their ability to hit long-range targets and lay suppressive fire was imperative to the mission's success and ability to get out alive. He just needed a third man. Having seen Joe shoot, he thought he had it.

Next to arrive was a big burly bald black man with a long gray goatee named Stewart, who arrived riding a big Harley Davidson motorcycle. Napier guessed the man was 8 to

10 years older than himself, and he was 44, making Stewart the elder statesman of the group. In this business, one didn't get to be an old man by accident, and frankly, Napier respected any man who lived to see 50 years old in their business. In addition to his age, Winter had told him Stewart had once been a member of the elite Marine Force Recon. Thus, Napier knew the man would have been trained to be an expert at observation and reporting of details. Respecting his background, Napier introduced himself to the man. Wanting to see what made the man tick, as he would with all the men for whom he was unfamiliar, Napier asked if later that evening if Stewart would be interested in going into Kansas City with him and doing a recon of the restaurant. Though it was phrased as a question, both men understood the request was an order.

"Just tell me when you want to go," Stewart answered plainly.

Over the next hour, the rest of the team arrived one by one. Each man claimed a bunk in the barn before finding their way to the impromptu gun range. The last to arrive went by the moniker, Cypher. According to Winter, Cypher was a technology wizard who would be required to run the comms and other electronic equipment needed on the mission. When Napier had objected, saying he needed trigger pullers more than computer nerds, Winter had assured him that the man was more than capable in that department as well.

With some coaxing, Winter had let it slip the man was born in the Soviet Union and had been trained in the dark arts by the FSB, the Russian equivalent to the CIA, after the regime's fall. The man had been tasked to Ukraine as part of a team whose mission was to gather intelligence and recruit assets to the Russian cause. Their ultimate goal, to retake the Crimean Peninsula from the Ukranians, long an interest of President Vladimir Putin. In 2015 when Putin was forced to admit that he had intelligence assets operating in Ukraine, the man known as Cypher's cover had been blown, and he had barely escaped with his life from Ukraine. Enraged at Putin and the regime the man simply did what he had been trained to do, he disappeared abroad. Since then, he worked as a freelancer and had proven quite valuable to Winter the last handful of years.

If he had not known the man's background, Napier would have never guessed when he first saw the man walking up to the range. The man didn't look like anything special. Maybe 6 feet tall and 180 pounds with an oval face, a thin straight nose, light-colored eyes, slightly long sandy brown hair, and horned rim glasses. He even spoke perfect English without any trace of an accent, like he grew up in the Midwest somewhere instead of Mother Russia.

By the time of his arrival, the gun range had become an impromptu gaming den. The men were taking bets amongst themselves in an array of shooting contests with a variety of weapons they had gathered for the upcoming mission. Joe and the Brockton twins had been the primary victors of most matches and were happily letting the rest of the group know it when the Russian walked up to the group. As the men continued to show off their shooting skills, Cypher remained at the edge of the group watching the show quietly, seemingly content to be an observer and save his money. That changed, however, when the twins announced a challenge with pistols. Bets were placed, and the men took turns firing 10 rounds at paper plate targets 25 feet away. Cain and Able each placed shot groups in the targets that could be covered with the palm of their hands. Their skills had been matched, if not bettered, by their young Mexican friend, the Butcher.

Having watched the men fire their sidearms, Cypher asked for his target to be moved back to 50 yards so that it was a fair contest! The audacity of request drew a few snickers from the crowd, nonetheless, Joe and Stewart stepped off the distance, placing the target as requested. While the pair worked to secure the new target, Cypher began taking bets from any of the others who wanted in on the action. By the time the target was set, the Russian had

$5,000 worth of bets taken, including $250 of Napier's own.

Taking a Russian made MP-443 Grach from his shoulder holster Cypher calmly extended his right arm and methodically fired 10 rounds from the 18 round magazine. While the target was being retrieved and replaced with a new one, he released the magazine from the weapon and began to feed more 9 mm rounds into it. When Joe brought the target in for all to inspect, Cypher's 10 bullets had not only all hit the target but were all within a three-inch circle. As the men all gawked at the target, Cypher slammed the magazine back into the weapon, let the slide slam forward and brought the gun to shoulder level with his left hand, and emptied the magazine in less than 3 seconds. The men stared as he calmly ejected the magazine, slammed home another from his belt, and began to walk downrange. Quickly the group joined him. It was impossible to tell how many of the rounds had actually hit the target, but all the men thought it was sufficient that the entire center of the target was gone. While the group stared in wonder, Cypher placed his left hand back into his hip pocket, removing a small vile which he removed the cap on before raising it to his nose, taking a bump into each nostril before putting it away.

"Not here," Napier had chastised him.

"Don't worry, friend, it's just to take the edge off." The man had replied before adding, "If you gentleman would be so kind as to bring me my cash to my bunk, I will unpack."

Watching the man walk away, Napier said, "Stewart, you ready. The rest of you finish cleaning out the barn. I want it ready for mock-up by the time we get back."

*****

September 12, 6:50 pm

Scouting the place had proven easy, and Napier was happy that the details provided in the plan were relatively accurate to what he and Stewart had found. Driving to the restaurant, the pair took the time to circle the area a few times from different directions using different streets to familiarize themselves with the city. Having never been to Kansas City before Napier was surprised the city was built upon rolling hills. He had always assumed the area was flat.

True to the plan, the two-story restaurant sat atop one of the prominent hills. Seeing it for himself, Napier was even more positive that Joe and the twins could control the battlefield from the structure's second floor. The trio would have relatively good fields of fire, though the man covering the front of the building would be slightly disadvantaged because of the taller three and four-story structures across the street. Those buildings would be prime positions for the FBI and City to place their own snipers once organized. Nonetheless, Napier had an idea for helping the man defend the front as well.

Satisfied with their view of the area, they made their way into the parking garage's lower level, entering from Eighth street. Parking the car they had borrowed from the Deen's, the two walked by the HVAC systems and saw the gate leading to the tunnel was where it was supposed to be. They also noted a security camera, but it appeared to be directed more at the floor of the parking garage than the gate. Napier was sure that the three men entering the tunnel could park and walk to the tunnel's entrance by hugging the garage's exterior wall and escape detection by the camera. The lock and chain both looked substantial, but nothing that would prevent the team's entry.

Making their way inside the restaurant, they were seated in a booth along the western wall. Ordering food and drinks, the two lingered over them. All the while, they were counting tables, chairs, guesstimating distances, checking on the number of staff, and finding possible weak spots that would need to be addressed for the betterment of the plan overall. After finishing their food, the two ventured upstairs after ordering another round of beers. Upstairs, the two played a game of darts, again as an excuse to view the space.

As his background indicated, Stewart was incredibly skilled at the work, making several sensible suggestions that would require minor tweaks to the plan to ensure the mission's overall success.

While they were playing darts and nursing their beers, Napier asked him, "So how does one go from being a Marine to this?"

"A man's got to make a living."

"Without a doubt. But not to pry or anything, from what I was told you left the service after 15 years. Hell man another five, and you would have retired."

"You really want to know why I left the Corp?"

"Call me curious. It was always my experience that anyone who got past the second enlistment was riding it out to at least 20."

"You were military?" Stewart asked dubiously.

"Army," Napier replied simply.

"Yeah, what did you do in the Army?" the big man asked the way combat veterans do; a subtle dig that there is an incredible difference between the Army of the infantryman and the Army of a dental assistant.

"I was a combat medic with the Second Ranger Bat outta Ft Lewis."

"You see combat?"

"Deployed to Afghanistan in 02 and again to Iraq a year later."

The big man took a minute to consider his response and then pursed his lips and nodded, apparently satisfied with the answer. "Yeah I was in Iraq in 0-3 for the initial push, helping to take the airfield and then went back in 0-5. While we were there, my platoon was sent on a fucking diplomatic mission to escort some fucking oil executives for some political bullshit. While we're there, this Iraqi asshole in a suit tells this new young L-T that they wanted to deviate from the designated route of travel to show the executives the reestablished oil fields that were being rebuilt after Saddam lit those motherfuckers up at the invasion. I'm the platoon sergeant, and I told the guy no, but he keeps after the L-T who hadn't even been in the country very long and the kid tells him we would do it. I tell the L-T he can't do that bullshit, but the little bastard pulled rank on me. So here we go off the protected route, in four semi-armored Humvees with two goddamn unarmored Land Rovers between us. We ain't off the course a mile when shit hits the fan. Two RPGs hit the lead truck with the L-T in it. While the rest of us start taking small arms fire from all around. I call in a bird, but I can't get the dumbass on the other side to understand we are off the designated route before the radio goes out. For the next 20 minutes, it's bad. We are fucking pinned down taking fire, the damn Land Rovers are shot to shit, and our Humvees aren't much better. Finally, an airship gets in and opens up with those 20mm guns, and the baddies go running. Afterward of the twenty men in the platoon, six were dead, including the L-T. Eight others were wounded, and all the oil guys were dead. I am sure you know shit rolls downhill and as the highest-ranking member left, that shit fell to me. When the company commander decided to read me the riot act about it, it pissed me off, and I beat him within an inch of his life before they pulled me off of him. I spent three months in the brig and was unceremoniously kicked to the curb. Now I do this, but I don't follow blindly, ask me to do some dumb shit, and I will put a bullet in you myself."

At least the man's threats weren't subtle.

After paying the bill, the two returned to their car and left the garage. Before leaving town, the took the time to drive up Eighth street to Main and then Main to Delaware Street. It wasn't lost on Napier that both Main and Delaware Streets still featured the trolley car system's exposed rails in the street. Parking in a large parking lot at the corner of Seventh and Delaware, the two men crossed the road to get under the overpass. It took a bit of searching since the instructions hadn't been clear on what they were looking for, but they found their point of exit: a manhole cover that was placed between two of the enormous concrete columns that helped to hold the colossal bridge that allowed cars to cross over I-35.

Satisfied, they returned to their car, got onto I-35 north, and made their way back to the barn.

Maybe it was the beer or the fact that he had already started talking, on the return trip Stewart continued unprompted, "In the Brig, I had a cellmate who was a Seal. Real crazy sumbitch. Anyway, he gives me this number and tells me that when I get out to call the number if I want to put my skills to work. I been hooked up with Winter ever since."

*****

September 12, 8:45 pm

Back at the barn, Napier was pleased to see that the men had finished cleaning it out as he had ordered. He would not tolerate men who didn't do as he told them. Nonetheless curious, Napier asked Fish for his opinion on how well the team had all worked together in his absence. Fish, who was short and so skinny that it appeared the wind would blow him over, had long bleach blonde hair, albeit with his roots showing he resembled a dirty Q-tip. His physical appearance belied how incredibly intelligent the man was. Still, having worked with the man previously, Napier was quite aware of the man's intellect and generally trusted his opinion or trusted it as much as anyone on the team.

Fish told him that once he and Stewart had left, the team went right to work cleaning the barn. He reported that each man did their fair share of the work, and it went pretty smoothly overall, minus one minor quarrel between the Russian and the twins who had tried to renege on the bet they'd made with the man. That, however, had been quickly defused when the rest of the team called the pair out, and they begrudgingly paid the man.

Happy that the team had been able to work together, he then inquired how they had managed to move the motor. At the mere mention of the motor, Fish began to laugh uncontrollably. After managing to collect himself, he told how twins had tried to move the piece of old rusted steel themselves. Try as they might, the two had been unable to budge the hunk of heavy metal. Unable to do anything with it alone, the two recruited the help of Joe and Butcher to assist them. The four men combined only managed to move it a couple of feet before they were utterly exhausted. So frustrated with it, they had even asked Fish if he could blast the thing in half. Apparently, having watched the group struggle for long enough, the big Englishman Winter had hired, Turley stepped in. Turley, who was bigger than even Stewart, stood at least 6'4" and weighed an easy 275 lbs though there wasn't any fat on the man, just massive arms, chest, shoulders, back and thighs. He had a prominent forehead, which stopped at his very short wiry hairline, sunken eye sockets, a large fat nose that had obviously been broken multiple times, and a square jaw that appeared acne scared. A pretty man he was not. Combined with his sheer size, the man was apparently freakishly strong as Fish continued. "He walked over to the barn wall and selected two chains from amongst odds and ends hung there. Securing the chains around the machine, the then squatted and wrapped the chains around his humungous forearms. Then he simply stood up straight, lifting the motor from the ground and walked it outside without seemingly any more effort than it would take you or me to take out the trash!"

Fish said he had later measured the distance and discovered the brute had carried it nearly 48 feet.

"How did the twins take getting shown up?" Napier asked him, knowing how fickle and petty the two brothers could be.

"Not bad. I mean I don't think the Englishman has said more than four words since he's been here honestly. Since he hasn't really rubbed their noses in it, they've left it alone."

"Good. We don't need any fighting amongst ourselves."

*****

September 13, 7:00 am

The next morning, the team was ready to build their rudimentary mock-up using not only the intel that Napier and Stewart had gathered the previous evening but also with the added information provided by the Russian and Fish. The two men had apparently pulled an all-nighter fueled by energy drinks and cocaine, using their computer to access the city files for the building, the block, and the surrounding area. The data provided them more exact dimensions of the rooms inside the building and ranges for prominent landmarks that would allow the twins and Joe to work more effectively from their nest. While the two men completed their quest, the Russian and Fish had established a kinship of sorts. The two had discovered that not only were they easily the smartest men on the team, just ask, and they would tell you, but other mutual interests as well. In addition to their mutual appreciation of the powder, they were both into computers, the latest technological marvels, and enjoyed 3-dimensional chess.

Individually each man had proven to be an asshole, which Napier was already well aware of regarding Fish. But now that morning had come, and the two were coming down from their high and beginning to tire, they were even more pricklish. Since the construction began, the two men had done nothing but alienate or anger the rest of the team individually as both Fish and Cypher had a habit of talking down to the other team members, openly belittling them. But when joined together, the pair was totally insufferable, so much so that even Napier pondered putting a bullet in their heads himself just to rid himself of the aggravation. He knew under different circumstances he probably would have, but the two men were too useful to waste. Yet!

After a morning of brutal work in which Napier pushed the team unmercifully, they finished recreating the barroom. The team was now ready to begin running through the plan and different scenarios. At least Napier knew as they trained throughout the day Fish and Cypher would remain separated from one another because Fish's assignment would primarily be in the tunnel he wouldn't be required for their run-throughs. Though he insisted that he be allowed to check the team's work regarding how they set the mocked up explosives during each run-through, claiming it was imperative to the mission that it was done precisely to his specifications.

Napier wasn't sure about all that, but it was easier to agree to allow the man to check their work than to argue with him.

Unfortunately, yet not unexpected, the two nerds as the team had dubbed them were not the only irritants in the group. The twins, too, were a constant annoyance to everyone, always telling everyone how they could have done this or that better than the man who had done it. In addition to their claims of being the best shooters amongst the group, they also claimed that they were the best carpenters and coffee makers. The best looking and the best, well anything. Their constant need to promote their superiority to the others was as bad if not worse than Fish and Cypher's annoyances. The brothers had also managed to piss off every man in the room. It got so bad towards the end of the morning Napier thought he was going to have to pull his gun to separate them from Turley. The man looked poised to battle both men at the same time, proving he was as fearless as Winter had claimed but also brought into question the man's commonsense. But similar to Fish, Napier was equally satisfied that the twins would be mostly separated from the group along with Joe, as they practiced the scenarios since they would be isolated in observation point/sniper tower on the second floor during the majority of the operation.

Mockup complete, Napier went to the house and told the Deen's they would be ready for lunch in approximately an hour. Meals for the team had been part of their agreement as he did not want the team to be seen around St. Joeseph or the surrounding area even so far north of the city. As they awaited lunch, they ran through the basic mechanics of the raid twice. In the exercises, the men then started to show their worth, quickly orienting to one another and showing the ability to move as a team, not perfect but passable.

For lunch, the Deens had brought out hotdogs and chips. Hungry, most of the team, began to attack the fare with a vengeance. Except for Cypher, who claimed, "I don't eat that processed stuff."

The statement brought a snicker from the man called Joshua. Joshua, Napier observed, was one of those people who a person could just look at and tell that the picnic basket was shy a sandwich or two. He had a pale hatchet-like face with a thin nose crooked from having been broken and not reset properly, which somehow emphasized that his dull green eyes were set too far apart. His jawline was covered in a wispy brown beard that matched the bushy eyebrows and male-patterned bald head that he wore long like James Taylor. To top it off, he talked to himself. The man's every stream of thought played out like a second grader reading a book who hadn't yet figured out you could read without moving your mouth. And because of prominent pair of gapped buck teeth, he naturally whistled as he spoke.

"What's so funny?" Cypher demanded of the man.

"You," Joshua responded point-blank.

"Why is that comrade?" the Russian said, losing control of his perfectly controlled English.

"You snort the drugs that were processed who knows where and cut with who knows what, but you are afraid of what they may have put in hotdogs." Joshua whistled.

His observation brought a snicker from the entire group. Napier thought that the Russian was on the verge of responding when Deen interrupted, apparently in an effort to defuse the situation. "Did y'all hear about how my brother was killed by the US Marshals out here?"

When the team declined knowing about it, Deen told the story once more of surviving the raid by a US Marshal swat team. He methodically told them how a sniper called Ghost had killed his brother John while John had valiantly tried to fight his way out. The story produced the desired effect, relieving the tension in the air. But it had particularly caught the attention of Joe, who began asking Deen all sorts so questions about the event and the sniper. Seemingly with every response, Joe got more and more excited by the story. After the story and explanations, Joe asked if Deen would be willing to show him where the sniper had been and where his brother John's body had been. The man agreed to show him later that evening after dinner.

"What's the deal?" Abel had asked him after Deen had left.

"Do y'all not know who he was talking about?" Joe asked the group.

"You mean his brother?" Cain asked. "I never met him."

"No, not his brother. The sniper. Do y'all know who the sniper was?"

In unison, the men shook their heads no. In disbelief, Joe explained excitedly. "Jack' Ghost' Kirby is damn near a legend in the world of snipers. They say the man could walk across a floor covered in bubble wrap without making a noise to get into position for a shot. And once in position, he doesn't miss. Like ever!"

"How do you know all this," Cain asked looking at the man like he had lost his mind.

"I always wanted to be a sniper. But when I tried to get in the Army and Marines they both said I wasn't mentally fit for duty because of my juvenile record. I mean damn who knew they looked at that shit ya know?"

"What did you do as a juvenile?" Fish asked.

"Nothing much, I snuck out of my house a few times and got caught after I shot a bunch of sheep and a couple dogs of some farmer."

"That kept you out of the service?" Stewart asked, clearly not believing the man's explanation.

"Well not the shooting so much as the getting caught painting doors with the blood and hanging the sheep's caucuses on some porches around town."

"Why the fuck would you paint doors with blood and hang sheep around town." the ever quiet Turley chimed in.

"I was marking the houses of the people to be saved."

"Saved from what?" Napier asked, now truly curious.

"From me! The voices in my head gave me a list of people I needed to kill, but I didn't want to kill anyone I wasn't supposed to. I remembered the Bible story of Passover, where

God told the saved people to mark their porches with lambs blood so the angel of death would pass them over. Well I decided that to save the people who weren't on the list, I would use the sheep's blood to paint their houses' doors. But once it got dark, I couldn't see the blood unless they left their porch lights on. So I started hanging the sheep instead. I could see them alright, even in the dark. The cops got me hanging the last sheep before I was going to go up on the ridge and start shooting. They took my rifle, 3,000 rounds of ammunition, and sent me away to the hospital for five years. When I got out, I tried to join up, but they wouldn't take me. Said they couldn't take anyone on the meds I was on."

"Are you on medications now?" Cypher asked before anyone else could.

"No way, man! The meds make me feel funny, and I can't hear the voices with them. The voices are my friend, ya know."

Jesus Christ, Napier, thought having heard the story. But it didn't seem to bother the twins any and the three spent the remainder of the day in the loft, sharing stories about the great shots they had made and planning to recreate the Ghost shot to prove they were all just as good as some government sniper.

*****

September 13 9:45 pm

By the time the men had finished drilling that night, they were tired of running through scenarios and tired of one another. Though he had planned to run one more set, Napier had decided to call it a day when he had been forced to pull his gun to prevent Turley from killing Fish.

After their last walk through which had been sloppy on several fronts, Fish had called the man stupid for having left a lead off the Play-Doh they were using to simulate the Semtex explosives they would be using. Not appreciating the little man's critique, the big man quick as a cat had him around the throat with his big left hand pinned against the wall holding him at shoulder level as if he were no more than a minor inconvenience. As the little man's blue eyes began to bulge from his head, Napier pulled his gun, telling the big man to let him go. Releasing his grip, Turley allowed Fish to fall to the floor in a heap where he gasped for breath. The big man walked away without so much as a backward glance.

Once recovered, Fish had demanded that Turley be replaced by another member of the team. Unfortunately for Fish, the big man was the obvious choice to handle the explosives. Unlike the others, the large Brit had previous experience working with the stuff, could read a schematic, and was tall enough to place the charges high along the targeted walls as intended without a ladder, so the two men would simply be forced to work out their differences.

Nonetheless, Napier had called their work for the day complete. He even had Deen bring in a few beer cases with dinner, hoping a few drinks would allow the men to relax. The beers failed to have the desired effect. The twins, out to prove they were also the best drinkers, were soon drunk and arguing with the other men and making enough noise to wake the dead. They kept on late into the evening when finally, Turley had enough. "Be quiet so I can sleep you bloody fools." the quiet man barked.

"Or what? You think you can make us big man?" Cain said tauntingly.

"He don't look so tough," Able added.

Any other time Napier himself would have liked to have seen the trio fight and settle their differences. One big man against the two smaller twins in stature had perfected the art of tandem fighting years ago and knew the two were even dangerous drunk.

Just as Napier was getting ready to intervene, Cypher asked, "Have either of you two nitwits ever heard of London's underground bare-knuckle boxing?"

"I have," Stewart said before either brother could answer. "It's fucking brutal. Two men without any padding or gloves on their hands meet in some makeshift ring and toe the line in the ring's center while everyone takes bets. When the referee gives the signal, the two men start to fight. The rounds last as long as it takes for one man to knock or throw the other man to the ground, and the match lasts until a man is knocked out or refuses to get up."

"Yeah, so what?" Cain said.

Cypher continued, "Our comrade Turley here is a legend in da sport. I recognized him as soon as I arrived. Won a few pounds on da man myself before he killed some bloke by striking him that he broke da guy's jaw and drove it through his skull into his brain."

Napier noticed again that when Cypher got excited, his native accent would return.

The Russian continued, "And before either of yous gets any ideas, I should probably tell you I went to a match one night where dey had paired up our comrade here against two big tough lads from Dublin. He had to fight the two at da same time after people began to refuse to get in the ring with Turley or bet against him. Both of the men were tough, experienced fighters who had trained together special for da match. The fight lasted less dan 2 minutes. The two boys started out ok, flanking Turley here and playing a game of cat and mouse. One vood feint while de other would sneak a punch or two in. Da two had even cut our man here on the forehead above the right eye, causing him to bleed into his eyes. The strategy looked sound and da people who had money on dat side momentarily started to feel good about der bets. Until..." Cypher snapped his fingers.

"Until what?" Able asked, now thoroughly captivated by the story.

"Dey tried the same trick one time too many. Da man on Turley's right feinted in, and Turley simply ignored him and caught the man on the left coming in with that big right hand of his square on the chin. Technically the referee should have ended the round there. But before he could step in Turley here whipped back around with his elbow, catching de other man in the temple, ending his night as well."

The twins looked again to the big man, who smiled and shrugged before asking, "Can I go to sleep now?"

The twins agreed that allowing the man his sleep was the wise course of action.

CHAPTER 7

September 18, 3:15 pm

Veteran FBI Agents, Seth Trenton and Kevin Moore were sitting in the office of their new boss Special Agent Jon Pearson at the Kansas City Missouri FBI Field Office Complex at the corner of 13th and Summit Streets, near downtown. The pair had just wrapped up their latest investigation into a human trafficking ring, from which they and the US Attorney's office had just gotten pleas from all those involved. They now sat quietly in front of their new boss, awaiting a new assignment, as Special Agent Pearson hurriedly typed on his computer. Trenton and Moore had worked together for nearly three years and had developed easy chemistry together to sit together comfortably in the silent room without feeling the need to fill the time and space with idle chit chat. Clearly, their silence made Pearson uncomfortable, however, who had tried and failed a couple of times to start chit chat with the duo since their arrival.

Trenton was a 38-year-old white male of medium stature with short-cropped sandy brown hair and blue-green eyes who looked so much like Steve McQueen the guys in the office had "Bullitt" embroidered on the back of his rec league softball jersey. Trenton had been with the Agency for 12 years and in the Kansas City office for the last 8. He was a walking encyclopedia for Bureau procedure and regulations for investigations, who had applied to be an Agent while in his last year at Drake Law School. He had a wife and two kids at home, who took up all his free time with their sporting events, scouting trips, and other extracurricular activities.

Moore was a 41-year-old black male of similar stature with a shaved head and neatly maintain goatee that was prematurely grey. A former police officer in Dallas, Texas, he had been an Agent for nearly a decade. He had been transferred to Kansas City three years prior. He was streetwise and used the knowledge he learned patrolling the streets for the job. A proud lifelong bachelor, he spent his off-time watching old movies and playing trivia with a team of other agents at various bars and charity events in the metro area.

Despite their differences, the two made a very capable team, Pearson knew having reviewed his predecessor's performance evaluations of all the Agents and partnerships under his command. Having just moved to Kansas City from the Knoxville Tennessee office less than a month before taking the promotion, he was still getting comfortable in the new role and getting to know the Agents under him. As a rule, he had no issues when assigning work and cases to his agents. Still, he also felt it was generally best to assign cases and details commensurate with an Agent's experiences and abilities. It was efficient, helped morale, and helped Agents grow. His respect for the two agents in front of him made the assignment he was about to give them a difficult task.

"Gentleman, I am not going to bullshit you. What I am about to ask you to do is going to seem like a task that is below your considerable talents as Agents and investigators. And quite honestly, it is. Unfortunately, it has to be done, and you two are the only agents available."

"Just get to it, boss, there's no need for apologies," Trenton said.

"Yeah, sir, you order, we follow." Moore added sincerely.

"Ok. Thank you both. As you are both certainly aware, we played a role in the indictment of Richard Primovero. Now the US Attorney is not feeling as strongly about the case as they were a couple weeks ago, since the sudden disappearance of Samuel Caynor, who they had been working through the parameters of a deal with for the last few months. Caynor was going to be the lynchpin to their case. Now I think it is safe to assume that Mr. Caynor is no longer with us."

"So you want us to investigate the disappearance of Mr. Caynor," interrupted Trenton.

"Nah, man, he wouldn't have apologized beforehand if that were the case," Moore corrected.

"I'm afraid Agent Moore is correct. What I need from you is far less exciting. Tomorrow morning at 11 am, Joseph Cabrini, who used to work for Richard Primovero in a similar capacity as Mr. Caynor, is set to be released from Leavenworth Penitentiary. I need the two of you to be there when he is released. I want you to follow him and watch him. If he so much as litters or does anything else that can be considered a parole violation, I want him arrested. Then we are going to lean on him and see if he retains any useful information regarding his former boss that the US Attorney's office can use to put him away."

"So, you want us to harass a felon?" Moore asked rhetorically.

"No, he wants us to catch the US Attorney's Hail Mary," said Trenton.

"I would say you are both correct in your summations," Pearce concluded.

CHAPTER 8

September 18, 7:30 pm

Logan was two hours east of Albuquerque traveling home, having reached a milestone of sorts. Having just killed his twenty-fifth man since becoming a contract killer 6 years prior. Despite being confident he had made a clean getaway, he reviewed every detail of thee just completed the mission as he drove. Always a perfectionist, he critiqued his own performance, identifying several items that could have been performed better, determined not to repeat any mistakes on future assignments.

The contract had been for a man named Salvador Galvan. Ironically, the man had been marked for death because he made the same mistake as many of those he had ordered retribution against, thinking he was too big, too untouchable. Everyone has a master for whom they serve, and Mr. Galvan acted against his boss's express direction when he ordered the execution of a local activist named Maggie Ortega, who had garnered some recognition leading a public crusade against Galvan's businesses. Because of Ortega's death, a $250,000 price had been placed on Galvan's head. A contract Logan had readily accepted.

As with all contracts in every business, his business contracts often had particular requirements to be filled to garner full payment. Galvan's deal was no different as it included a unique stipulation, the solicitor had explicitly requested that Galvan be injected with Saxitoxin. The same toxin has been used to kill Ortega. Having never heard of the poison before, Logan did a quick internet search and discovered Saxitoxin causes paralysis and death by respiratory failure. The substance it turned out was even somewhat infamous as the CIA had given it to a pilot named Francis Gary Powers, who was flying spy missions over the Soviet Union in 1960. Powers had been given the poison with instructions to inject himself before allowing himself to be captured to ensure any secrets were taken to the grave. However, when the plane was shot down by the Soviets, Powers refused to inject himself. The poison was then discovered by his capturers. He was convicted of espionage by a Soviet court and subsequently served in a labor camp for nearly two years before being released as part of a prisoner exchange. Upon returning home, he was heavily criticized for not using the poison but served in the CIA for another eight years working as a test pilot. In a sad twist, having survived being shot down over a hostile land and years of piloting experimental aircraft, Powers died when the helicopter he was piloting crashed in 1977. He was working for a news station covering wildfires in California.

The poison stockpiles were supposed to have been destroyed. Regardless, Logan had been provided the location where two auto-injectors of the poison would be left to pick up upon his arrival in Albuquerque. While he had little experience with injectables, he knew the process was simple enough; get close to the target stab the needle into a fleshy portion of the body and press the plunger. The biggest challenge was finding a way to get close.

It had taken him over a week of study and some trial and error. Still, Logan had finally managed to get close enough to his target by impersonating a caterer at an event Galvan was hosting. Having cut his hair and shaved his beard, he acquired a catering uniform to fit in with the service staff. Helping the caterer's during their set up, he finally caught the opportunity he was looking for when he was asked to take a coffee service to Galvan and his special guests in a conference room down the hall from the main banquet room.

Pushing the cart down the hall towards the only open door near the end of the hall to the left, Logan overheard the men in the room discussing security for the night's festivities. He couldn't help but smile at the irony. Pausing in the doorway, he saw three middle-aged men sitting at a conference table with stacks of papers and open laptops in front of them. A much younger man sat nearer the door, looking bored without a computer or paper before him.

Standing at the table's head was Galvan, who, upon seeing Logan with his coffee cart, said, "Oh great. Gentlemen, why don't we take a break and let this young man get set up."

At his suggestion, the other four men rose from their chairs and exited without giving Logan a second look. Too good to look the servers in the eye, Logan thought thankfully. Entering the room fully, Logan double-checked the four corners of the room to see if anyone else could have been lurking.

Misinterpreting his look Galvan pointed to the corner near the window saying, "Please put it in the corner out of the way. And if you would bring me a cup with cream and sugar that would be wonderful."

Logan was somewhat taken back by the man's manners though he supposed many people would say he was well mannered too. Following Galvan's directions, Logan pushed the cart across the room, parking it in the corner near the window, behind Galvan. In the glass reflection, he saw that Galvan had sat down, returning his attention to his laptop. Taking the opportunity, Logan pulled the auto-injector from his pocket and rotated the cap a half turn releasing the needle lock. He laid the now active apparatus on top of a linen napkin. Choosing a cup, Logan turned it over, sitting it on a saucer before filling it with coffee, creamer, and sugar. Using a silver spoon, he stirred the drink. He carefully picked up the cup and saucer with his right hand while he palmed the poison pin and napkin with his left.

Walking carefully across the space, ensuring he didn't spill any of the hot coffee, he stepped to the man's right, who barely gave him a second glance. Leaning forward, Logan sat the coffee on the table with his right hand and began sliding it towards Galvan, who instinctually reached to meet the cup halfway. As Galvan reached forward, Logan's left hand shot out to meet him, the head of the auto-injector catching him squarely in his long tan neck. Upon contact, Logan heard the audible click of the spring injecting the needle forward, which pierced the skin sending the poison directly into the man's bloodstream via the jugular vein.

Galvan quickly jumped back, his hands moving to his neck, spilling the coffee all over the table and Logan's pants. Ignoring the burning he felt on his leg, Logan clamped his right hand under the man's jaw, forcing it up so that he couldn't scream out while holding the injector steady to ensure all the poison entered the man's system. Holding the man still, Logan looked his vicitm directly in the eyes. He expected to see surprise, fear, or even questions in their depths, but there was only unabashed hatred. In less than ten seconds, Logan felt Galvan go completely limp, while his eyes softened. His hate leaving with his soul, Logan told himself.

Letting go of Galvan's jaw Logan laid the man back into the chair, his head staring at the ceiling, the auto-injector still lodged fully into his neck. Turning the chair towards the window, Logan heard someone approaching from the hallway. Calmly straightening, Logan stepped back to the corner opposite the coffee cart near the door. Placing his hand in his pocket, gripping the handle to the razor-sharp, Benchmade knife, ready.

Galvan's bodyguard entered the room calling Galvan's name as he entered. To his credit, the man immediately sensed danger and instinctually began to turn towards the corner where Logan stood, reaching for the weapon in his shoulder holster. Before he could get to his gun, Logan's hand was out with the knife sweeping forward from his hip. As his hand approached parallel with the floor, he let go. The knife flew true, covering the short distance between the two men in less than a blink of an eye, the four and a half-inch blade hitting the man squarely, slightly left of center in the upper abdomen just below the ribs, burying itself to the hilt. Not confident the knife was sufficient to get the job done, Logan followed the blade's path towards the man. Grabbing the man under the chin with his right hand Logan bodily forced his head back and slammed his body onto the table. Holding the man flat against the table,

Logan grabbed the knife handle with his free left hand, pulling it down and away, opening the man's belly and allowing the blood from the obviously pierced aorta to gush from the body freely.

Moving quickly, Logan placed the knife back inside its sheath in his pocket and stuck his head out the door, looking both ways down the hall: clear. Locking the door handle, he pulled it shut behind him and turned left away from the main banquet room and walked away.

Though he had made it away cleanly, he chastised himself for several mistakes he felt he had made on the job since he had gotten in the car. He knew there was no such thing as a perfect job, and ultimately he was graded as pass-fail only and that his solicitor would consider the job a success ensuring he would get his fee. Nonetheless, he was incensed that he had to kill the bodyguard who wasn't part of the contract even though Logan knew the man was likely the man who had actually killed Ortega, and most certainly had killed others at Galvan's direction. It was still unnecessary, and only the second time he had ever had to kill someone other than the target while on an assignment, the first being a man who had tried to kill him to get out of paying the contract, and it rankled him.

Preparing to exit I-40 to get on US 54 to return home, his phone rang. Taking his eye off the road momentarily, he saw that it was Paige calling. Paige was his friend, handler, and confidant. He had worked with her since coming into the business 6 years prior. The arrnagement had been profitable for them both.. He knew the reason for her call, and he didn't particularly want to have the conversation at this time, but he knew it was necessary.

"Hello."

"Is it done?" Paige asked.

"It is. I just finished the job this evening, and now I'm on my way back home," he answered.

"I assume there were no complications?" she continued.

"Nothing for you to worry about. You know me better than that."

"I do, but I have to ask," she said. "I'll make sure your fee is sent to your account."

"I appreciate it," he stated dryly, hoping to end the conversation.

"Before I let you go, I wanted to give you a heads up to be careful when you get home. I don't know anything specific, but the grapevine is abuzz that Winter and Napier are working together in K-C. Apparently, they have recruited a bunch of mercenaries for something big. No one knows what it is, but it will be bloody judging by the names involved."

"You don't have to worry about me. The only thing I am going to do is go home and sleep. Tomorrow Michele and I will go have lunch, and then I am going home to sleep some more."

"Alright, you guys have fun, but keep your eyes open."

"I always do."

"Okay, hun. Drive safe and let me know when you are ready to work again."

"Sure thing. I'll talk to ya later." Ending the call, he settled back into the seat. Hitting play on the rental car's CD player, he resumed listening to the audiobook version of a graphic novel he had really wanted to read but had never found the time, ready to get lost in the rest of the storyline and the 10 hours drive ahead.

Unfortunately, as much as he tried, he could not focus on the story emanating from the speakers. Instead, the mention of his lunch plans with Michele the following day triggered an avalanche of thoughts and emotions he had been avoiding since he had left home nearly 10 days prior.

As was his standard operating procedure after Logan had accepted the contract on Galvan, he began inquiring with comic book dealers and other contacts he had to see if there were any rare comics available in the Albuquerque area that he could acquire to display and sell in his own comic book store. Owning and operating his comic book store was his true passion in life, and as it turned out was the perfect cover for his other work as a hitman. The comic store gave him an excuse to travel all over the country regularly looking to add rare inventory to his store and an easy way to launder the money he made from the jobs as he needed it. His search of the Albuquerque area just happened to reveal several books he was interested in, including a semi-rare and highly collectible book from 1990. The book was the debut for four characters that were now well into their second decade as a cultural phenomenon. Their distinctive faces had been featured in many movies and television shows and had all kinds of merchandise available. The quartet was featured on everything from their own line of action figures, t-shirts, board games, video games and even vitamin gummies. But what set this first issue apart, making it so collectible, was that these well-known characters used guns in the issue, instead of using their own individual trademarked ninja weapons. Since the issues release their twin Katana, Bo, Sai, and Nunchaku had become as synonymous with the characters are as much as their individual personalities.

And since he was going to be in the area anyway, Logan decided to use the opportunity to knock out another of his bucket list items. An avid rock climber, a hobby he had picked up in Afghanistan, he had always wanted to visit The Land of Enchantment to climb, having heard repeatedly from his fellow climbers how great the climbing was there. Logan hurriedly did some research online, looking for guides and locations near Albuquerque. After calling a handful of guides unsuccessfully, he finally found a guide who could take him on a climbing tour on short notice. However, Logan had to be willing to join another group of climbers whose 3-day climbing tour of the Sandia Mountains, the chain of mountains that bordered Albuquerque, was scheduled to begin in two days. Happy that the timing would work out, Logan quickly agreed and sent the man a non-refundable deposit to ensure his spot in the group.

Excited about the prospects of getting his hands on an issue that had eluded him for years and getting to climb while he was at it, Logan sent a text to Michele, the woman with whom Logan shared as much of his life with as he could, thinking she would be happy for him. It proved to be a gross miscalculation. He knew she had been less than completely satisfied with the terms of their relationship for the last year, dropping hints consistently that she was ready to advance the relationship to the next level, be it marriage or cohabitation. To protect her from his other life's reality, he had evaded her suggestions, deftly changing the subject, or simply ignoring it when she brought it up. No sooner had he hit send, then his phone rang: Michele.

"Hey babe," he answered, thinking she'd be happy for him.

"What the hell do you mean you're going to New Mexico to climb and get some comic book? And what am I supposed to do while you're gone? Do you think I am just going to sit around and wait for you?" She exploded.

"Wait. What? It's business. I've been looking for that book for the last 5 years. I finally got a line on a good one. I'm going to go see it and hopefully buy it." Logan tried to explain.

"Hopefully? You mean you don't even know that you're getting it? But you already have that climbing trip booked, don't ya?" she yelled at him louder.

Still unsure why she was upset he said defensively, "Yeah, I mean, I was going out anyway. Why wouldn't I?"

"Why wouldn't you is right." She said sarcastically. "I don't know what's worse, that you decided to take the trip without asking me or that you don't understand why it bothers me. Do you even own a calendar."

A calendar? He thought, shit, what am I forgetting? He wasn't sure, but he had the sinking sensation. Obviously, it was something significant to Michele, and he knew better than to ask what.

He was trying to think of a way to apologize, though having a hard time doing so when he didn't know what he was apologizing for when Michele added coldly, "Logan maybe when you get back you can find the time to come to my house and get your shit out of my backyard."

"Your backyard? I don't have anything in your backyard."

"Not now, but if you go to New Mexico, you're going to," she said before the phone went dead.

Logan was stunned how he had instantaneously gone from happy to completely upset. It confused him. He thought himself to be generally a very level headed guy. Hell, he was even level headed while he stared death in the face during his combat tours of Iraq and Afghanistan. But Michele could toy with his emotions like it was sporting fun for her. Never was there a person he so wanted to protect every hair on her head and yet at the same time made him ready to pull his own hair out.

The more he thought about her getting upset with him, the more angered he was by it. "Does she not understand everything I do for her?" he asked the empty room. "I've been helping her since we met."

Due to his feelings for her, Logan did everything he could to help her as much as he could with everything he could. After all, he thought, he had bought her her own pistol, though he knew he did that to get her to go to the range with him more. Logan had helped her clean up and restore her house, again acknowledging he did it as an excuse to spend as much time with her as he could. He had helped and encouraged her to finish her degree in accounting because he knew she wanted it. Then helped her again get her first job and had even offered to help finance a space as she considered starting her own shop. He thought all that, and she got mad because he needed to leave town for a business trip of his own. The more he considered it, the more upset he got.

Then as he drove to the Duke City, his phone rang just as he got through Wichita. Looking down at his phone, he saw that it was Michele. Still upset from their prior conversation, he had genuinely considered letting it go to voicemail but knew that would only make things worse.

"Hello," he answered hesitantly.

"Where are you at?" she asked pleasantly.

"I just made it through Wichita and headed towards Dodge City."

"Wow, you left early. You didn't even say goodbye."

Say goodbye? Yesterday you forbade me from going, he thought but nonetheless answered, "I didn't want to wake you."

"That's sweet, but I wish you would have. I was laying in bed kinda hoping to send you off right," Michele said in a manner that left no doubt about what she meant.

The statement left him dumbfounded as the blood in his brain considered heading south at the mere suggestion, but he recovered by responding, "Well, you could have come over and stayed last night."

"I was still mad and jealous that you were leaving last night. I'm sorry. I know you sometimes travel for the store and like to go climbing. I just wish you'd take me with you once in a while. Or at least ask me to go."

Now he felt like a complete jackass. "I am sorry, babydoll. I tell you what, next trip, I will definitely plan to take you along. Or hell, maybe we can just plan on a long weekend or something sometime soon."

"That sounds nice. But right now, I would settle for a simple afternoon out at our spot when you get back for our anniversary."

While he knew "our spot" was referring "The Peanut", a downtown Kansas City bar and grill they regularly frequented as their spot after they had eaten there on their first date before attending a concert nearby at the Sprint Center. Unfortunately, he was entirely unsure by what she meant regarding their anniversary but tried to hide the fact that he didn't know what she was talking about by saying, "That would be great. I promise when I get back, we will go get some wings and have a few drinks. Then after we can have a sleepover."

"Thank you, honey, as long as you are back by the 19th. Now drive safe, I need to finish getting ready for work myself."

The line went dead, and Logan continued to stare at his phone. I will never understand women, he concluded.

Then each day that had followed seemed a big jumble of mixed messages. Each time his phone buzzed, he was unsure what the message would read. Periodically she would text him telling him how much she missed him and how she wanted to have her way with him when he got home. Other times her texts would say that they needed to talk about things going forward. Then yet other texts asking if he remembered to clean out his fridge or if he needed anything from the store. So confused was he that he was unsure if he should be excited or apprehensive about seeing her the next day.

The clock in his bedroom read 6:54 am when Logan finally walked in. Determined to get home, Logan had just driven 12 hours from Albuquerque, New Mexico, to his home in Kansas City, Missouri, making only two stops along the way: one for gas and one to exchange the rental car for his beloved VW Golf GTI. Completely exhausted from the trip, he ensured his alarm was set before collapsing his long and lean 6 foot 3 inch, 185-pound frame into his bed after kicking off his shoes and letting his pants fall in a heap the floor, not even bothering to brush his teeth.

CHAPTER 9

September 18, 9:15 pm

The rest of the week was much of the same on the farm for Napier and his team. Their days were filled with repeated drilling in preparation for the job at the Peanut. The teams went through every plausible scenario they could imagine. While running through the scenarios, the men got better and better, each man knew not only his own job but also the job of every other man as well, each ready to cover down should one be lost.

When not drilling, however, they continued to argue and bicker amongst themselves. Napier considered it a miracle that no one had been killed in the feuding. Thus far, he had been able to keep them in line through sheer force of will and promises of imminent death, as not a man amongst them doubted his willingness to shoot them should he have too.

While all the dust-ups were an incredible annoyance, the most constant feuds were between Butcher and the last of Winter's men: Joshua. Butcher was the youngest man on the team at 23. A good looking Hispanic kid with bronze skin and wavy black hair the color of a raven's wing who had an obsession with knives.

Since their arrival to the farm, Napier had yet to see him when he wasn't sharpening, playing with, or throwing one of the many he carried.

Napier had used him on two recent jobs he had done on the twins' recommendation who had somehow befriended the man in Mexico. The kid had proven himself capable in a fight when it was just the two of them with a willingness to take orders without argument. However, amongst this group, the Butcher apparently felt the need to prove his manhood to the older men. His braggadocios stories and constant jeering of the others when a mistake was made during a run were quickly grating on everyone's nerves but in particular, the man Joshua.

Because of his odd looks, strange mannerisms, and high pitched whistling voice, Joshua had become the target of fun for the Butcher. Because of his youth or his ignorance, the Butcher didn't understand, like everyone else in the room did, that Joshua would kill him simply to amuse himself if he so desired but had managed to not do during their week-long stay.

Just as Napier thought he could finally exhale having gone to the main house, paying the Deens the last of their money and telling them the team would be leaving the following morning. Yet returning to the barn, he saw Joshua and the Butcher circling one another, each with a blade in hand. The others sat back, watching seemingly hoping they killed each other. Enraged Napier drew the pair of Kimber 1911 .45 ACPs from the speed holsters on his legs and stepped between the pair a weapon aimed at each of their faces. "We're leaving tomorrow for the job. Tomorrow night you fucking idiots can kill each other after it's over. I don't care. Hell, I will ensure the survivor gets the other's share. But anything before then and I will not only kill you both, I will hunt down anyone, and everyone you care about and fucking kill them too. You got me?"

Both men expressed their understanding of the threat and put their knives away.

"Chinga tu madre; you lucky sombeech," Butcher took one last taunt at Joshua as they separated from one another.

"I think when this is all over, you and I will meet again amigo. Then we will see who is lucky." Joshua said as he walked away, out the big barn's door into the dark.

Napier decided to follow the man to ensure he wasn't getting some other weapon and come back to take them all out. Outside, he found Joshua leaning against the side of some old piece of equipment that Napier couldn't name in the halo of light from a big light hung from a pole between the barn and the family's house. As he neared the man, he saw the man was again holding the knife from the barn and mumbling something to himself, though he couldn't make out the words.

Without even looking in his direction, Joshua said, "I think I am going to kill that Mex."

"Not until we finish the job."

"I will wait. I'm good at waiting."

"That is between you two. But I just need you to hold it together for one more day. Like I said after that, you can gut each other if you want."

"I am good at waiting," the man repeated himself.

Thinking that was about as good a response as he could expect, Napier turned to return to the barn when the man began to speak again.

"When I was twelve, my dad got me a new stepmom. She was so pretty. She used to walk around our house half-naked, teasing me. The old man he used to knock me around pretty good when she would tell him she saw me lookin. But she wanted me to look, the slut. For three years, I waited. Then on my 15th birthday, she came into my room wearing the short little robe she always wore. So I took her. She screamed at first, but she was liking it. I could tell. But the stupid bitch's screams were so loud she woke my dad. He came in and saw me on top of her, and he got mad at me. Not the dumb whore. When he came at me, I picked up this knife, the birthday present he had gotten me, and stuck it in him. Right in the middle of the belly, right below the ribs. When I pulled it out, the blood shot all over the place. I mean, it covered my walls, the bed, me, even my stepmom, who was really screaming then. The screaming didn't bother me, though, there was no one else to hear her then. So I finished with her. After all those years of teasing me, the bitch had it coming. After I finished. She curled up in a ball in the middle of the bed and said she was calling the police, so I cut her damn throat too. Stupid slut."

Napier remained still momentarily, unsure how to process what he had just heard. Satisfied the deranged killer was done talking Napier returned to the barn. He reminded himself he just needed to keep the group together for a little more than 24 hours, and then he'd be a half-million richer and could wash his hands of the entire mismatched group. Whoever was left, that is. Napier was under no illusions that people were going to die the next day. A lot of people.

CHAPTER 10

September 19, 6:00 am

Joey had been told the longest night of his life would be his first night in prison, but that was bullshit. The longest night had been last night, his last night in prison. After eight years, two months, and sixteen days spent wandering the halls and prison yards of Leavenworth, the papers he was given two weeks prior declared he would walk out of the place at noon. A free man. He spent the entire night unsleeping, thinking about the next day and the days beyond, all the possibilities.

In the days, weeks, months, and years prior to getting the parole letter, he always imagined that his last night in prison would be analogous to how he felt as a child on Christmas Eve, anticipating Christmas morning: what would Santa leave under the tree? Unfortunately, as with Santa, Christmas morning wasn't so joyful for bad little boys who received a lump of coal in their stockings. Joey certainly had reason to fear his day would be one filled with coal.

Since receiving the notice of parole, seconds had seemingly taken minutes and minutes took hours for a number of reasons as he considered what he hoped would be a long future and the roadblocks to the possible future. Lying awake, he wished he could imagine all the possibilities beyond the next day. But his reality was he couldn't allow himself to think beyond the next day and the meeting with Primovero.

The questions were endless: how would he get to the meeting? Obviously, a car, after all, it was a short drive from Leavenworth to Kansas City. He also knew that he would be a rather high priority for his former boss, so he wouldn't just want anyone to fetch him. No, it had to be one of his trio of most trusted lieutenants: Cuppari, Lessons or Wentz, who he knew through the prison information system remained in positions of influence and power within the family. He quickly eliminated Cuppari as a possibility because he would be needed to drive Primovero himself to the meeting. That left either Lessons or Wentz as the man likely tabbed for the job. He acknowledged that he had respect for both men, but of the two, though, he reminded himself Wentz scared him more. While Lessons would kill him on orders without thinking twice about it, the man was generally civil and could care less about the conversation, which would likely mean a quiet ride. Wentz, on the other hand, was completely unpredictable. Notorious for his hair-trigger temper, the man could be having a friendly conversation one minute and a minute later get mad at any perceived slight and beat a man half to death for it. Yet he would insist on filling the time on the road talking. And that was before even getting to the restaurant. It was enough to drive him crazy, to many variables to the equation to calculate a proper answer.

To complicate matters further, yesterday he had been taken from the cell he had called home for the last two years, with its familiar concrete bed topped with its thin, lumpy mattress and blankets where he had grown accustomed to sleeping. He was moved into a new strange space used for "transitioning personnel." The space was a bare 8 x 8 room with a similar yet different bed and blanket that he simply could not get comfortable on, making time slow all the more. Every second of space between the second hand's audible clicks on the room's analog clock, emphasizing it was really happening.

Despite no sleep, when the lights came on, Joey immediately got out of the bed. His body responded automatically, having been conditioned to do during his time in prison. However, his routine was interrupted when he went to step outside the holding cell for headcount only to find the door locked. A moment later, a voice came over the loudspeaker above the door, telling him that he would be taken to breakfast and then to the shower inside the hour. With nothing else to do, he began an exercise regimen of pushups, sit-ups, and air squats.

Following breakfast and a long solitary shower, he returned to the new space. Still only 9:30 am with nothing to do but watch the clock, he laid down hoping to sleep again, but it continued to elude him as he pondered what the rest of the day would bring. As much as he would have liked to have thought about the days, weeks, months, and hopefully, years ahead, he knew he couldn't overlook today and the upcoming meeting with his former boss. Would Primovero really take his new beginning away from him before it even began?

Mercifully, at 11:45 a guard name Zimmerman came to get him for out-processing. Joey followed his directions to the letter, as he always had. The guard searched him for contraband one last time, drawing it out to humiliate him, a final parting shot he was sure. Search complete, the guard led Joey down the hall to another room with a wired window and pass-through slot, above which read "Out-Processing" in hand-painted block letters. At the window, Joey filled out what felt like a mountain of paperwork. The guard at the window took his time scanning the papers to ensure they were all completed satisfactorily then gave Joey another folder containing information regarding his parole officer, felon services, and outreach groups.

After 45 minutes, he exchanged his prison garb for the clothes he had worn to his sentencing hearing. A conservative blue suit, which had been perfectly tailored to fit his body, a similarly custom made white button-down shirt, brown shoes, matching belt, a checkered silk tie, and matching pocket square. Primovero's tailor put the entire ensemble together for him, saying it made him look like an honest man, the implication being he wasn't. Pulling it from the bag, it was embarrassingly wrinkled, but he had no choice but to put it on having no access to an iron. The time working out in the prison yard over the last 8 years showed. He was 5'9" and had been a soft 168 pounds when he walked in; leaving he was a lean and toned 172. While still fitting, the shirt was now slightly tight through the chest and shoulders: his trousers, a little loose in the waist. Cinching the belt tight to keep the pants up, he put on the shoes and finally the jacket, which he was afraid to attempt to button thinking he could rip the coat which he hoped could be altered. He didn't bother with the tie, instead, putting it in his hip pocket.

Fully dressed, the guard named Zimmerman asked him if he was ready. "Yes, sir," he responded automatically. The guard pushed the buzzer alongside a large steel door and nodded into the security camera mounted above it. There was an audible click, and the guard opened the door. As the door opened, Joey took a deep breath, telling himself this was it.

Stepping through the door, two men arose from the plastic chairs that were of the same vintage as those in the visiting room that sat against the small space's wall. "Oh shit," Joey muttered to himself, recognizing both men instantly: Lessons and Wentz! He had anticipated, even expected that one of the two men were likely to have been sent to fetch him, he had not expected both. Quickly Joey tried to determine what it meant that they were both here. Complicating matters more, he remembered the two men did not really like one another, and yet here they were together. Not good, he thought, wondering what their presence meant for the rest of the day and whether he would even make the meeting with Primovero.

Standing in the doorway to freedom, Joey swallowed hard, knowing he was about to get into a car with the two men. He quickly pondered asking the guard if he could stay until the pair greeted him in unison like they were all long lost friends, "Joey!"

Forcing a smile to his lips, Joey exhaled, "Chad. Tony. It's good to see you both."

"You look good. No worse for wear," Tony said jovially.

"Thank you," he responded to the pseudo compliment, not wanting to get off on a bad foot with the man. Sensing the man was satisfied with the simple reply, Joey asked, "So where to?" intending to get the record statement, knowing the jail was recording the entire scene.

Seeing through his simple ploy, Lessons replied bluntly, "The car's outside. We'll talk there."

"Don't mind him, Joey. Chad didn't get much sleep last night and is even crankier than usual." Wentz joked sardonically.

Feeling defeated, Joey followed the two men out the heavy metal doors across the parking lot to a big black Lincoln Continental. Unlocking the doors with a key fob, Lessons climbed into the driver's seat, while Wentz took the passenger seat. Before joining them, Joey turned and took one last look at the place with its concrete and steel exterior surrounded by chain-link fencing topped with razor wire. Lifting his right arm, he raised his middle finger in an angry mock salute to the place. Arm extended, he said, "I guess you won, after all, you bastard."

CHAPTER 11

September 19, 11:00 am

Four hours after his head hit the pillow, Logan was awoken by the alarm on his cell phone. Rolling over stiffly, he fought with the screen and shut off the alarm before falling back into the bed. Laying there, Logan stared at the ceiling while his body reminded him how easy it would be to return to his slumber. However, his mind convinced him to get up, knowing he had promised to take Michele out for their anniversary; though he was still unsure what it was the anniversary of, it wasn't like they were married or anything.

Trudging across his bedroom to the bathroom, Logan started the shower to allow it to warm whilst he relieved his bladder. That finished, he put his hand in the water and found it still too cold for his liking. Continuing to wait for the water to get hot, he studied himself in the mirror. Having cut his near shoulder-length dark hair to a close-cropped buzz cut and shaven his beard during his trip to New Mexico to alter his appearance to throw off his target's security detail, Logan saw a younger version of himself staring back. The only thing missing he decided was one of his old Army uniforms, and he could have still passed for a man in his twenties. He wondered what Michele would think of the new look as she was the one who had suggested he grow his hair and beard after seeing Jason Mamoa's rendition of Aquaman.

More than just the new look, he wondered what the day would bring for them. Their fights had seemingly become more and more frequent and always seemly triggered by his inability to commit to her fully. But how could he, after all? What was he supposed to do? Tell her he lived another life aside from running a comic book store? One where he took money to kill people? She would never understand. Hell, sometimes he didn't. Regardless, he admitted he didn't want her to not be in his life.

Stepping out of the shower, he toweled off, feeling somewhat better but craving coffee. Not wanting to make a pot, he got dressed in a pair of brown canvas pants, hiking boots, and a blue long-sleeved t-shirt with a bright yellow oval and black bat on the chest, the mid-September weather allowing him to forgo a jacket or his customary hoodie. Because he kept his work life and home life as separated as possible, he never carried a weapon on his person in Kansas City beyond the Brig Slide Belt he wore everywhere. The belt contained a dagger hidden within the buckle, a fire starter striker, an LED penlight, and the heavy leather strap itself, all of which could come in handy in a pinch, yet to an uninformed eye looked like a simple belt. Picking up his cell phone, wallet, and keys, he locked the door behind him.

He looked across the street toward's Michele's house from his front stoop as was his custom only to see her car gone. He paused mid-stride momentarily confused by its absence until he remembered it was Thursday, and she said she was working in the office before meeting him at the store. He really needed that coffee he reminded himself at the blunder. Climbing in the car, he backed out of his driveway. Putting the car in drive, he passed Michele's driveway as he exited the neighborhood. With his brain currently consumed with their relationship standing, he couldn't help but recall how the two had met, nearly four years prior, when she moved in across the street from him.

Logan lived near downtown Kansas City, Missouri, in a small 1950's tract style ranch house on a quarter-acre lot in a neighborhood full of similar homes. When he bought his house the realtor told him the neighborhood was going through a transition as younger people were to buying up all the small homes. The buyers then renovated the houses, wanting to all the modern amenities, while living closer to the downtown area. In the last decade downtown Kansas City had gone through a revitalization itself with the development of the Power and Light District, a bar and entertainment district that the city had long been missing to draw people downtown. With its success, more and more young people were moving closer to the once-abandoned inner city. In the first two years living in the neighborhood, the few homes that had become available were quickly sold after hitting the market.

Then the home across the street from his went on the market after the owner, an elderly woman named Martha, had passed away. Martha's children had immediately placed the home on the market. Logan and the other neighbors had all assumed that the house would sell quickly, but Martha's children had considerably overpriced the property and had done little to clean the house or to update it to help sell it. Thus it had sat empty for almost 8 months before the for sale sign out front was finally marked sold.

Almost a week after seeing the sold sign, Logan saw a bright orange and gray moving truck parked in the driveway as he came home from the store. Driving by, he noticed a short, blonde-haired woman in a bright pink T-shirt and grey sweat pants struggling to lower the moving truck's sizable metal ramp. Parking in his own driveway, Logan walked back across the street to where the woman continued heaving at the ramp with little progress to show.

"Need a hand?" Logan asked as he approached.

When she turned around to see who had spoken, he saw that the woman had blue eyes to accompany the blonde hair. The pair of features worked in unison to brighten an already pretty face, though he could see the look of concern on her face at the offer of help from a complete stranger.

To ease her concerns, he pointed back to his home, "I'm Logan. I live in the house across the street".

Looking past him, she saw his car sitting in his drive, and her face softened as she pulled a loose strand of the medium length hair back behind her ear, seemingly satisfied with his introduction. "Sure. If you don't mind. It's jammed or something."

Walking to the rear of the truck, he grabbed the ramp and pushed it slightly forward to release the catch before picking it up and walking it out till the hooks caught the bumper's end. Once extended, he sat it down and tested his weight against it by hopping up and down on it a few times. Satisfied it wasn't going to collapse with her, he said, "There ya go. Should be good now."

The blonde-haired woman walked up to him, took off her glove, and extended her hand, "I'm Michele. Thank you so much."

Shaking her hand, Logan saw she was at least a foot shorter than he was. Up close, he also couldn't help but realize that the baggy shirt and sweat pants she was wearing did little to hide all of her very well proportioned curves. It was the combination of her pretty face and those curves that had motivated him to remain and help her carry a few boxes and pieces of furniture into her new home more than any desire to be neighborly he admitted.

After only a handful of trips back and forth between the truck and the house, a van pulled up alongside the curb with a large decal on its side that read, "Jed's Drywall Service." Out of the van climbed an overly muscled crew of 6 meatheads all in tank tops or t-shirts that were a size two small showing off their overdeveloped chests, shoulders, and arms. The man who had driven the van walked up to Michele and gave her a one-armed hug and kiss on the cheek, eyeballing Logan the entire time.

Michele introduced the man as Jed. Extending his hand, Logan introduced himself to the man. As Jed took his hand, Logan saw an evil smile form upon the man's lips as he tried to crush Logan's hand. Jed, however, quickly discovered that Logan's own hands were even stronger than his. The years training as a wrestler, in Judo and, rock climbing had developed vice-like grip strength in Logan's hands.

Neither man openly let on to their little test of strength, but both knew what it was. It was at that moment Logan decided he didn't like the man. Releasing hands, Jed told Logan that his assistance was no longer necessary. At his words, Logan glimpsed to Michele to see her looking down and avoiding his eyes. Nodding, he said to her, "If you ever need anything, I'm across the street." At his words, she looked up and smiled, triggering a foreign sensation that swept across his body. It was something he had never experienced before or since.

However, the moment was shortlived as he saw the unmistakable look of anger flash across Jed's face. Satisfied with the result of his words on both Michele and Jed, Logan walked back to his house.

Once she was settled in, the two became cordial neighbors who would wave when they saw each other in their yards and occasionally say hi to one another at the mailbox or the local grocery. The few occasions that Logan had been able to speak with her, he found she had an understated sense of humor and dry wit, which made her even more attractive.

An avid observer of the comings and goings around his home, Logan couldn't help but notice that Jed's truck, also adorned with his logo, was often parked in front of her home. The pickup truck routinely remained late into the evenings and sometimes through the night. Unlike Michele, the few times he had seen Jed outside, the man had either given him a sneer or simply ignored him. He wondered to himself what anyone could possibly like about an asshole like that, though he reasoned many of the women he knew were attracted to assholes, especially assholes with muscles.

Michele had been living across the street for a few months when Mrs. Blair, a widowed, retired school teacher, who lived next door to Michele, told Logan that she had been hearing a lot of arguing and fighting coming from Michele's house. Logan said to her that a lot of people fight, but Mrs. Blair insisted not like those two, referring to Michele and Jed. The woman confided in Logan that it sounded like it was getting physical between them. Logan suggested she call the cops next time she heard such a commotion unsure of what else to tell her.

A few days later, on a very overcast day, as he was packing his car for a job, Logan saw Michele walking to her own vehicle wearing a baseball cap and big pair of sunglasses. When he waved to her, she looked away, like she was embarrassed to have been seen. The sight affected him more than he cared to admit.

Ten days later, upon his return, Logan was purposely driving extra slow down his street. Nearing the finish of the latest Harry Bosch audiobook by Micheal Connelly, Logan hoped to finish it as he pulled into his driveway. Approaching his driveway, he saw Jed dragging

Michele from her house by the hair towards his truck, yelling at her so loudly Logan could hear the man through his closed windows and radio speakers. The scene made him go instantly cold inside. Stopping his car in the middle of the street in front of Michele's driveway, Logan blocked the man's truck.

Climbing from his car, he said through clenched teeth, "Let her go."

Though Jed was a few inches shorter than Logan, he was easily the more muscular man outweighing Logan by at least 50 pounds. The size difference made him overconfident, and he laughed before telling him, "If you know what's good for you, you'll move your car and get outta my way before you get hurt."

Stepping around his car towards the brawnier man, Logan simply replied, "I've never really known what's good for me."

It took a moment for Jed to comprehend the meaning of Logan's words. When the words penetrated his thick skull, he released his grip on Michele and threw a haymaker right at Logan's head. Seeing it coming, Logan stepped inside the punch towards the man and under hooked the man's arm with his left and pivoted. Using Jed's own momentum created by the punch, Logan carried him over and across his hip in a classic Judo hip throw. Jed hit the ground flat and hard, forcing the air from his lungs with an audible whoosh. Logan stepped back nonchalantly, looking towards Michele to see her staring wide-eyed leaning against the truck.

As he was about to ask if she was alright, Jed got up from the ground enraged and charged Logan. Allowing the bigger man to come in, Logan grabbed the charging man by the shirt with his left hand, keeping his right arm free. Once again, using the force of the man's momentum against him, Logan simply dropped to his butt, placing his right foot in the larger man's solar plexus and rolled backwards. The momentum carried the bigger man over and across, helped along by the thrust of Logan's leg. A classic Judo sacrifice throw, that Logan's former Senseis would have been proud of. Jed again crashed hard into the ground flat on his back, while Logan calmly sprung back to his feet.

Jed was slower to arise from the ground the second time but was just as visibly angry. Once on his feet, the heavily muscled man pulled a utility knife from his belt, causing Michele to gasp. Her reaction caused the same evil smile Logan had seen the day they shook hands appear again on the man's face before he lunged towards Logan intending to gut him.

Logan simply crossed his arms at the wrists in an X and attacked the wrist wielding the knife, effectively blocking it down. Using the movement's momentum, Logan swept his arms across his torso, turning the bigger man's wrist over, curling the elbow with it. Logan flipped his right hand, twisting the elbow beyond 45 degrees to convert the move into a perfect wrist lock. Using his iron grip strength, he applied pressure, causing the man to drop the knife. Tired of playing with him, Logan continued to push the joint forward. Trying to escape the pain in his arm, Jed instinctively tried to flee but went no more than two steps before crashing into his truck. However, Logan never lost control of the arm, and with the larger man pinned against the truck, he continued pushing the arm forward until it broke with a loud snap, causing Jed to scream out in pain.

Logan leaned in close and whispered, "Remember that next time you want to lay a hand on someone. And if I see you again, I will do more than break your arm asshole."

Leaving Jed near his truck holding his busted arm, Logan escorted Michele across the street into his home, where she stayed fearful of Jed's return for a few days. During those couple days, the two became friends. After she moved back to her own home, Logan took her to his mixed martial arts gym and enrolled in some self-defense classes. Thereafter, they often carpooled to the gym together. He also took her to the range and taught her to load, fire, and clean a pistol. Once she had proven proficient with a gun, he bought her a Glock 26.

The pistol was the smaller version of his Glock 19 that he had taught her to shoot with.

The more the two of them hung out together, the closer they became. Then one night, she asked him to go to a bar with her downtown called the Peanut to meet some of her friends for drinks. That night they ended up in bed together. Both enjoyed the experience and agreed to a friends with benefits situation, which evolved into something more over time.

CHAPTER 12

September 19, 12:10 pm

Agents Trenton and Moore pulled into the minimum security prison lot at ten minutes past noon. Trenton parked in an unoccupied spot where they could see the main door from which they knew Joseph Cabrini would emerge. They were about ten minutes late after their morning meeting with the US Attorney regarding their recently completed investigation had taken longer than expected. Neither agent was concerned with their tardiness, knowing that the prisoners were never released precisely on time and more often than not 30 to 45 minutes after the prescribed time—one last jab at the men who'd been confined there.

They were under no illusions about the odds of success on their new mission. Nonetheless, they both acknowledged that they were looking forward to a few days on the low-pressure detail, after the time and effort they had spent on their previous case. Their tentative plan was to observe the man a few days to see if he led them to any new information. If that didn't work, they would approach him again about testifying against Primovero or at least inquire if he would offer insight into the ledger, which Pearson and the

US Attorney's office both insisted was needed for any hope of convicting Richard Primovero. But again, they held out little hope of getting any useful information from the man having spent the previous afternoon and evening reviewing Cabrini's file. During his incarceration, the man had been offered numerous deals and opportunities to turn against his former boss while he was in prison. He had never come close to taking any of the proposed deals. Now free, even if on parole, there was even less incentive for the man to cooperate.

Watching from the front seat of their government issued sedan, the two Agents watched Cabrini emerge from the prison with two men. Both Agents had worked in the Kansas City Field Office long enough to recognize the two men escorting Cabrini immediately: Chad Lessons and Tony Wentz. The duo were two of Primovero's heavy hitters. Though neither had been caught up in the latest sting or subsequent indictments, both men were near the top of the US Attorney's Person's of Interest List.

"I guess our boy is still in the game," said Trenton, who had chosen to wear a white shirt and red tie with his navy blue Brooks Brother suit, nodding towards the three men as they moved towards the Lincoln. "Otherwise, why would these two be picking up our boy." Putting the government sedan into drive, he prepared to follow the men out of the parking lot.

"Seems so. Maybe today won't be so boring after all", replied Moore who wore a similar suit though with a light blue shirt paired with a navy and yellow striped tie.

The Lincoln moved out of the parking lot and took a right.

After pulling onto the main road following the big luxury sedan, Moore suggested, "What do you say we let them know we're here? See if we can get them to do something stupid."

"Sounds good to me," Trenton agreed. Speeding up, he closed the space between the two cars, tailgating the big Lincoln for nearly four blocks until the vehicle in front of them stopped at the stoplight.

Seeing Cabrini turn around, the two agents both waved enthusiastically.

******

They had traveled less than a quarter-mile from the prison in silence. Joey began contemplating how his early parole was going to be a death sentence when Chad muttered, "Don't look now, but we got a tail."

Turning around in his seat to look out the rear window, Joey saw a dark sedan with two men inside. The car was uncomfortably close to their rear bumper, allowing Joey a full look at its occupants, a bald black and a white guy with short brown hair. The pair wore matching sunglasses and suit jackets but different shirts and ties. The car and men had feds written all over them and made Joey smile, 'maybe I ain't dead after all,' he thought.

"Who are these assholes?" Wentz asked.

"Not sure," Lessons answered, "but they followed us out of the prison lot."

As they approached a stoplight, the light turned yellow and then red. Lessons dutifully stopped. All three watched as the two men in the car behind them made a show of waving. "What the fuck?" Wentz stated.

"I don't know. How about you, Joey, those two friends of yours?" Lessons asked in an aggravated tone.

His glimmer of hope dashed at the killer's words Joey stated shakily, "No Sir. I've never seen them before."

"Yeah, well, for your sake, I hope you don't. I'd hate to have something happen to you now that you're free before we see the boss," Lessons said through clenched teeth as the light turned green.

The rest of the drive from Leavenworth to Kansas City, Missouri had been the longest of Joey's life; even longer than the day, he rode the prison bus from the federal courthouse to the prison after he was sentenced. Despite Nelson's words that Primovero wanted to see him and the presence of the presumed cops behind them, Joey wasn't able to find any comfort in the big plush sea. He had no difficulty recalling that Primovero had many cops on his payroll. Many of them were more than willing to look the other way, if not assist in his burial somewhere along the twisty country roads.

He was able to exhale once Lessons pulled off the desolate KS-5 onto the busier highway I 435 S. He knew the traffic would provide too many potential witnesses. However, he still knew that Primovero, Lessons, and Wentz all knew of safe houses and abandoned warehouses that they could quickly get rid of him inside the city should they want to.

Unintentionally, it was Wentz who subdued his fear of imminent death as they got nearer downtown. "The boss is excited to see you again. Wants to reward you for being a stand-up guy in the joint back there. He's kept tabs on you, ya know. Guys have told him that you did your time like a man and kept your mouth shut. I didn't know you had it in ya personally."

"Hey man, zip it. The boss said to get him there, not to talk to him. Keep an eye on those assholes behind us." Lessons admonished while exiting the highway into downtown, the federal car in tow.

The remainder of the short drive returned to one of silence, for which Joey was thankful as he pondered what was to come. More confident he would actually meet Primovero as Nelson said, Joey was pretty sure he knew what would occur at the meeting. First, Primovero would act happy to see him, in an attempt to get him to relax. Then when Primovero thought he had let his guard down, his former boss would mention what a strange coincidence it was for him to have been granted an early release the same time he was facing indictment. After that, he would demand to know what he had told the cops to secure his release. It was utterly predictable, even a reasonable calculation from the man's perspective. The question was how he would answer the man? Appreciating the man's paranoia, Joey doubted the truth was going to satisfy the man.

Before he had come up with a satisfactory response, the car pulled into a curbside space near the entrance to "The Peanut." The Peanut is an institution onto itself in Kansas City. Known as the oldest bar in the city, it began as a speakeasy during the prohibition years. After the 21st Amendment was passed to repeal prohibition in December 1933, the speakeasy became a highly successful bar. So successful, there are now multiple locations throughout the greater Kansas City area, including one on 9th street in downtown, not far from the original. The 9th street location is in a two-story brick building that is easily identifiable by the large green awning that runs the building's length with "The Peanut" stamped across it in bright white letters. The awning provides shade to the tall glass windows and keeps the inside in perpetual shadow, a nod to its speakeasy roots. And while the newer location lacks the original's history and atmosphere, the downtown location remains a popular spot for people who live and work in the area to get great wings and cocktails throughout the day.

Getting out of the car, Joey looked the place over. 'Wow! It hasn't changed a bit in 8 years.' He felt the corners of his mouth rise at the thought, which he quickly subdued, recalling what awaited him inside.

******

The light on the stoplight turned green. "I would say he knows he is being watched now," Trenton said. Pushing the accelerator, he continued their less than subtle trail of the car and the three gangsters.

"If not, he isn't as smart as we thought," Moore joked straight-faced, as was his way.

Never more than two car lengths away, the two agents remained glued to their quarry for the 20 miles of rural road built along the rolling hills of Eastern Kansas. The two-car convoy traveled along backcountry roads until they reached I-70. Merging onto the highway, they continued into Kansas City, crossing the border into Missouri until they exited near downtown on the Oak Street exit. From the exit ramp, the lead car proceeded further into the heart of downtown, the FBI Agents close behind. The Lincoln finally parked in a single unoccupied spot on 9th street near Washington Street. Despite the traffic behind them, Trenton stopped the car. The two agents watched as the trio exited their car and walked straight into The Peanut, a local bar that had received accolades for its food and drinks menu, particularly its wings. It was a place they were both very familiar with as it was less than a mile from their offices at the FBI field office and less than another half mile from the Federal Courthouse, thus they had both been in the place before.

"Whaddaya think?" Moore asked.

"I think I haven't had lunch yet, and some wings sound pretty damn good to me," Trenton replied.

"Works for me. I'll go in and get us a table while you park."

"Ok. But be careful. Those are some bad dudes."

Nodding in agreement, Moore climbed from the car and followed the trio into the bar.

After finding a parking spot on the nearby parking garage roof, Trenton hustled back to the bar himself.

CHAPTER 13

September 19, 12:20 pm

Grabbing a large black coffee from a nearby Starbucks, Logan drove to his place of business, The Funny Pages, a small comic book store located not far from his home. The shop was in a good but not great location near the campuses of the University of Missouri, Kansas City and Rockhurst University in a small strip mall near Troost Avenue and 56th street. It was in one of those neighborhoods stuck between the swanky part of town where the money people like to visit and the run-down part of town, where many are afraid to venture out at night, with his store space nearer the latter. The store's location, combined with the prominence of its barred windows and the locking cage door on the storefront, had oftentimes intimidated customers when they first saw the place. But even after seven years, the sight of his sign still triggered his sense of pride.

The space had previously been occupied by a beauty salon and then florist before Logan had signed a lease with a desperate landlord. After signing the lease, it had taken him nearly 2 months of solitary and tireless hard work to prepare the store for its grand opening. On opening day, he was gushing with pride from the accomplishment. He had even managed to convince a local radio station to do a remote for his grand opening to help draw in customers and kick off a small advertising campaign. That day was one of the most profitable days the shop would have early on.

Despite his best efforts, the store barely broke even in the first month, and it went downhill from there. For the next 8 months, the store leaked money, and Logan was scarcely able to keep the lights on, going deeper and deeper into debt to save the place. Then one night, as he was about to close, two young men entered the store, both wearing jeans and oversized hoodies. One of the men immediately approached the counter while the other began to look over the merchandise. Though he had been in business only a short time, Logan was instantly on alert, knowing this was a typical maneuver used by tandem shoplifters that had been used successfully against him a few times when he first opened. The guy at the counter would start asking a bunch of questions to distract him while the other would pocket whatever the target item or items were.

Logan was preparing to deal with the questioner when to his surprise, instead of asking him a question, the man pulled a small pistol from his sweatshirt's pocket. So shocked by the action, Logan did the only thing he could do: He laughed, a deep full belly laugh.

Confused or shocked by his reaction, the gunman said, "What the fuck are you laughing at man. Give me the money from the register."

The demand only made Logan laugh harder, so much so he was on the verge of tears when he responded, "There is no money in the register, see for yourself." Reaching out, he hit the button opening the register, the empty drawer sliding out entirely—a loud hollow metallic clank sounding as it caught against the metal stop.

The man with the gun leaned in, peering into the empty drawer unbelieving. Looking over his shoulder, the guy said, "Can you believe this shit."

Logan took the opportunity, grabbing the man's gun hand, pushing it away with his left hand while reaching across the man's other shoulder for a handful of the hood on his sweatshirt with his right and jerking it down hard, smashing the man's face into the glass display case. The sudden impact causing the man to drop the gun behind the counter at Logan's feet.

Seeing what had happened to his partner, the second man rushed forward. With his hand still on the back of the man's head, Logan used it as a prop to hop over the counter like a farmer would a rail fence. Timing his vault perfectly, he kicked the second man in the solar plexus as he came to his partner's aid, sending him backward into the aisle and on his back.

Logan allowed his momentum to carry him forward, following the man into the narrow space between the tables of milk crates and comic books. "Did you know in many countries they still cut off people's hands for theft?" Logan asked cryptically.

At Logan's words, the would-be robber's eyes grew large as he tried to back away. But before he could move, Logan was on top of him, sitting atop his chest his knees atop the man's biceps pinning his arms wide. "Lucky for you, they frown upon that in this country." Logan continued before grabbing the man's left hand with his right and twisting the fingers until all four broke with a grotesque snap. The man on the ground screamed.

"At least you get to keep your hand," Logan said before pulling his phone from his pocket and calling 9-1-1.

The police arrived a few moments later and took the two men into custody as Logan held them at gunpoint with their own gun. While two officers took the men to the cruisers, a tall officer wearing a mustache with sergeant stripes on his shoulder and a name tape that said Forward asked Logan for the security footage.

Logan led the officer in the backroom, where he was also living at the time, sleeping on an old army cot, and preparing his scant meals with either a microwave or Instapot. Rewinding, the old school VCR that he had inherited with the space he readily showed the officer the footage of the two men trying to rob him.

Having watched the video 3 or 4 times, while Logan narrated the events, the man finally seemed satisfied, put up his notebook, and asked Logan for the evidence. Ejecting the tape, Logan handed it to him.

"Man, are you ok? That was a risky stunt you pulled off there," officer Forward said.

"It's not the first time I've had a gun pointed at me."

"Really?" the officer asked dubiously.

"Six years in the Army, with tours in Iraq and Afghanistan".

"Oh. I was in Iraq too, 3-15 Infantry, 3rd I-D, Fort Stewart." the officer admitted. "What unit were you with?"

"1-22 Infantry, 4th I-D, out of Ft Hood."

"When were you there?" the officer asked suddenly more curious.

"I was there in 0-3 for the initial push and was in the Stan in 2005 with 173 Airborne Brigade."

"You were the guys who found Saddam! Were you there?"

"We were, and I was. I was part of the group pulling security along the river as they pulled Saddam from his hole. But really man, by then, things had settled down compared to when we first crossed the border."

"I hear ya, we took the airfield. You guys were further north and west of us. But capturing Saddam will always be a part of history. That is awesome. Thank you for your service."

Always unsure how to respond to the statement, Logan said, "It was a means to an end. I bought this place with the money I saved over there."

For the first time seemingly, officer Forward began looking the place over. Suddenly realizing that he was standing in Logan's living quarters, he asked, "How's business?"

"Could always be better," Logan replied.

"I'm sure," Forward said soberly.

Once the officers left, Logan pretty much thought the entire affair was over, but he couldn't have been more wrong. The event turned out to place him on a path he never could have imagined. The next morning, as Logan went to unlock the front door and open for the day, he noted three people waiting. One man in jeans and a flannel shirt held a big fancy camera, while a pretty woman wearing a smart suit held a microphone. Logan recognized her from one of the local news stations. The third person was a wise-looking older gentleman in jeans, a wrinkled shirt, and poorly knotted tie. Looking beyond the trio, he saw a local news van and a car with the Kansas City Star decal on the side.

By that evening, the story of his disarming the would-be robbers was big local news and had also made the national news. The short-lived notoriety was good for business. Essentially it had been free advertising and provided a small uptick in business. More importantly, the national story had been seen by one of his former army buddies, Billy Hendrix. Hendrix would ultimately make the introduction to Paige. That introduction became one of the most important of his life, leading him to take his other job, one that allowed him to save the struggling store.

Now a handful of years later, the store had become successful, turning a tidy profit for Logan without the supplementation from his work with Paige, though it still required a lot of work on his part. Enjoyable work made easier by his two employees, Eric and Ryan, but work nonetheless.

It was still early in the business day for the store, but Logan was happy to see two cars and a bicycle parked out front already as he pulled into the parking lot. Taking an unoccupied spot near the front door, in front of a window display that his two employees hated, Logan took a brief moment to look around. He recognized the red bicycle and the late model blue Honda Civic as belonging to two regular customers. Subconsciously checking the calendar in his head, he knew that Tyrone, who owned the bike, had ridden over from school on his lunch break to get the latest edition of a small indy comic book about a fugitive from justice during an intragalatical space war. Meanwhile the man in the Honda was on his way to his office at UMKC and checking to see what, if any, collectible copies the store had brought in that he may want for his growing collection. However, the new Lexus sedan sitting directly in front of his store he didn't recognize.

Climbing out of the car, he stretched once, again still tired from his drive, then retrieved a rolling case from the trunk of his car with the new inventory he had acquired during his trip to New Mexico. Carefully carrying the case and the large coffee, which was still too hot to drink, walked through the store's front door.

Entering the room, he heard the electronic door chime sound, a comforting sound for his employees who appreciated the security system. However, Logan still would have preferred the old fashioned bell he used to have. Inside the door, there was an ample open carpeted space where Logan sat various promotional displays the comic book companies sent the dealers. Today, to the right was a cardboard cut out from a major distributor depicting a dark-haired man almost as tall as Logan himself. The cutout figure held guns in either hand and was clad in all black, but the most prominent feature was the large skull emblazoned on the man's T-shirt. To the left was another cut out of a lesser-known character from a small indie publisher that was one of Logan's new favorites. The cutout was of a pink-haired voodoo priestess whose face gave off the distinct impression of someone you didn't want to mess with.

Beyond the displays were the original five waist-high rows of milk crates where newest comics were alphabetically displayed. Each row featured a different publisher or publishers. In the middle aisle stood Tyrone, the young man with the bicycle, wearing his customary blue Royals baseball cap over cornrows and his Pembroke Hills wrestling sweatshirt right where Logan assumed he would be. "How's it goin, Mr. Spencer?" the young man asked respectfully.

"Good Tyrone, how about yourself?"

"Good."

"When does practice start?" Logan asked, referring to wrestling, a sport Logan had excelled in while he was in school and was still passionate about it.

"First practice is in 3 weeks. Actually, I wanted to ask you, are you going to be at the gym this weekend? Maybe we can spar a little." the young man asked sheepishly.

"I should be there Saturday morning. Come on by, and we can roll some." Logan answered happily.

"Thanks, Mr. Spencer."

Along the walls were t-shirts, posters, and collectibles that could all be bought in the store. Standing near the right side wall, the man with the Honda, Jimmie Andersen, a stoop-shouldered, red-headed man wearing khaki pants, a plaid button-down shirt, blue square bottom tie, and tweed sport coat browsed the inventory, as Logan expected. The seemingly haphazard outfit seemingly fit perfectly for his job as a law professor at the nearby UMKC law school.

"Jimmie, aren't you running late?" Logan joked as he walked by.

Glancing at his watch, the man smiled, "No, my class doesn't start until one today. And my office hours aren't until after that."

In the back of the showroom, the register sat atop a sizeable glass display case that ran nearly the room's length. Inside the case, Logan displayed the more expensive collector's items. Behind the display case stood Ryan, one of his two employees. As tall and thin as Logan himself, the man had bleach blonde hair and thin round-rimmed glasses, making him look eerily like John Lennon. Because of their similar statures, many of his customer's assumed Ryan was his younger brother. He was not, but the two were close, and Logan knew the man had three real loves in life: comic books, bad jokes, and pot. Despite his tendency to wake and bake, the man never missed a day of work and related to most of the customers on a level that Logan could never match. However, this morning, he spoke with a tall, middle-aged man in a nice suit whom Logan guessed was not like most of the store's clientele. The man driving the Lexus, Logan, presumed.

After placing the case and his coffee on the counter, Ryan said in a manner to meant convey the importance of the man, "Logan, this is Mr. Murray, and he wants to talk to you about your trip."

"About my trip?" Logan asked guardedly, surprised by the statement.

"Yes sir," the man in the suit interjected before Ryan could explain, "As Ryan here said, My name is Moses Murray, and I understand you just procured a certain first edition comic in New Mexico. I'd like to buy it."

"Wait. You care to explain how you know I just bought a first edition in New Mexico?" Logan asked curiously since he hadn't told either Ryan or Eric, his other employee, where he was going or what he was buying.

"Because I have been trying for years to find that book myself and when I finally got a lead on one and get ahold of the guy he tells me a comic dealer in Kansas City had just bought it. So I called around a bit and determined that had to have been you. Since I live in St. Louis, I decided to drive on over and make you an offer."

"You drove over here in that suit to buy a comic book?" Logan asked dubiously.

"I have some other business interests over here as well. Today seemed as good a time as any to check on those too. Two birds with one stone if you will."

"What kind of business interests?" Logan asked, trying to change the subject and slow the man's momentum so he could think.

However, the man would have none of it, instead, waving him off by saying, "Mostly real estate and asset development properties. Nothing fascinating unless you understand the zoning laws and underwriting markets so that you can exploit them. But I am not interested in any of the property around here." The man said almost insultingly as he waved his arms around. "I am just trying to get you to sell me that book."

"Ok. But you should know I haven't even had this thing graded yet." Logan responded in an effort to slow the man down once again.

"But you bought it. From what I've heard about you and what I have seen in here, you don't buy stuff unless it is the real deal," the man said in a flattering way apparently aware of how his previous comments could have come out as condescending. "Plus, I have it on good authority from the person who referred me to the guy in Albuquerque that the book is legitimate. I'm willing to give you seven grand for it right now sight unseen on those facts alone."

The man's offer reinforced Logan's wariness of the man and situation as the offered amount was precisely what he had paid for the entire group of comics and was what he had hoped to get for the copy once he had it graded. Now he was wondering if maybe he wasn't underselling himself based on the man's evident enthusiasm for the issue. Besides, there was just something about the guy that Logan didn't like thus, he responded, "That is a very generous offer but I wouldn't feel right about selling it for that much without getting it officially graded. I know a grader and can have him take a look at it in the next day or so. After that, I will be ready to consider a fair price for it."

"Are you sure? Seven thousand is a lot of money and a fair deal if you ask me. I mean, if someone said I could recoup my investment after only 3 days, I sure wouldn't turn it down."

If the comment was designed to make Logan reconsider, it backfired completely. Logan did not like to negotiate with people much, to begin with, and he certainly didn't want to negotiate with people who had inside knowledge of his deal. "No, sir, as you said yourself, I have a pretty good reputation in this industry, and I wouldn't want anyone to ever think they got a bad deal from me and ruin that reputation. Let me have it graded first, and then we can talk numbers." Logan deflected, trying not to let on he was bothered by the insider trading knowledge the man revealed having.

"You're sure? If it grades low, I might not be willing to offer seven large any longer."

"I guess it's a chance I'll just have to take then," Logan said definitively.

Murray stared at Logan unspeaking for a moment, before nodding. "Ok then, I can respect that. Let me give you my card, and you call me after you have it graded."

Reaching inside his jacket, Logan tensed ready to pounce, until the man's hand came out with a card held between his index and middle fingers. Taking the man's card, Logan placed it in his pocket. "I'll have it graded this week."

"I look forward to hearing from you."

After the man left, Logan started unpacking the case he had carried in, while Ryan rang up Tyrone, who had brought his new issue to the register. Sale complete, Ryan asked, "Man, did you really just turn down seven grand just like that? Like the man said, what if it doesn't grade well?"

"Don't worry, the book is legit, and it's clean. It will grade as high or higher than any other first issues he is going to find. He knows it, and I know it. I figure he is good for at least another two grand easy and maybe more. Plus, I just didn't like the guy, which is going to cost him at least an extra grand all by itself. I hate when people try and tell me how to run my business. Ya know?"

The younger man looked awed for a moment at his words but quickly recovered and said dryly, "Oh man, I guess I won't tell you any more about putting up those ugly posters in the front windows then."

Logan laughed at his young friend's sardonic wit, "Shit man, I do that to hear you and Eric squawk as much as anything. Lets me know you two are paying attention is all."

"Speaking of paying attention, what all did you do in New Mexico?" Ryan asked, rubbing his own head to emphasize Logan's new look.

"Well, you know, cut my hair, bought some comics, climbed some mountains, and ate some good food. What else is there?"

"Why did you cut your hair though, you were looking like a dark-haired Thor when you left and come back looking like GI Joe again."

"Man, it got hot on the mountains. Besides, it'll all grow back."

"You and those mountains, I just don't get it. Of all the joys nature has to offer, and that's what you do." Ryan laughed at his own thinly veiled pot reference.

Ryan and Logan were finishing logging the items that Logan had brought back from Albuquerque into the computer's inventory and were putting them in the display case when the door chime sounded once again. Looking up, Logan saw Michele walk in and instantly felt the wave of warmth that she inspired in him every time he saw her.

Having worked that morning, she was wearing a pair of hip-hugging khaki slacks, and a sky blue 3/4 sleeve blouse unbuttoned just enough to give a hint of cleavage. The outfit accentuated her blonde hair and blue eyes perfectly, as Logan knew she intended. Upon seeing her, Ryan immediately stammered an awkward hello, which made Logan laugh, knowing his friend was uncomfortable around women, to begin with, and even more so with attractive women. Though Michele had been coming to the shop a few times a week since Ryan started working there, he still always got tongue-tied around her.

Hearing Logan chuckle at Ryan's greeting, Michele stared at him teasingly as she marched directly to the counter, stood up on her toes, and gave Ryan a hug and a kiss on his cheek causing the man to simultaneously blush and smile broadly.

"Great now, he is going to be daydreaming the rest of the day, and I won't get any work out of him," Logan joked.

Before Ryan could defend himself, Michele jumped in winking at Ryan, "You two work in a comic book store, this place is all about daydreaming. Ain't that right, hun?"

Clearly embarrassed, the young clerk sauntered off towards the back, carrying the empty roller case to the storage room.

Watching Ryan almost float across the store, still smiling, Logan looked at Michele and asked, "You ready to go?"

"Are you kidding, I've been looking forward to this for a week."

Meeting her at the corner of the counter, he bent down and gave her a kiss. When he went to straighten, she placed her hand on top of his head. "What did you do?" she asked.

"The heat got to me," he lied in a literal though maybe not in a figurative sense. "Don't worry, it'll grow back."

"You better hope so. You look like a psycho with your hair so short."

"Oh, I can be psycho," he stated dryly with a wink as they left the store hand in hand.

Outside, Logan walked around the car with her, opening the passenger door. Seeing the backpack in the passenger seat, he remembered it still had a few thousand dollars of traveling cash inside along with the spare needle of poison that he hadn't needed for Galvan. Not wanting her to sit on it or look inside, Logan nonchalantly tossed it into the back seat before allowing her to sit down. "Your chariot, my lady," he said playfully.

CHAPTER 14

September 19, 1:28 pm

Joey followed Wentz and Lessons into the bar bypassing a young waitress and the occupied tables. He followed the two men as they walked directly towards the far left rear of the room where a table and booth sat empty. Both tables had "reserved" signs sitting atop them. Moving past the table and into the booth, Wentz picked up the cardboard sign, wadding it up before throwing it back down on the table and sliding into the left-hand side. Joey went to the right and slid in himself only to be told, "keep sliding" by Lessons. Sandwiched between the two killers, Joey reminded himself to stay calm.

No sooner had they sat down than the young waitress, who upon closer inspection had red hair and freckles, stepped up to the table. Nonchalantly removing the balled up sign, she began reciting the day's specials.

Having not seen a woman outside the few women who worked at the penitentiary, Joey took a moment to watch her. He began internally debating with himself whether she was truly pretty or merely an average looking girl; he was overestimating from being locked up.

Completing her reading of the day's specials, she asked, "What can I get you to drink?"

To distracted gauging her beauty to hear what she had said, Joey didn't respond to her question until Wentz elbowed him in the ribs. At the prompt, Joey quickly asked for a large draft of Boulevard Unfiltered Wheat, which had been his usual order nearly a decade prior. The girl, who Joey decided was beautiful, wrote down the order and asked the two killers what they were drinking. Both men ordered sodas.

The pair's drink orders caught Joey's attention, the way a slap on the back of his head from his grandmother had when he was growing up. He cursed himself under his breath for being distracted by the pretty girl, not realizing the error he had made ordering the beer. It was well known that Primovero did not drink and abhorred drunkenness in general. His former boss believed alcohol clouds the mind and that mankind only sits atop the food chain is because of his mind and use thereof. Thus, Primovero saw anything that interfered with his mind as an absolute detriment.

It was equally well established that there was no drinking or use of any recreational drugs while on the job with Richard Primovero. People caught drinking or intoxicated while on the clock working for him were dealt with swiftly and harshly in all his business ventures, legitimate or otherwise. In fact, Joey recalled when he had escorted Primovero to one of the bars, he controlled to collect money from a man named Romero. Romero was a two-bit thug that Primovero had inherited when he came to be the head of the family who ran a bookie operation out of the bar's back room. There had been a big championship fight on this particular night, and the betting had been heavy all over town. Primovero didn't want to let the money sit overnight in the bars, afraid someone might attempt to steal from the family's new man in charge. It would be the last stop of the night for them, and Joey even recalled Primovero telling him that they would be in and out and then go grab breakfast at one of the family's controlled diners before heading home. Walking in, they found the staff cleaning the place after what had obviously been a busy night while Romero sat at the bar. Nearing the man, they saw a duffel bag and two longneck bottles before the clearly inebriated man. Before Romero's alcohol-soaked brain could see through the fog to recognize Primovero, so enraged had Primovero become at the sight he simply picked up one the beer bottles by the neck and swung it directly into the man's ear. Romero fell to the floor holding the side of his head, where Primovero proceeded to systematically kick in his ribs. Two things happened afterward, Romero never worked for Primovero again, and the men and women in his employ understood not to drink on the bosses time.

"We're working, go ahead and enjoy the drink but take it slow, you haven't had one in a while. The boss will be here soon, and I doubt he will mind just don't get another one before you two have a chance to talk," Lessons responded to what must have been a concerned look on his face.

Joey nodded in response, still chastising himself for the apparent faux pa and rationalizing the need for the beer to calm his nerves until all this is over. When the drinks arrived, Joey quickly put the large frosty mug to his lips; taking a long pull hopeful the golden liquid would work its magic. The cold beer was crisp and slightly sweet with a hint of citrus; eliciting an appreciative smack of his lips. Joey, who himself never had been a heavy drinker nonetheless knew he would now forever associate the taste with freedom. He hoped it was a taste he would get to enjoy after the meeting with Primovero.

Taking a second, smaller drink from the heavy mug, Joey exhaled and began to think through his present situation. For the first time, he began to look over the interior of the barroom. Much like the exterior, the inside had remained much the same since his last visit, dark paneled walls with various pieces of drinking propaganda and sports memorabilia hung all around. Its familiarity helped bring a sense of calmness to the situation, giving him the strength to remind himself: Everything is going to be ok, surely the man wasn't brazen enough to murder him here.

Joey was shaken out of his thoughts by Wentz asking him, "Hey man, so what are your plans now that you're out? If you need a girl or anything, let me know. I know some people, and I'll spot you the costs."

"Thanks, Tony, I appreciate it, but I think I will be ok in that department."

"Are you sure? I mean you been without for a while assuming you didn't change teams inside".

"No, Tony, I am heterosexual." Joey responded then quickly added to clarify, "I like women."

"Good, but just you know this world has changed since you been away. I mean, the last girl I took out told me she don't 'do that on the first date'" Tony said using air quotes. "But you know what I told that bitch? You don't get many second dates do ya?" I bet she will think twice about that the next time after she had to find another ride home and pay the bill when I walked out on her," the man boasted while trying to stifle a laugh at his own humor.

Joey, who had always been nervous around but respectful of women, was dumbstruck at the statement. To fearful of saying anything to the notorious brawler about how reprehensible that statement was, Joey took another pull on his beer.

Lessons, however, had no such fear, responding contemptuously, "Tony, you ever think that is why you have to pay for it? No lady is going to put up with that crap."

Giving the lean killer a sideways look, the little brawler said, "Don't mind him, kid. Chad here is just in love with some broad named Jenni, who manages the boss's house even though he won't say it. He wouldn't know what to do with another woman ifin he even had the chance. He is kinda touchy about it."

"Watch it, man, I am not one of the girls or little crackheads you usually slap around. You will respect me, and I would prefer you keep Jenni's name out of your mouth as well, or the two of us may have to discuss this outside after the boss gets here." Lessons said his eyes locked on the shorter man, his face expressing the seriousness of the threat.

Swallowing hard under the icy glare, Wentz said, "See what I mean kid. Real touchy,"

*****

Inside the restaurant's door, Moore awaited Trenton's arrival. To the door's right was a long dark wood bar that ran nearly the length of the room, with bar stools spaced evenly along its length. Behind the bar, along the wall, was a long mirror, almost as long as the bar itself. Shelves were mounted to the mirror and were full with an array of liquor bottles of various vintages. The remaining floor area was filled with white laminate topped tables and chairs, many of which were occupied by patrons. A quick study revealed a rather diverse group as expected in a downtown bar. There were older men and women in suits who were trying to eat without getting anything on them. Other patrons wore blue-collar service uniforms, enjoying late lunches. There were even some bikers enjoying a few beers, while a pair of younger guys in jeans, T-shirts and baseball caps, sat at the bar talking to the barman.

Moore quickly cataloged the scene in his mind before returning his gaze to the three men they had trailed from the prison. He had watched the trio take seats at the reserved booth in the back corner of the establishment, which reinforced the place's selection had been decided in advance. But why? He asked himself.

Agent Moore continued his stakeout as the men spoke to the waitress, and the waitress made her way back across the room to the bar. Summoning the bartender, he heard her tell the man she needed two sodas and a tall beer.

She waited while the man behind the bar filled two tall plastic cups with ice and soda before removing a tall frost-covered mug from the freezer. From the tap, the man expertly filled cold glass, leaving nary a head on the golden liquid. The waitress took the tray and returned it to the men's table, where the three men continued to talk. He noted the fact that Cabrini received the beer, while the two gunmen got sodas. Not an unimportant observation knowing the reputation given the rumors of Primovero's dislike of men drinking who worked for him.

After what seemed to have taken much longer than necessary to Moore, the door opened, and Trenton walked inside. "What took you so long?" Moore asked his partner.

"The garage is nearly full. It took me a minute to find a spot," said Trenton, breathing heavily, having jogged back to the restaurant from the parking garage.

Satisfied with the explanation, Moore waved his partner to follow, and the pair crossed the room, eyes fixed on the three men the entire way. They choose the empty table nearest the second reserved table, not wanting to provoke an unnecessary argument with the restaurant staff. The table left the two Agents close enough to watch the three men but not so close to hear what they said as they spoke in hushed tones.

No sooner had their butts struck the wooden chairs than the waitress arrived to go over the day's specials and take their orders. Both men ordered the special, a dozen wings, along with diet sodas.

Once the waitress left, Trenton asked, "So what do you think we are doing here?"

"I don't know. This certainly wasn't listed in Cabrini's file, and I've never heard of Primovero or his crew operating down here, but the table they are sitting at had a reserved sign on it too, when they walked in." Moore answered, pointing at the sign on the table that separated them from the three men.

"So they didn't pick this place at random?" Trenton said, following Moore's own line of thinking.

"No, they didn't. But why here and why now?

*****

It was a short uneventful drive from the comic book store to downtown, during which Michele unloaded a week's worth of office gossip upon Logan. While he had only been to her office on a couple of occasions, he felt he knew all her clients as intimately as she did from the regular updates she provided him.

Parking on the top floor of the crowded parking garage near the restaurant, Logan climbed out of the car. He was about to lock the doors when he saw the backpack in the back seat. Opening the door again, he crawled inside and fetched the bag, sliding it over his shoulder.

When Michele asked him about it, he told her truthfully that he didn't need the bag but was more concerned about the potential damage a thief would do to his car breaking in to get the backpack than losing it. Thinking it over, she agreed, taking his hand.

Hand in hand, the pair walked back through the aisles of cars and out of the garage through the ninth street entrance. Passing the alley between the restaurant and the parking garage, Logan was surprised to see four motorcycles parked together: a pair of crotch rockets and two shiny Harley Davidsons. The four bikes filled the entire opening, making it virtually impossible for a vehicle of any sort to enter or exit. He couldn't recall having ever seen anything parked in the alley before other than the occasional delivery truck. In the back of his mind, the sight sounded an alarm, though he was unsure of what it meant in his tired state. He considered bringing it up to Michele but decided against it as she would think it trivial and seemed excited to get inside.

Walking in from the bright afternoon sun into the dimly lit atmosphere, Logan paused a moment inside the doorway to allow his eyes to adjust. Standing just inside the door, he studied the scene as his eyes grew accustomed to the space. It came as no surprise to Logan that the establishment contained more than a handful of people enjoying a late lunch even at the odd hour. At the bar, near the back corner where the window to the kitchen allowed the cook to pass food to the bartender and waitresses where he and Michele usually sat two men: a good looking young Hispanic kid and a peculiar looking slightly older white guy. Behind the pair was the hallway that led to the bathrooms and staircase leading upstairs. Both men wore bulky vests of some reflective material. They looked like vests many motorcyclists wear at first glance, but to Logan something about them seemed wrong. Again, he could not determine what his tired mind was trying to tell him. After all, there was nothing abnormal about the t-shirts, jeans, boots, and baseball caps, the men wore. On the ground between the two, Logan noted two backpacks and sleek full-faced motorcycle helmets. Both men had near empty baskets of food and half-empty draft beers on the bar in front of them. Again nothing unusual about that. The pair were talking with Martin, the lone barman working. Martin wore the bar's standard uniform of a logo'd green t-shirt and jeans. As regulars, Logan knew Martin was in his mid-twenties and was working his way through school at nearby UMKC. He assumed the two crotch rockets belonged to the pair of men. But where were the guys with the Harleys? He wondered.

Seeing him looking, the bartender raised his hand in a half wave to say hello. Logan returned the wave, and Martin began placing coasters and silverware out near the two vested men, anticipating Logan and Michele seating themselves near the two motorcyclists. From previous encounters, Martin understood Logan usually sat in that corner because it allowed him to see the door and the comings and goings from the kitchen and people going to and from the restrooms, not liking people being able to sneak up on him.

Still curious as to the other bikes owners, Logan turned his attention towards the remainder of the long rectangular room. Logan saw many of the tables and chairs, away from the bar, were occupied by patrons. A quick study revealed a rather diverse group, as expected in a downtown bar. Near the front of the room, a pair of square tables were pulled together, forming a long rectangular table allowing a bigger group to sit together. At the newly formed long table sat were three older men, two white and one black. All three men were well dressed in gray suits and had silvery hair. Sitting with them were three women. Two of the women appeared only slightly younger than the men, and wore expensive-looking black pantsuits of their own, looking as if they had just exited some board room. The third woman was much younger, with a mix of Asian and caucasian features, wearing a purple blouse and grey slacks, appearing uncomfortable in the company of the five older people. Logan guessed she was likely some kind of secretary to the others, though she looked young even for that. Still, he freely admitted he was never a good judge of women's ages. The man at the head of the table had a neatly trimmed beard. He somehow managed to not get any sauce in white hair while simultaneously eating and talking to the group. The four other older group members seemed content, allowing the bearded man to speak while they attempted to enjoy the saucy wings without getting any wayward drips on their pricey clothes. The young girl sat at the corner of the table between the bearded man and one of the older ladies. Before her was nothing in front of her but a glass of ice water, a notebook and a pen.

Towards the middle of the room, near the wall, at another table sat two men wearing some kind of matching work uniform made up of matching dark green shirts and pants with a white circular emblem on the left breast pocket and name tapes on the right. Logan knew the uniform meant the two worked for the city in some capacity. Both men appeared to be in their late forties and were both immensely overweight. The array of fried food before them showed that neither man was particularly worried about it.

To the immediate left, at the corner booth near the front window sat two men in biker's garb. The two Harley Riders he decided. Black pants, long-sleeved shirts, bulky leather vests, and boots. The man with his back to the window was a large, heavily muscled white man. The man had some sort of bandana around his forehead from which hung unnatural looking long black hair pulled back into a braid. The man sitting with him was a nearly as large black man who had a long funny looking beard and shaved head. Logan noted they each had saddlebags sitting at the table with them, and each man had a long neck bottle before them but no food baskets. For a reason, he couldn't quite identify it struck him as odd that the four bikes had been parked together in the alley, yet the four men sat at polar opposite ends of the room.

However, his curiosity was quickly forgotten when he looked at the cluster of men in the back left corner of the room. In the corner booth, sat three guys in suits, but they didn't appear board room types. The man on the left was short and nearly as thick as he was tall, with jet black hair slicked back, wearing a shiny maroon suit with a crisp white undershirt open at the collar lower than usual revealing a tuft of chest hair and a thick gold chain. Opposite him to the right was a tall stoop-shouldered man with a solemn face wearing a grey suit that even in the dim lights shone and looked expensive, with a light blue undershirt opened at the collar as well but not as severely as his counterpart. Between the pair sat a man of average size with a tasteful blue suit but even from across the room look wrinkled and untidy, like it had been packed away in a duffle bag or something.

Near the trio, a few tables away sat another pair of men. The two men sat at on adjoining sides of the table instead of directly across from one another. Though awkward by social standards, their position allowed them to both see the men in the corner booth. To Logan, there was no question that both were cops of some variety. He decided they were likely FBI or DEA based on their clothes and haircuts. Both men wore what looked like standard-issue government blue suits. One of the men was black, with clean-shaven bald head, and looked to be in good shape. With him was a similarly built white guy with short brown hair whose profile showed a severe expression that never seemed to waver from the corner with the three other men.

As Logan was finishing his study of the interior, Michele took his hand in an attempt to lead him towards the bar where Martin had placed the coasters and napkin wrapped silverware. Before they took more than two steps, however, Logan said, "Hold on a second. Let's go sit in a booth."

Michele looked at him with a questioning look on her face, to which Logan responded, "Trust me, I think this is going to be interesting."

Leading her to an unoccupied booth that left one empty between himself and the two bikers and two vacant booths between themselves and interesting trio in the opposite corner. Logan chose the seat that allowed him to watch the three men in the corner booth and the two cops in a way that wasn't overly obvious.

The seat selection did not go unnoticed by Michele, who again looking confused, knowing that Logan always preferred to have his back in the corner of a room whenever possible. "What's going on?" she asked.

"Nothing, I just thought we'd change it up," Logan lied, unable to say for himself why he wanted to see what was going on, just a gut feeling something was afoot. Usually, being a decisive person, he struck it up to still being tired from the previous week's actions and the long drive home last night.

It appeared Michele was on the verge of questioning the excuse when Julie, the waitress, appeared with napkins, silverware, and coasters. Having been coming here regularly for a few years, the three were familiar enough with one another to exchange pleasantries before the girl asked the pair if they were having their usual, skipping the reciting of the specials. Michele nodded, asking for a Tom Collins while Logan opted for "Just coffee and water," instead of the two fingers Maker's Mark over ice fingers that he traditionally had when they came out. The deviation from his standard order drew looks from both Michele and Julie.

"I'm still tired from a long drive last night," he said by way of explanation.

After Julie left them to get their drinks, Michele asked, "Did you find the book, you rushed off to the desert without me for?"

"I did. It's ungraded, but it's in really good shape, so it will grade out well. I picked it up for $2500, and I should be able to sell it for $7,000 easy."

"And how much did you spend on your trip? A couple thousand? So you're making what maybe $1500."

"I didn't spend that much on the trip, and I picked up a few other issues that will widen my profit margins too."

"I still don't understand why you have to always go run out for these things. Why can't you just use Paypal and UPS or eBay or something."

"C'mon Michele, we've been through this. There are too many fakes, forgeries, and scammers out there. It's too much money to buy these things sight unseen. I have to ensure they are authentic before I can sell them. Reputation is everything in this business."

"You could send Eric or Ryan once in a while," she retorted.

"You know I couldn't. I trust them with the store and some of the little stuff people bring in but nothing like this. Besides, Eric doesn't drive, and Ryan gets lost in town using a GPS."

Despite herself, Michele laughed at the comment knowing it was true. She had great affection for the two men who worked for Logan, but she admitted the duo weren't all that suited to manage the bigger deals she knew the store made the lion's share of its profits from.

Logan thought the conversation was over with as Julie returned with their drinks, and he and Michele both took a sip. But the moment of peace was short-lived, and as Michele suddenly asked, "But what about Paige, has she found you any more items to go galavanting off to find?"

The question surprised him, and he was unsure how to navigate the minefield she had just laid. He knew Michele had been jealous of

Paige, whom she had never met since she first saw her name on his phone's screen after they first started fooling around. Despite his assurances that nothing had ever occurred between them, Michele hated that Logan would seemingly go off at moments notice on Paige's whim a few times a year, despite his best efforts not to make it seem that way. Making it worse, he knew, was the fact that he never offered to take Michele along. In fact, he avoided even acknowledging her subtle hints about wanting to go. It wasn't like he could say, "Sorry, honey, you can't come because I need to kill a few people."

Sensing where the conversation was quickly going, a place he was hoping to avoid altogether, he was looking for the words to steer the conversation in another direction when he was saved by an entirely unexpected arrival.

*****

Agents Moore and Trenton were still discussing theories of why the men they had followed from the prison had chosen this particular bar, assuredly not a random choice they agreed, when suddenly the entire place went deathly quiet. Looking back over their shoulders towards the door, the two agents saw a man they both immediately recognized. It wasn't lost on Moore that apparently everyone else in the bar knew him too.

CHAPTER 15

September 19, 1:42 pm

Richard Primovero stood inside the restaurant's front door looking the room over. The man hadn't uttered a word, yet his mere presence had silenced the small crowd. Even without the pristine, perfectly tailored blue suit, gold Rolex, Prada dress shoes, and expensive haircut, he would have commanded the room's attention, just as he always had. Despite being a 56-year-old slim man of no more than average height, Primovero commanded any room's attention and always had, though few could identify why, himself included. Some claimed that it was his dignified face and head full of thick hair, once black but now a silvery grey that drew the attention. Others would tell you he simply had a magnetic ora about his person.

Regardless the reason, his soft features belied the dominance of his presence, which was undeniable. There wasn't a person in the bar who would have argued the point at that moment. But today was undeniably different too. Whereas people were customarily drawn to the man by that ill-defined magnetism, today, everyone stared for another reason altogether. Since the indictment, his picture and name had been all over the television, newspapers, and internet, with more stories coming each day. It seemed both the local and national media were fascinated by the whole thing. In fact, over the last few weeks, some prominent members of the nation's press had started referring to Primovero as John Gotti 2.0. The media exposure had forever changed Richard Primovero from a man of the shadows to a man of infamy.

The young waitress hustled towards the man but stopped when he raised an outstretched hand towards her. Always well-spoken, the lilt of his voice only reinforced the magnetism of the man. "It's ok dear, my party is over there," he said, turning his outstretched hand to point to the room's back corner. "Please bring coffee and cream to my table." Eyes forward, he walked across the room undisturbed by the fact that every eye watched him though even he acknowledged inwardly that hearing his name being whispered so openly was a somewhat new phenomenon.

Walking straight to the corner booth where Cabrini, Lessons, and Wentz were sitting, he stood a moment to allow Lessons and Wentz to move to the empty reserved table nearby. "Hello Joey."

*****

The sudden hush that invaded the bar's atmosphere took a second to penetrate Joey's busy mind. Refocusing to present, he looked up to see Richard Primovero walking towards him. The man hadn't appeared to have aged at all in the last eight years. Coordinated with the man's arrival to the table, Lessons and Wentz rose silently and moved to the table between himself and the suspected Feds who had trailed them from the prison. Remembering his manners, Joey stood at Primovero's greeting and extended his hand.

Instead of shaking his hand, Primorvero stepped in close and embracing him in a hug. The maneuver totally threw Joey off, which he suspected was Primovero's intent. Sitting down, Joey badly wanted to take another large gulp of the beer but instead managed to stammer, "It's good to see you, sir."

"You too, Joey. Eight years is a long time."

"It certainly is".

"But not as long as it could have been, right?"

Shit here we go, Joey thought. "I suppose so, though no one serves a full sentence anymore outside of those who get life without parole."

"That's what I hear. You may know that I have suddenly taken more of an interest in the subjects of prison sentencing and time served."

Unsure of how to respond this time Joey, took a large gulp of the golden liquid from the tall mug before him and watched as Primovero smiled, not a friendly smile, like a cat toying with a mouse smile. Just make it through this, and you have the rest of your life ahead of you, he reminded himself.

"Beer, Joey? I am sure you remember I don't allow the men who work for me to drink on the job."

"I'm sorry. I didn't realize I still worked for you?"

"Joey, you never stopped. I assume the money you extorted from me is still making you money after all?"

The line caught him flat-footed. Taking another sip of the golden liquid, Joey asked, "What are you talking about?"

"Joey, please, do you really think I'm stupid? You of all people should know better. I always knew you were skimming some of the cream from the top of the milk for yourself. But you did such a good job for me, I allowed you to do so. It wasn't until you were gone, and Sam took over managing the accounts that I realized how much you had stolen. How much did you get over the years? Three, four, five million? I figure with your skills, natural inflation, and interest you've probably earned at least another million or two on top of whatever you took from me even with the market volatility unless you completely lost your touch. I mean, I've never seen anyone who could play the numbers like you could, before or since. Thus, giving you the benefit of the doubt, I am guessing you owe me 6 million?"

Joey stared at the man. "Six million dollars?"

"Yes, Joey, six million dollars. Normally I would give you some time to give it back to me or let you work off your indebtedness, but thanks to the government freezing my accounts, I don't have any money currently, and I have bills coming due shortly. So you can appreciate my dilemma."

Joey swallowed hard, and Primovero reminded him, "Joey, you know there is only one way to resign your position with me."

The statement made an empty pit in Joey's stomach. How upset will he be when he finds out I don't have that much money to give him? He wondered.

*****

Agents Moore and Trenton watched in stunned silence as Primovero made his way across the room, only to have their view obstructed by Lessons and Wentz, who stood and made their way to the open table between themselves and the booth. The pair sat in seats with their backs towards their boss. The two killers stared directly at the agents and the rest of the room. Once seated, Wentz even touched two fingers to his brow and brought it forward in a mock salute towards the agents.

"The plot thickens," Moore whispered.

Trenton nodded in agreement.

"Think they would agree to scoot over so we can spy on their boss?" Moore joked.

Trenton was on the verge of responding when he was interrupted by the distinct sound of the front door opening again. Curios, the two agents peered over their shoulders behind them. Moore recognized the man standing in front of the door filling the space immediately: Primovero's personal driver and bodyguard, Thomas Cuppari. The man looked as if he were going to a funeral wearing a black pinned striped suit and fedora, Moore thought. Despite the expensive clothes and the years beginning to catch up with him, Agent Moore knew Cuppari had the reputation for being as dangerous as either Lessons or Wentz. After a quick study of the bar's interior, Cuppari walked further into the room to join Lessons and Wentz, Walking by Moore and Trenton without a second glance.

Cuppari leaving the doorway, allowed two more men to step inside the room. Both men had short-cropped hair, blue suits, and crisp white undershirts: FBI Agents Cliff Eldridge and Rui Gram. Moore and Trenton had never worked directly with either man, but he was aware both men were still in their twenties and had only graduated from Quantico in the last 2 years. As unseasoned agents, the two were part of the team tasked to maintain surveillance on Primovero. As junior Agents, they were assigned the daylight hours, the least interesting of shifts. Following Cuppari into the room, Agents Gram and Eldridge joined Moore and Trenton at their table, sitting so that they all faced the three bodyguards, Primovero and Calibrini.

"Howdy boys," Eldridge said by way of greeting, while Gram simply nodded.

"Glad y'all could make it to the party," Trenton responded to the pair before the group began a silent staring contest with the three men at the next table.

*****

The developing scene before him was not lost on Logan. There were now 25 people by his count in the room, including Julie, the waitress, and Martin, the bartender. He assumed there was at least another 1 or 2 in the kitchen—26 or 27 people in all. Amongst them there was at least 3 cold-blooded killers, four if he counted Primovero along with another four guys who could only be Federal Agents who he was sure were also armed. It seemed this date could be one to remember, anniversary or otherwise.

It took a few minutes, but after the initial excitement of Primovero's arrival, Logan could feel everyone in the restaurant let out a half breath. After another handful of seconds, the bar began to return to its normal rhythm, though there was still an undeniable sense of something imminent in the air.

Julie returned to their booth. "You two want your usual, or are you going to make my life hard again?" she said sarcastically towards Logan.

Michele laughed at the quip, while Logan put on his best mocking hurt face before confirming their usual was fine: a dozen buffalo wings for Logan, a BLT for Michele and a basket of fries to share with a side of ranch dressing. Smiling at his effort, Julie left to put their orders into the kitchen.

Following Julie's departure, Michele leaned forward and asked in a hushed serious tone, "What's going on?"

"I'm not sure, but something seems to be happening. I assume you know who the guy is who walked in a few minutes ago."

"I've seen him on the news. He's the mobster guy right?" she asked. Even more quietly than before, like the words were dirty.

"Yeah, his name is Richard Primovero. He pretty much runs organized crime in Kansas City. I assume the three guys at the next table work for him, or are his bodyguards or something, and the four guys in the suits next to them are cops. I would wager they are FBI or DEA. I don't know who the guy is in the wrinkled suit sitting with him is, but he looks like he would rather be anywhere than here."

"Why do you think they're here?" she whispered again.

Taking a moment to consider the question, Logan answered, "I honestly have no idea."

Looking around the room, Logan saw that he and Michele weren't the only ones enamored with the newly arrived guests. It seemed as if everyone was stealing glances towards the corner while lingering over their food. Even the table of older executives had ordered another round of drinks when Julie was clearing their empty baskets of food.

CHAPTER 16

September 19, 1:53

Sitting in the booth, the Chieftain felt as exposed as he ever had in his entire life. Every eye in the room had looked his way in the minutes since his arrival. He knew everyone in the place was judging him. They don't even know me, he reassured himself.

Even now, looking around the room, he could see the other patrons stealing sideways glances in his direction, with no one seemingly in a hurry to leave the show. In fact, it appeared that many were intent on lingering, judging by the waitress bringing another round of drinks to the table of suits she had just collected the food baskets from.

Well, that can't be helped. They certainly weren't being held hostage. Not yet anyway, he thought, requiring him to stifle a laugh at his own cryptic sense of humor. Feeling somewhat guiltily, he reasoned that if they just listen, there shouldn't be much collateral damage.

Stealing a look at the clock behind the bar, he saw that if everything was on schedule, then the show would soon begin. He just needed to keep this idiot, who he had nothing but contempt for, engaged for a few more minutes. Then the real fun would commence.

*****

Logan's phone buzzed in his pocket. Afraid it was the store, he dug it out and saw it was a text from Paige. He considered ignoring it, thinking she was trying to get him to take another job already initially. Still, then he was struck by the thought that maybe his previous employer was trying to renege on paying his fee. He really didn't want to have to go hunting for someone who refused to pay his bill. The one guy who tried to stiff him on a contract previously had seen the error of his ways, and Logan didn't really want to have to make an example of another.

Opening the text, it read, "Napier in KC with the Brockton twins. Doing a Job for someone called the Chieftain, be careful."

Well, at least she wasn't telling him he was going to need to go hunting, he hated killing people when there was no money in it. However, it made him consider again what Napier and the Brockton twins could be doing in Kansas City. There wasn't anything that jumped immediately to mind, but he knew in his tired state he wasn't operating at full capacity. Nonetheless, he knew enough about Napier and the twins' reputations to think, I don't know what they are up too, but it's going to get messy.

"What is it?" Michele asked, bringing his mind back to the present.

"Nothing," Logan answered, returning the phone to his pocket.

Julie had returned to top off his coffee and water when Logan heard a loud snapping and grinding metal sound behind him. The already shaded room grew even darker, and the restaurant went eerily quiet as everyone within tried to determine the source of the sound. The onset of the sudden silence was interrupted by the sound of compressed air releasing from what Logan recognized as airbrakes from large trucks.

Seeing Michele's eyes grow large and her mouth agape, his eyes moved to Julie, whose face looked even more disturbed than Michele's as they both looked towards the window at his back. Turning his hips in the booth to see what had occurred, a deep voice commanded from behind him, "Everyone stay where you are." Looking over his right shoulder, Logan saw the pair of bikers each holding submachine guns covering the room.

As the events unfolded, everything seemed to go into slow motion for Logan, a sensation he had first experienced in Iraq during his first real firefight. Beyond the two gunmen, Logan saw the light of windows had been blocked out by the canopy hanging over the glass. Its frame was in tatters, destroyed by what appeared to be two large trucks judging by the size of the tires Logan could see from the small portion at the bottom of the window that had not been blocked out. Logan knew they had to have been at least the size of garbage trucks and parked on the sidewalk itself to have hit the canopy like that. Looking closer, he could see that the two trucks were parked nose to nose in a coordinated manner, effectively covering the restaurant's entire face.

Pivoting his head back to check on Michele and Julie, he saw one of the two men with the bulky vests at the bar also had a weapon in hand. His suddenly revived his brain registered the weapon to be an H&K MP5 submachine gun with the longer 30 round magazine. Logan continued to watch as the young Hispanic man directed Martin from around the bar to an unoccupied table. Well, that cleared up the mystery of why the four bikers hadn't been sitting together, Logan thought. He chastised himself for having not listened to the warning alarms that had gone off in his head.

Turning his gaze to the middle of the room, Logan could see the mobsters and FBI Agents had all been caught flat-footed as well; nary a one had made a move, let alone, draw a weapon of their own.

Then a loud crash from the front of the room pulled Logan's attention to the suddenly open door where four armed men entered the restaurant in a single file line. The men were all wearing identical black tactical gear: boots, cargo pants, long sleeve shirts, gloves, and tactical vests, complete with magazine pouches and modern first aid pouches. Each man also carried a large duffle bag on his back. The quartet would have looked like a paramilitary swat team, if not for their face coverings. The first three men inside wore sleeves around their heads and lower faces, similar to what runners or construction workers wear that disquieted their features leaving only the space around the bridges of their noses and eyes exposed. The face shields were all different, allowing the men to identify one another; a knight helmet, an American flag, and a Confederate flag.

The two men with the flag face masks each carried big rifles. The man in the American flag had a sniper rifle outfitted with a scope and bipod. Judging by the barrel's size and the magazine protruding from the weapon, Logan guessed it was a .50 caliber. The man with the Confederate flag carried a distinctive looking weapon that any Army veteran would instantly recognize as an M249 or SAW. The SAW is a belt-fed automatic weapon capable of firing 725 rounds a minute. Serious firepower, he thought, watching the two men move in and draw down on the crowd, reinforcing the bikers. The Confederate masked man walked over to the two bikers behind Logan, making sure not to cross in front of any of the other men's muzzles. There he removed his bag, laying it on the table.

The man in the knight mask had a pistol in his left hand, but an MP5 of his own dangled on the right side from a strap on his vest. The Knight took off the large duffel bag and carrying it directly behind the bar, yanking the bartender out of the way, "Go sit down or else!" Opening the bag, he began removing some kind of electronic equipment, ignoring everything else in the room.

The fourth man and the last man to enter wore only a backward baseball cap and a pair of crimson shooter's glasses to disguise his features. From under the sides of the cap, Logan saw blonde hair, though, on his face, he wore an unnaturally dark goatee, which Logan gathered was a more subtle part of the man's disguise. He didn't appear to be carrying a weapon in his hands, though Logan saw he wore a pair of speed draw holsters on each leg that both carried big pistols. As the door closed behind him, the man lifted his right hand into the air revealing a small black box, about the size of a garage door opener. In a slow, deliberate manner, with everyone's eyes in the room upon him, the man in the sunglasses pushed the button. Almost instantaneously, a loud bang and flash of light showed in the windows, and the two large trucks both crashed flat to the ground, their chassis now destroyed.

A smile appeared on the man's face as he announced, "Now that I have your attention!"

Napier! Logan thought, watching as the man crossed the room to drop his own duffel bag at the biker table.

Quickly Logan looked back to check on Michele again, finding she had gone completely pale. Over her shoulder, his mind also registered Primovero in his corner booth smiling sadistically. Of course, the men were here for Primovero. But why? An enemy wanting to put him down before the man cut his own deal? He reminded himself it was none of his business, he had only one priority now, getting Michele out of here to safety, no matter what it took.

Reexamining his surroundings searching for options to get them out of there, Logan couldn't help but notice the room remained filled with stunned silence. Looking around, Logan noted the men in the flag masks with their rifles were already moving towards the back. Given their equal size and the weapons they carried, he assumed they would be the Brockman Twins. Bypassing the kitchen door, Logan realized they were moving towards the staircase to cover the street from the windows on the second floor, understanding that it made complete sense from a tactical perspective.

As the initial shock and awe of the moment past, Logan searched his memory for what he knew or had heard about Napier and the twins, trying to determine their play here. Unfortunately, through the fog of his mind, he couldn't come up with anything other than all three men weren't afraid to leave a path of death and destruction in their wake, which was uncomfortable, to say the least, sitting unarmed directly in their path. He could tell he wasn't alone in his discomfort seeing the looks of fear, worry, and anger on his fellow patrons' faces. And those poor folks didn't even know who these men were or their earned reputations.

The room's stunned silence was broken when the door from the kitchen crashed open, and a man in a greasy apron came skidding across the floor, apparently shoved by the man following him into the room. The newcomer wore the same paramilitary uniform the others had along with a blue and red mask in the form of a British flag across his face. The man carried another large duffel bag across his back and a large rifle that Logan could not identify slung across his chest. The odd-looking man from the bar emerged from behind the new arrival, submachine gun in hand and now wearing his own face mask: a skull. "The alley and back door are secure, and the kitchen is clear," the man announced in a distinctive high pitched voice.

Seeing the two men, the other three bikers donned their own masks: the Hispanic kid, a devil mask; the black biker, an evil clown; and the biggest man, a panda.

While the room was distracted by the cook's sudden arrival, Napier raised his nose towards the stairs. The nod was clearly a silent communication intended for the man in the British flag mask as the newest arrival stalked off, apparently intent on joining the twins upstairs. Napier then turned his attention to the man in the knight mask behind the bar. The Knight appeared to be studying a laptop which had been connected to three other machines: one square box about the size of a shoebox with an antenna, one small satellite dish maybe a foot high and six inches round and a separate square panel that looked like a guitar amplifier. Satisfied with what the laptop was telling him, the Knight gave Napier the thumbs up.

Turning back to the room, Napier commanded, "Everyone place their hands on the table in front of them. We are going to go table by table, person by person, and you will remove any weapons you have on your person slowly and give them to my men."

"The hell I will!" came an angry retort from the man in the maroon suit as he stood reaching inside his jacket. His hand never found what he was going for as the Skull pulled the trigger on his weapon twice. The sounds of gunshots were so close together they sounded as one filling the room. The rounds hit the man in the maroon suit just above and below the right eye leaving small angry holes upon entry. There was no distinguishing the exit wounds however, as the back half of the man's skull was gone, covering the wall and table behind him in a pink and red mist as blood, skull, and brains from the man's head found a new resting place.

"That's ten bucks, Mex. I take cash, check, or credit card," the Skull whistled, feint blue smoke curling up from his weapon.

"What the fuck are you talking about, you crazy son of a bitch?" the Devil asked.

"Don't you remember I said I bet you ten dollars I'd kill the first person today."

"What?" the Devil asked again.

"It's ok," the Skull whistled, "we'll just go double or nothing. You hear that people one of y'all is worth an Andy Jackson."

*****

The sound of the metal crashing had taken everyone in the room by surprise, including The Chieftain, and he knew it was coming. While recovering from the crash's shock, he was surprised to see the four men from inside the room with weapons in hand, covering the room before anyone else had reacted to the crashing sound. That hadn't been a part of his plan, but he appreciated the deviation. The tactic had caught, Lessons, Wentz, Cuppari and the FBI Agents off guard, eliminating the possibility of a gun battle and unnecessary injuries to the hostages. Of course, in his original plan, he had surmised that at least one or two of the people on his list would have been killed during the initial shootout. Nonetheless, they could easily be disposed of later. He couldn't afford witnesses who would be able to put it all together when it was over.

Seeing the men in their tactical suits enter the room, he couldn't help but feel a sense of relief, though he knew he had to hide his joy from anyone who could be watching. He consciously tried to mimic everyone else's facial expression in the bar who saw the newcomers as a sign of perilous danger even though to him, they represented freedom. No more prosecutors and lawyers. No more police officers. No more loose ends.

He continued watching the man in sunglasses, who he assumed was Napier, make a show of triggering the explosions on the trucks. He appreciated the theatre of the maneuver; how the action captured the undivided attention of everyone despite the other gun-toting men. The Chieftain also enjoyed how the trucks effectively placed a barrier between the cops and first responders that were assuredly on their way and the group inside. The police now wouldn't be able to view the actions going on inside, and to get in, they would have to come through the bottleneck between the trucks and building. That bottleneck could be easily defended by one or two men.

He continued to watch mesmerized when the sunglassed man announced, "Everyone place their hands on the table in front of them. We are going to go table by table, person by person, and you will remove any weapons you have on your person slowly and give them to my men."

Shit, he thought instantly, realizing he was sitting behind Wentz and knowing the hot head's reaction. It was as if everything in the world suddenly slowed to a crawl. He was in the midst of ducking for cover as Wentz rose from his seat shouting, "The hell I will." He hadn't evened hit fully behind the table when the loud crack, crack of the weapon filled the room. His ears registered the sound while he simultaneously felt the warm and sticky blood hit him on the side of the face.

He laid still a moment in the relative safety of the bench's cushioned seat. Not until he heard the man announce, "Anyone else object to giving up their weapons?" did he rise back to a seated position. Fully erect once again, his eyes were immediately drawn to Wentz's body lying on the floor beside the overturned chair the man had been sitting in only a minute prior, its once white cushion soaking up the blood from the man's corpse.

One down, three to go, he counted in his mind.

Taking his eyes off the corpse, he looked to his lunch companion to see if he had been hit. The man appeared unharmed but for having Wentz's blood all over his face and suit coat. He couldn't help but suppress a grin watching the man take a napkin and clean off his face.

*****

Napier watched the man's head explode into a mist of skull, blood, and brain matter. Stupid shit should have never gone for a gun against nine armed men, he thought. He certainly wasn't going to lose any sleep over it. In fact, looking closer at what was left of the man, he was satisfied that he was one of the men who had been marked for death: Wentz.

Nonetheless, he would need to remind his team about shooting too quickly, especially Joshua, as those rounds had nearly hit one of the men seated in a booth behind the deadman. That could have been a real problem as the man paying all their fees sat there. Napier assumed it was a safe bet that they would not get paid if they killed the man, accident or not. He wanted to yell the fact at his men but held his tongue. The instructions had been explicit on the fact that the man wanted to remain as anonymous as possible within the group until the last possible moment when he would reveal himself.

Looking at his watch, he decided it was going to be a long five hours until dark.

CHAPTER 17

September 19, 2:03 pm

Agent Moore sat at his table, unbelieving. The combination of seeing the man's head explode from sudden gunfire and the Skull's cryptic words caused the people in the room to react. Some began crying in fear, others gasping in sheer surprise, and still, others seemed to believe it was all just a show, unbelieving they could be living this. At Moore's own table, Eldridge had cussed in anger under his breath at the sudden, senseless violence, while Trenton and Gram both appeared shocked beyond words. Making it worse, Moore knew they all felt powerless to prevent it.

The crowd's sounds were quickly extinguished by the man in sunglasses raising a gloved hand, palm extended. As if they were all preschoolers, everyone did their best to quell the noise. When the room returned to relative quiet, minus a few gasping sobs coming from one of the older women, the man in the glasses continued, "Anyone else object to giving up their weapons? And don't worry about your cell phones. We are jamming the signals, so if you want to try to call for help, it will do you no good."

On cue, two of the masked men, the Skull and Devil moved to the double table where the crying woman sat, while the men in the clown and knight masks covered the room. All the while, the man in the panda mask began pulling, long cords of a gray looking substance from the saddlebags off the floor. While not an expert, it didn't take much imagination to understand the cords were some type of plastic explosive. Not good!

Moore's attention returned to the executives' table, when the man in the skull mask with the funny voice said, "Weapons." The group all in unison started shaking their heads no. Minus the woman who had been crying who now began to hyperventilate and struggle for air, her eyes going back and forth between the man in the skull mask and the body on the ground.

"Shut up, lady," the man in the devil mask shouted at her. When the older man at the head of the table tried to explain that she was scared, the Devil kicked his chair from beneath him, causing him to hit the floor hard. Before the older man could recover, the Devil was on top of him. Reaching behind his back, the masked man grasped a green handle that had been covered by his motorcycle vest. Removing a large square bladed knife, the man waved the weapon in the older man's face but intended for all within the room to see.

"Do you know what this is?" the Devil asked, knowing he had captured the audience's full attention. The gentleman on the ground emphatically shook his head no while the remainder of the room watched in silence, the only sound in the room the woman's continued gasping. The Devil continued, "This is a combat cleaver custom made by Chaos Bladecrafts. It's razor-sharp." To emphasize the point, he grabbed the old man by his chin. Forcing the man's head back against the floor, then with a flip of his wrist, the Devil took off part of the man's mustache and beard in one quick stroke, before continuing, "It weighs almost four perfectly balanced pounds and can cut one of your goddamn arms off in a single swing. If any of you want to see for yourselves, just step out of line one time and I'll show you."

The man in the sunglasses calmly added, "It will be in your best interest to speak only when spoken too."

Putting the large blade back into the sheath, the Devil stepped back, and the pair of masked men next approached the men in the green uniforms. "Weapons," the man in the skull mask said again. This time both men nodded in the affirmative. The man in the skull mask pointed to the man on the right who slowly pulled his right hand back towards his waistline and removed a Leatherman multitool from a black case on his belt and laid it on the table. The Skull picked it up and threw it to the man in the panda mask who caught it without comment, putting it down on the table beside the duffle bag as he worked cutting the gray cord into equal lengths.

The Skull then nodded towards the man on his left. The man mimicked the actions that his lunch partner had just performed, removing a relatively large folding knife from his pocket, though it appeared small in comparison to the combat cleaver they had just seen. Handing it over to the masked man, the uniformed man damn near dropped it when there was an explosion from the room above.

Based on the fact none of the masked men reacted to the sound Moore theorized the masked men must have all been anticipating it. Taking the knife from the fat man's shaking hand, Agent Moore could sense the smirk on the Skull's face hidden beneath the mask as he said in a provoking manner towards the Devil, "A lot of good a knife does you against a gun amigo."

"Cut it out," the sunglassed man said as he placed two fingers to his right ear, a sign the group was using comms. "The boys are through the wall upstairs and have their positions set. Now move along before we have company."

*****

In the right hands and circumstances, a knife can very effective gun or no gun, Logan told himself wishing to feel the hilt of his own blade riding comfortably in his pocket, so that he could show the man exactly how wrong he was. Then he reminded himself where he was and who he was with. Looking at Michele, he mouthed, "Just do what they tell us, and we will be ok." Hoping the words would reassure them both.

The Devil and Skull finished with the two large men in green uniforms and were looking for the next table to search when the room's quiet was disturbed again by the distinctive sound of a rifle shot coming from the floor above the main room. The sound of the big .50 cal was the most intimidating sound of any weapon for a single man to carry and it showed as Logan's eyes could see the shock and fear deepen on the faces of every hostage inside, even the men in the corner with the killers. The first shot was followed by 5 more, evenly spaced shots, indicating the shooter was taking deliberate aim at some unknown target.

"Good job. Keep me posted," Napier said conversationally into his throat mike as the last round's sound was fading into nothingness. Napier then raised his voice to address the room. "The first cops showed up but the boys upstairs persuaded them not to get too close. I suspect we will see the swat and tactical units here shortly."

The statement struck Logan as odd. Why tell the room that?

As Logan considered the possible intent of Napier's words, Napier nodded towards the two masked men telling them to continue their search. The Devil and Skull moved on to the table where Martin, Julie, and the cook sat. The men repeated the routine, asking for weapons. The three shook their heads no to say they didn't have any weapons on them. The Devil appeared ready to move on to the next table, but the man in the skull mask lingered, saying to Julie in a menacing tone, "Are you sure I don't need to frisk you red? I mean, you certainly have something hiding under that shirt."

Julie started shaking her head emphatically no, backing as far back into her chair as physically possible as the Skull extended his hands towards her. His efforts were halted when Napier shouted, "Enough! Now search the rest of them." Even threw the mask, Logan could see the look of disappointment on the man's face, or was that something else? Nonetheless, the man moved on without argument.

Next, the pair of masked men went to the table with the four men in the blue suits whom Logan suspected were police officers of some variety. "

Weapons?" the Devil said.

*****

Moore watched the two men approach their table. He knew what was coming. Taking his eyes off the pair of masked men, Moore looked at his three fellow agents and did his best to convey to them not do anything stupid with his eyes. Meeting Trenton's eyes, he was fairly certain they were in agreement knowing the man as he did. Similarly, Gram seemed to understand the vibe he was trying his best to deliver. Of Agent Eldridge, Moore was less assured. He just hoped neither man decided against playing hero and getting them all killed.

"Weapons?" the Devil asked. For the first time, Agent Moore recognized that the man was speaking with a strong Hispanic accent, a reminder that he needed to be taking as many mental notes as necessary so that they could get these guys when this whole ordeal was over.

Taking the lead, Moore slowly raised his hands to shoulder level, spreading his fingers as wide as they would go. Carefully he used his left hand to pull back his suit coat, revealing the shoulder holster. Using his right hand, he grasped the weapon at the bottom of the handle as far away from the trigger guard as he could and pulled the weapon in a measured manner holding it above his head. The man in the skull mask quickly snatched the pistol from him, thrusting it in his pants' waistband.

The man in sunglasses then approached the table. "Why are you carrying a weapon?"

"They're FBI," Primovero stated contemptuously before Agent Moore could respond.

"That right?" the sunglassed man asked, gesturing with his hand. "Let me see."

Repeating the same process, Agent Moore opened his jacket with his left hand and removed his wallet from the inside the inner breast pocket with his right. Handing it to the man, he carefully returned both hands to the tabletop.

The man with the sunglasses opened the wallet and took a moment to study the credentials inside. At the same time, Moore said a silent prayer asking that the Lord look after him and three fellow agents, asking him to dissuade the man with the sunglasses from executing the four of them.

Agent Moore considered the prayer answered when the man dropped the wallet on the table before announcing to the room, "Well lookie here, four of our nation's finest FBI Agents. You boys may want to be extra careful. My guys don't too much like cops and would love to have a reason to shoot a few, especially Feds. Understand?"

"Yes sir," Agent Eldridge answered gruffly, while the other three men simply nodded.

"Don't call me, sir, son. I work for a living," The sunglassed man responded. "That goes for all of you. You may call me Napier, should you have reason to address me at all, though I reiterate you may speak only when spoken too. Understand?"

The entirety of the room bobbed their collective heads in the affirmative.

"Now carefully, you three remove your weapons one at a time." Napier directed.

Following his example, each of the three agents cautiously removed their service pistols, which the man in the skull mask took, handing each gun to a different member of his mercenaries.

Once complete, Napier asked, "Are you sure none of y'all are wearing a backup? Should I have my men frisk you?"

"We are clean," Moore answered for the table.

"You better be. Otherwise, my men will not only kill you but one of the other hostages in the room, if I catch anyone of y'all with a weapon, as a matter fact that goes for the entire room. Anyone caught with anything that could be used as a weapon, not only gets you killed but also gets someone else killed. Capeesh?"

Again Moore and his fellow agents conveyed their understanding with a collective nod of the head. Seeing it, the rest of the room also acknowledged their understanding. Seemingly satisfied his point had been made, Napier and the two masked men moved off to the next table, while Moore searched his head for what he could recall about a man named Napier.

*****

The man in the skull face mask then walked over to Logan and Michele's table, stepping over the body still lying on the floor, while Devil lingered at the FBI table glaring at the four men.

First, the Skull looked dismissively at Logan and then took a long appraising look at Michele. Even threw the mask, there was no hiding the intent of the man's gaze. Allowing his eyes to linger a little too long on her, the man in the sunglasses said, "Let's go."

"Weapons," the Skull mask said mockingly.

Slowly reaching in her handbag, Michele removed the 9mm Sig Sauer Logan had gifted her. Laying it gently on the table, she gave the masked man a look of hatred Logan had certainly never seen before. The Skull picked up the weapon, never removing his eye from her obviously amused.

Never one to hold her tongue, she snapped, "What are you looking at?"

"You mama. When we are done here, I was thinking I could show you what it means to be with a real man."

"You think carrying that gun and scaring people makes you a real man? All I see is a scared little boy, trying to act tough to make up for your um obvious shortcomings," she said, contemptuously nodding towards the man's crotch.

Despite himself Logan felt himself smile at her comment. However, the smile immediately disappeared from his face.

The man grabbed Michele by the back of her head and smashed her beautiful face into the table. As she picked her head up from table, Logan saw blood coming from her nose and mouth. The sight of it made him feel a hatred inside that he hadn't felt in a long, long time.

You die first, Logan decided. You are all
gonna die!

CHAPTER 18

September 19, 2:17 pm

The Chieftain continued studying his saviors' actions as the room was systematically cleared of weapons by the men in the skull and devil masks. Seeing the man get shaved was particularly amusing, and he had to try hard to suppress the grin from his face during it. He was also amused by the disarming of the FBI Agents, though he wondered if Napier announcing his name was wise. However, the Chieftain wasn't a fan of the skull masked fellow's actions towards the good looking waitress nor his smashing the blonde woman's face into the table. Though he understood the violent action would be remembered by everyone else in the room, helping to keep them all in line until they could get out of here, he nonetheless wished the men would have made examples of someone other than the women.

Leaving the woman holding a stack of napkins to her bloody face, the two masked men approached the table with Lessons and Cuppari. Though he could not see their faces fully, he could tell by their posture that neither man was happy to be giving up their weapons.

Cuppari was first. In a move the Chieftain knew was to show he wasn't intimidated, Cuppari stood allowing him to look down on the two masked men. Reaching inside his sport coat, he ceremoniously removed the large .357 revolver he always carried from his shoulder rig. Handing it over to the Skull, Cuppari said, "Careful with that asshole. Wouldn't want you to shoot your dick off or anything."

"That all you got old man?" the Devil mask taunted in return.

Bending over, Cuppari hiked up his left pant leg and then pulled another much smaller pistol from the ankle holster there. "This is probably more your speed," he said, tossing it to the Devil.

The Devil eased back the hammer of the little pistol, placing it directly on Cuppari's chest. In response, Cuppari swatted the man's hand away before nonchalantly sitting down summarily dismissing the man.

Next was Lessons turn. "Pat him down." The man in the sunglasses ordered, confirming the man had heeded his warning in the original plan.

"You heard the man stand up and put your hands behind your head," the Skull sneered at Lessons. Lessons did as he was told and stood placing his hands on his head, giving two men an icy stare that was enough to bring the room's temperature down a few degrees.

Patting him down, the Skull removed a pistol from his belt and a fixed blade knife from its sheath hidden in the Lesson's pants' left hip pocket. "That's all you got," the man in the devil mask sneered.

However, lessons didn't take the bait remaining silent and perfectly still with his hands on his head.

"Sit your ass down, boy," the Skull whistled at him menacingly.

Wordlessly Lessons sat, staring straight ahead, the icy stare in full effect; now boring a hole into Napier and the Knight behind the bar.

*****

Napier watched as his men finished clearing the room of weapons. Though it was still very early in the assignment, he was satisfied with how things had gone thus far. For the most part, the instructions and plan had been good. Very good even especially with the touches he and his team had added. That wasn't to say there were not a few developments that were bothersome.

The plans provided by the man calling himself Chieftain had warned him that there would likely be some cops in the room, but he hadn't mentioned the possibility of FBI agents. The feds he knew would be much more difficult to evade after they were away because they would take it personally and had nearly limitless resources at their disposal to hunt down any and all survivors. Of course, the feds had been hunting him for years anyway without any luck. But the point remained it was a possibility which should have been shared.

Napier had also been told there would be multiple armed bodyguards in the room who would each need to be eliminated before the job was over. The instructions implied that the Chieftain expected a handful of the men marked for death would be taken out during the shootout that would have taken place during his team's storming of the building. This part of the plan was never sensible to Napier. Why expose himself and his team to unnecessary gunplay? Thus he had staged four of his men inside the room to get the jump on anyone who would consider fighting back against his invading force. Plus, the plan was dependent upon having hostages. The hostages would be valuable commodities before this ordeal was over he knew. Not having to shoot it out inside the bar minus the dumbass who had went and gotten himself killed trying to draw a weapon against a room full of armed men had extended their negotiating power when the time came.

Regardless of his changing the plan, to this point, he imagined his benefactor was happy overall with their results. The man had given no indication otherwise. Napier was actually thankful that the man hadn't objected to his changing of the plan. An untrusting sort of guy, Napier wasn't so stupid to ignore the fact that it didn't take a big leap to consider himself and his team would become targets of the Chieftain as well before this was all over. With that in mind, he had changed the plan slightly for a couple of reasons. First, the changes made tactical sense while continuing to work towards the Chieftain's overall goal of confusing the cops and eliminate anyone in the room who could implicate the Chieftain. Secondly, he had put a few unexpected elements into the plan so that he and his men were not overly predictable, should the man try to double-cross him. He needed the Chieftain to feel comfortable but not so comfortable that he thought Napier was no longer needed.

Finished with the mobster's bodyguards, Napier watched the Skull and Devil turn towards the corner booth where the last of the restaurant's patrons sat. Stepping towards the table, the Skull said one last time, "Weapons."

Looking at him cooly, Primovero said, "You will find no weapons here, gentleman. Carry o'' about your business, please."

The calm response from the gangster confused his two men, causing them to look to Napier for direction. Taking a moment to decide whether a search of the two men would alienate the man paying his fee, he waved off his pair of henchmen deciding it wasn't worth the risk.

"Now that that's done, Panda, do me a favor and take this body back to the freezer, I am sick of looking at it."

Wordlessly Panda walked to the body, crouched and picked it up, throwing the limp carcass over his massive shoulder, the way a farmer would carry a bag of feed corn. As the big man walked away, Napier added, "Now ladies and gentlemen, if none of you want to join your friend in the freezer, I advise your continued cooperation, though I believe there is room in there for all of you should it be necessary."

CHAPTER 19

September 19, 2:22

The entire bar heard the sirens in the distance. It had taken almost 8 minutes for the police to initially respond to the pair of exploding vehicles and subsequent shots fired. And now the sound of multiple sirens indicated the full cavalry was set to arrive. As the noise grew louder, Agent Moore could sense everyone suddenly holding their breath, wondering what was to come. They were not held in suspense long as the sound of the machine guns opening up above them filled the room: da..da..da...da...da..da...da from the firing of bullets mixed with cling...cling...cling...cling as the expended brass hit the floor above.

The men above fired their weapons for about 30 seconds. The display obviously had the desired effect as once the machine guns' noise stopped, the sirens no longer seemed to be approaching. In fact, the sirens stopped sounding at all.

I hope they are okay out there. That was stupid anyway, the first responder had already taken on rifle fire, Agent Moore thought.

The silence that followed was as maddening as it was tense. Studying the room, Moore looked at each and every individual in the room, hostage and masked man alike, each person silently conveying the thought of "what's next?" Then the unexpected happened. From the room's corner booth came a stifle of laughter, like a kid trying not to laugh at something inappropriate in front of their parent. The sound then grew as both men in the corner began to laugh. They were joined by Napier and then seemingly at once the masked men and finally the loudest of all the tall man accompanying the blonde lady with the busted nose joined in.

Before Agent Moore could work up the courage to say anything, Primovero stood and slammed his hand upon the tabletop. Still snickering, he said, "That'll teach those boys to mind their own damn business for a while."

"Don't get too comfortable." Agent Moore said, unable to hold his tongue any longer, "They aren't just going to sit out there and do nothing."

His words drew a slap on the back of the head from the Panda who was working with some wiring and electronics at the table behind them. The slap nearly drove Moore's face into the table, causing him to literally see stars and hear ringing in his ears.

Despite the ringing, he heard Cabrini advise, "Quite right. I'd be willing to bet that they will shut down the power in here within a few minutes and hope that the darkness and the lack of air conditioning will help draw us out. After they cut the power, they will attempt to make contact and ask for the list of demands to begin negotiations."

Agent Moore and the other agents all looked at one another, knowing the man's words were correct.

"He's right," Primovero jumped in, "Leave it to cops to be unimaginative and do everything straight by the book." Then redirecting his gaze towards Napier and the masked men, the mob boss added, "I hope you and your men have prepared for this as well."

"You know we have," Napier answered in a sadistic tone.

*****

September 19, 2:36 pm

The Chieftain wasn't surprised when the lights went out, casting the entire room in eerie false darkness despite the mid-afternoon hour. Some of the hostages gasped at the sudden extinguishing of lights. Meanwhile, he heard cussing from near the front of the room where the Panda and Clown had been running the corded grey material, and wiring harnesses.

His ears then detected what sounded like rushing feet coming from the hallway, followed by a sudden crash. Then a male voice with a hispanic accent yelled loudly, "Get off me you dumb son-of-a-bitch."

"Fuck you, man, I didn't see you." came the Skull's distinctive whistle.

"Cut that shit out, you two." Napier's voice sounded as two lantern looking lamps were suddenly lit near the bar.

In the light, held high by the Knight, the Chieftain could see the Clown and Panda, weapons in hand, near the window. The two men covering the space to the East of the building adjacent to where they had been working. On the opposite side of the room, the men wearing the devil and skull masks were lying in a heap upon the floor. The Chieftain surmised they were supposed to have been covering the gap for a possible rush from the swat team. But in the darkness, the pair had gotten tangled up. Now in the low light, the pair engaged in a staring contest.

"Devil, take your ass and hang the lanterns before you two idiots do something stupid," Napier commanded with more than a hint of anger in his voice.

"You heard him, boy. Go sit down," the Skull provoked the Devil once again whilst he uncurled himself from the floor and the Devil below him.

"Who you callin boy Ese?" the Devil responded, pulling the cleaver from under his vest once again as he got to his feet.

"You!" the Skull said evenly, turning his submachine gun on the man.

The argument was broken by the sound of three rapid gunshots, fired into the ceiling by Napier. "Goddamn it, that's enough!" he yelled, for the first time genuinely raising his voice. To emphasize his point, he aimed the pistol in the direction of the two men.

The Chieftain and the hostages all stared at the scene before them. It was apparent that both of the masked men were calculating their odds. Seemingly simultaneously, both men determined that their boss was not joking and would shoot them for any further digressions.

Seeing the men were not going to challenge him, Napier's voice returned to a conversational tone, "Now Skull take your ass up stairs and make sure those three are okay. Then come back and sit on that window. Devil hang the lights and then help those two finish running that Semtex. And I am telling you two assholes right now, if I have to break you two up again, I am just going to shoot you and be done with it. You understand me?"

Both men grumbled they understood and then went off as directed. Watching the pair storm off, the Chieftain hoped the police remained calm intent to wait them out, otherwise, any more stress and the Chieftain was sure these dumbasses would kill one another, leaving him all alone.

*****

When the lights went out, Logan heard Michele gasp. Logan knew she was never a fan of the dark and kept a nightlight on in her bedroom, hallway, and bathrooms at both their houses. He was sure the added stress of the armed men and the scurrying feet certainly weren't helping.

Then came a crash and cussing men. Taking the opportunity, Logan quickly leaned over, unzipped the backpack and removed the spare auto-injector from the Albuquerque job, slipping it inside his left cargo pocket. Not the greatest of weapons, but it was better than nothing. He just needed to make sure that he remembered there was only enough for one if he got the opportunity to use it.

When the lights came on, he was happy Napier had stopped the fight between the Skull and Devil. He didn't much care about the man in the Devil mask, but the man in the Skull mask was his, even if he had to track the man to the end of the earth. Or more likely, he'd have Paige find the man for him. She was a magician with things like that.

CHAPTER 20

September 19, 3:24 pm

With the battery-powered lanterns hung at various points throughout the building's entire interior, the room was aglow in an eerie light. The lights allowed Agent Moore to see clearly enough though there were definite shadows and blind spots within the space that remained. The scene reminded him of Rick's Bar in Casablanca, all that was missing was the piano playing in the corner.

An old fashioned black phone with a cord, cradle, and 12 buttons rang behind the bar with the metallic clanging sound that one associates with old phones, breaking the silence. It reminded Agent Moore of the phone in his grandma's house when he was a kid, and in his mind, the sound fit the spooky atmosphere. On the third ring, Napier answered, "Hello."

Moore listened intently to the half of the conversation that he could hear from where he sat. It wasn't difficult in the room's silence. Nor did it appear the killer cared that he spoke loud enough for all to hear.

"Of course, I expected your call. It was so predictable, Marshal Grube."

It was Moore thought since Cabrini had told them all a half-hour prior that the police would cut the lights and then call. He would have questioned if the person on the line was qualified to be speaking to the man since the local crisis negotiator had been their former boss whom Agent Pearson replaced, but he recognized the name Marshal Grube.

Marshal Grube was Nancy Grube, a US Marshal who was a trained crisis negotiator. Trained by the FBI's Crisis Negotiation Unit, she had a reputation for being very calm and levelheaded, which was definitely preferable to the alternative, having seen how easily the men in the hostage-takers could be provoked. He hoped it also meant that the local US Marshal Special Operations Group were on location as well since the FBI's own Hostage Rescue Team was in Washington DC and couldn't be here for hours, and Agent Moore distrusted the local and State police units to manage the situation.

"What do I want? Well, Marshal I think we all want world peace, a place to call home and food on the table do we not."

Fuckin Asshole, Moore thought, though he knew it was Grube's job in this situation, to attempt to understand the offender and show them that she was listening to hopefully empathize, build trust, and eventually get the person to surrender voluntarily. However, it didn't take much insight to see that these guys were not planning to surrender anytime soon.

"Well, Ms. Grube, if you can't give us world peace, I'll tell you a few things we do need. First, I need the list of witnesses who provided testimony at the indictment of Mr. Primovero. You may call me at any time with that list. Secondly, I need 25 million dollars wired to routing number 187307288-47 account 3004872685. And finally, I need your team to arrange to have a fully fueled helicopter landed on the roof of this building. The helicopter must be capable of carrying 12 passengers. The pilot will land the helicopter and then exit the vehicle and retreat across the roof to the east and get off the roof on at the corner of Bank and 9th Streets. We will allow one fire truck passage down 9th street traveling east to west to extend his ladder to allow the pilot to exit. If the truck comes from any other direction. Or if anyone should try to leave the truck. The pilot will be shot, and the truck will be fired upon. Before you object, I am told the roof of this building will support the helicopter's weight. I have my own pilot who tells me that the building is large enough for a skilled pilot to land without any problems during the day. However, it's really tight, so it would be much more difficult at night. I also advise you to move quickly on these items, patience is not something my men are good at."

This guy is crazy; surely, he knows they will not give him any of those things, thought Moore. Though he knew that Agent Grube's job was to convince him that she was on his side and there to help him, not criticize him.

"Show of good faith?" Sure I will give you a show of good faith. Give me 20 minutes, and I will release some prisoners."

Shit, that's the best news yet. Hopefully, he will let all the civilians go, Moore thought. Looking around the room, he could see that everyone had certainly perked up at the statement.

"How many you ask? Oh, let's say a handful."

Moore looked around the room and really counted for the first time. The bartender, cook, and waitress, the two city workers, the table of older ladies and gentlemen in suits and their administrative assistant and the blonde and her lunch date. That was 14 without counting himself and the other Agents or Primovero, Cabrini, Lesson or Cuppari, whom he didn't imagine Napier would release regardless. Even being as generous as possible, he couldn't imagine "a handful" would free all 14 of the others either."

"Marshal Grube, I have no more time to talk. I advise you get your people working on that list. Once the sun goes down, I will stop playing nice."

"No, Marshal Grube, I will not keep talking and my good faith effort just shrank. Now get me my list of names, money and helicopter." And with that, he placed the phone on the cradle gently.

Moore wasn't a hostage negotiator, and he certainly wasn't an expert on criminal profiling, but there was something about what had just happened that felt wrong. Napier had been entirely to calm, to measured on that call. Obviously, he knew what would happen. The man had prepared and rehearsed precisely what he was going to say. The specific directions about the helicopter showed that. But why rehearse those demands? The man surely had to know that the people outside would never actually give in to those demands. Right?

Something else was going on here, but what? God help them if these guys actually were considering turning themselves into martyrs and going out in a blaze of glory.

*****

September 19, 3:40 pm

"Ladies, please stand," the Clown said.

Logan watched Michele's eyes grow large at the summons as she looked at him questioningly. Nodding, he tried his best to reassure her it was ok.

Michele stood along with the other four women in the room: Julie, the two older executive types, and the young assistant. Upon standing, the same woman who had started to hyperventilate previously began to do so again. Leaning over the table, the gasping woman supported herself with one hand, while clutching herself with the other. The young girl rushed to her side and began whispering in her ear that it would be alright while patting her on the back to console her.

"Calm down damnit, we're going to release you! This is about to be over for you," the Clown said, seemingly trying to add to the effort to reassure the woman.

Once the younger woman was able to get the lady calm enough to stand on her own, the Clown gathered the women in the middle of the room. "We will let you go one by one every thirty seconds. You will go out the front door and turn left. Once clear of the truck you will veer into the middle of the street and walk to the barricade to your freedom. I advise you to walk slowly and directly with your hands up so that the officers can see them. Understand?"

The women all began nodding their heads in unison acknowledging they understood.

Hearing Michele was about to be released brought a sense of relief to Logan. Knowing she would safe and out of the way would make what he would do go much more smoothly.

"Wait a minute!" Napier interrupted. "All women, they are going to think us sexist. We can't do that. Whatever would Marshal Grube think of me? She seems to be a woman of equality. Let's show her we are too." Pointing to the young girl who had consoled the older woman, he said, "You sit back down."

The command immediately brought the hyperventilating woman into a full panic, as she clutched her chest and looked to be on the verge of a full heart attack. The young woman stepped to her and tried to reassure her, "Grandma, it'll be ok."

"I'll stay." Michele then volunteered. "If you need one of us to stay here, I'll stay is that ok?" she asked Napier.

Logan felt his heart sank at her request, wanting her safely out of the way.

Shrugging, Napier answered, "Fine by me. Have a seat." Turning to the room, he crossed his arms and placed his chin in his right hand in an over-exaggerated manner to indicate he was thinking. Then suddenly, he pointed at the older mobster in the black suit who had carried the big revolver, "You will be going with them."

"Me?" the man said, pointing to himself confused.

"Yes, you," said Napier.

"I'm not leaving the boss." the big man declared defiantly.

"You're acting like this is a request. It is not. You are going with the women, or you will be joining your friend in the freezer."

"It's ok Tom, go." Primovero broke in.

Looking towards his boss, the man looked confused, even hurt.

"You will go out with the prisoners, and you will have everything ready for when this is all over. Understand?" Primovero clarified.

It took a second for the words to sink in, but the man suddenly smiled a not so lovely smile and nodded affirmatively. Getting up, he joined the line of women at the door.

The man in the clown mask organized the five hostages, setting them in a line within the room near the front door. First, Julie, then the hyperventilating woman, the granddaughter, the second executive, then the mob man.

Apparently satisfied with the arrangement of the hostages earmarked for release, Napier began dictating what the other people in the room's jobs would be as the group of hostages were released. He set his men up in a defensive posture to thwart any type of assault should the group outside get any ideas.

However, Logan knew it was unlikely the police outside would not want to do anything at this juncture when Napier appeared to be cooperating. Though Logan himself was suspicious of the man's motives.

*****

Observing the arrangement of the prisoner's release playing out, Moore decided this had all been preplanned. The Clown's seeming initiative to choose five hostages for release without having been told to do so didn't fit the modus operandi the group had displayed overall in the first hour. From what Moore had seen thus far, none of the mercenaries did anything wihtout seeking the glassed man's approval first.

Then following the Clown's selection of the prisoners, the man calling himself Napier had again tookover, seemingly because he didn't want to appear sexist ? It made no sense to

Moore. Nonetheless, from the point he replaced the woman with Cuppari, Napier apparently couldn't help himself and began micromanaging the situation again.

Pointing towards the larger of the two workers in the green uniforms, Napier placed the obese man to the left of the front door. He explained to the man his job was to open and close the door at the designated intervals to allow the selected hostages to walk away. He was advised that he needed to stay down to leave the men inside a clear line of fire should anything happen during the release. Napier then directed the other big man in the city's uniform to place himself in the window on the southwest corner. Behind the man, Napier ordered the Clown to position himself to guard against the possibility of the police using the prisoner release as an opportunity to assault the building. In the southeast corner, he set one of the men wearing suits who had been sitting at the double table. Behind the man, Napier placed the Skull, who patted the man on the shoulder with his machine gun's barrel.

Looking over the arrangement, Napier then ordered the Knight from behind the bar to take up position behind the man at the door, to act as an extra layer of protection should an assaulting force manage to breach their defenses to that point. The Knight vehemently protested the assignment saying, "I have to monitor the equipment to make sure it remains online."

To Moore, the excuse was a convenient one for the Knight, who sounded put off by the assignment, almost as it were beneath him. Napier, however, would have none of it. He pulled a pistol and pointed it at the man saying, "Comrade don't think you're not expendable. That equipment will be fine on its own for a few minutes. Plus, Panda and Devil are still setting the Semtex."

Hearing the contempt in his voice, Moore wondered if maybe Napier hadn't tasked the man to monitor the door simply put him in his place. The man appeared to have a purpose with every action and command; thus far, Moore didn't think this was any different. The Knight gathered his submachine gun with a huff and positioned himself behind the large man at the door.

Smiling at the man's bending to his orders Napier stated, "Ok fat man squat down and get ready with that door!"

The man did as he was told. Even from afar, the large man was obviously uncomfortable maintaining the squat because of his girth. Agent Moore also wondered if the man's discomfort wasn't exacerbated from the realization he positioned to be a human shield and door barricade should a gun battle ensue.

He was certain Napier was aware of it and had chosen the large man specifically for that reason.

"On the count of three you go", announced Napier pointing towards the waitress. "1...2...3!"

On the word "three," the fat man pulled the door open wide by duck walking backward. Staying low, as instructed, the man gave enough room to allow the first hostage passage outside. The pretty waitress walked through the door and turned to her left precisely as ordered.

The Clown provided play-by-play of the scene from his observation post in the corner. "She's in the open and moving towards the middle of the street with her hands raised. She's nearing the police barricade. She stopped. They are having her turn all the way around. Her hands are down and they are letting her through."

"30 seconds and you go." Napier said to the next woman in line.

The woman who had hyperventilated twice already appeared on the verge of doing so again, sobbing softly. "Just do what the waitress did, grandma," the young girl tried to reassure her lovingly.

"And go," Nappier commanded foregoing any type of countdown apparently unwilling to listen to the woman for any longer.

The woman moved forward through the door and made the same left turn. It took what seemed an eternity, but the Clown finally announced, "She is in the open. She is moving toward the street. She is nearing the barricade. They stopped her. Oh shit, she fainted!"

"Jesus Christ," Napier mumbled under his breath. Moore watched as the man threw his hands in the air while spinning away from the bar stalking off down the hall.

Focused on the picture before him and unaware that Napier had just left the room, the Clown continued, "The cops are confused. Ok, now they have someone coming across the barrier."

A pause, "He's checking her over." Silence again as everyone in the room seemed to hang on his every word. "Ok. He's getting her back to her feet." A sigh of relief was felt if not heard from the hostages' audience hearing the woman was apparently ok. Finally, the Clown stated, "They're through."

Looking around the room, Moore saw the smiles on the other hostages' faces and felt that everyone within the walls was silently applauding the woman's success, though none were as elated as the woman's granddaughter who was next in line.

Agent Moore had watched the girl from the moment her grandmother walked through the door. The emotion was evident every moment as the Clown called the play by play of her granmother's journey. Her face wrinkled and relaxed, her lips alternating between smiles and quivering with every word the Clown uttered. When the woman had hit the pavement, he thought the girl was soon to follow suit but to her credit she held on. Only when the Clown said her grandmother was up and had made it across the barricade did the girl appear to get a bit of her own strength back. In fact, she seemed to be overly amped to leave when the Knight reminded her, "Devushka do not go until you are told to."

Returning to the room, Napier waited much longer than 30 seconds before saying anything, which ratcheted the tension in the room back up. To make matters worse, he slow-played the countdown when he spoke, "3, Mississippi... 2, Mississippi... 1 Mississippi... and go!"

Agent Moore couldn't help but smile at the girl's resolve who, before stepping through the door, touched her fingers to her lips and waved to him. Moore was happy that Napier laughed and let her go. Based on the Clown's description, the young girl didn't let the grass grow under her feet between the door and the police barricade either; maybe realizing that antagonizing the killer wasn't a good idea.

"Clear!" the Clown declared. Moore and many others in the room seemed to exhale at the announcement, which triggered the 30-second clock again.

The final of the four women made it out the door without delay or hijinks. As the woman made her way across the no man's land outside Knight reminded Cuppari who had stepped near the door, "No funny business."

"Don't worry, I'll do what needs to be done," the faithful bodyguard responded matter-of-factly looking like he was about to take a simple evening stroll.

When the Clown reported the woman had cleared the barrier, Napier said, "Okay, Mr. Cuppari, you're up."

For some reason that Agent Moore couldn't wrap his head around the statement sounded odd to him. He tried to work through what was bothering him about it as he continued to take in the fascinating scene, awaiting the man's release. Again the prescribed 30-second mark elapsed without Napier beginning a count down or granting permission to exit. Instead, the man pulled a phone from his pocket. "When you get over there, give this to Marshal Grube," the man in sunglasses said, handing the phone to

Cuppari. "Tell her she can communicate with me using this. My number is the only number preprogrammed on the phone, and she can text me. I don't like having everyone hearing my side of the conversation."

Cuppari stared at the phone for a brief moment and took it, giving a half shrug, "Whatever you say." Turning, he walked through the door, marching proudly from the room into the evening light.

As the fat man hurriedly closed the door and struggled to rise, it suddenly struck Agent Moore., How did he know the man's name was Cuppari? But Agent's Moore's train of thought was completely derailed by a concussive explosion from outside that sounded more like a crack of lightning than a gunshot.

"Damn boss, he just got blown in half," the Panda announced from behind Moore!

"What the fuck just happened?" Moore asked aloud despite himself.

*****

Check Cuppari off the list. Two down six to go. Napier thought as he looked through the window at what remained of the mobster's body. Turley had been right; the small phone bomb had nearly ripped the man in two. Impressive what such a small amount of Semtex can produce.

The bar phone's ringing pierced the silence of the shocked room once again with its metallic clang. Taking his time walking to the bar Napier picked up the line on the fourth ring, knowing without a doubt who was on the other end. "Hello, Marshal Grube."

"What was that?" Marshal Grube asked.

"Oh, that was simply a little display. Our friend was carrying less than an ounce of Semtex that detonated in his hand. You saw the results. For reference, we have wired this building with 50 pounds of it. You and your officers try anything funny, and the entire block will be nothing more than a hole and a memory Marshal Grube. Now, as I look at my watch, it is a few hours before dark. I have yet to see any of my requested items. No list of witnesses, no money, and no helicopter. I suggest you make that happen and soon unless you want to see a fireworks display that the city will never forget."

CHAPTER 21

September 19, 4:22 pm

The room's morale had risen with the release of each hostage, helped by the accompanying play by play of the big man in the clown mask. Seeing the young girl blow the killer a goodbye kiss, had even provided a feel good moment to those in the restaurant. But the reality of the situation slapped everyone in the face again with the death of the mobster. The pronouncement he had been blown apart by a mere ounce Semtex of which there was over 50 pounds in the building, slapped them all into their frightening reality.

Once the initial shock of the bomb detonating and killing Cuppari had subsided, the remaining individuals were consolidated to the two booths and two tables in the back corner. The hostages were herded easily, exhibiting their understanding of what upsetting the men with the guns would mean.

Agent Moore and his three fellow agents had been moved into the booth adjacent to the booth occupied by Primovero and Cabrini. Joining Cabrini and Primovero were the woman who had volunteered to stay and her date, the tall man in the superhero T-shirt. The three executives had been put at the table with Lessons nearest the wall. While the two fat guys, the bartender and the cook sat in the table nearest to Moore and his fellow agents.

Agent Moore understood the practicality of the move. It allowed the mercenaries more hands to work, placing the last of the Semtex along the walls and cover the possible approaches of assault. Clustered together allowed them to be covered by only a single man, the Knight at the bar who alternated between watching the group and checking the machine's screen perched before him. Agent Moore could tell by the man's body language the man was getting antsy about something. Having a nervous man with a gun pointed at them didn't make Moore feel better about the situation.

*****

Logan was disappointed that Michele had volunteered to remain in the name of equality, though his level of respect for her went up even higher if that was possible. But that didn't mean she needed to be here. It actually pissed Logan off even more. Napier agreed to her staying when his plan all along had been to kill the mobster as a demonstration to the police outside what he could and would do. Making matters worse, that demonstration had a profound effect on Michele. She now seemed more afraid of being blown up than being shot, a phenomenon he had seen a lot in Iraq and Afghanistan, though he had kinda always thought dead was dead. To her credit again, though, when they were directed to their new seats, she walked there ramrod straight without any sideways glance. Logan was glad for it, as she would have seen the man in the Skull mask staring at her with each step. Exercising what he believed good judgment, she slid into the booth next to the man in the rumpled suit, leaving the open space next to Richard Primovero for him.

"Welcome to our little party," Primovero said as Logan sat down.

"If this were the old country, my grandmother would have prepared a feast in your honor," the man in the wrinkled suit added boyishly to Michele.

Not wanting to be rude Logan, replied back, "Thanks for having us." The remark drew a snicker from one of the nearby tables causing Napier to remind everyone to be quiet.

"We were just making our new guests comfortable, Mr. Napier. You have nothing to worry about." Primovero replied back, drawing a long look from the killer. Primovero matched the man's gaze in what appeared to be some test of wills. Finally, Napier looked away and said to everyone, "The next person to speak without my permission is getting his fucking tongue cut out. Understand?"

Not letting the moment pass, Primovero said quickly, "Perfectly."

Obviously irritated at the man getting in the last word again, Napier spun on his heel and went straight to the bar where he spoke in hushed tones to the man in the Knight mask, looking over his shoulder and pointing to the crowd. The Knight man nodded in affirmation to whatever was said, and Napier walked down the hall, out of sight.

Once he was entirely out of sight, Logan heard Michele exhale. Looking back towards her, he could see how uncomfortable the scene between the two men had made her, and once again, he wished she had just gone with the hostages outside. Her presence was going to make what he was about to do that much harder.

*****

Napier left the room walking upstairs, knowing he needed to step away from Primovero before he gave in to the urge to hurt the man. Obviously, the man was toying with him and playing with the deference he had shown him to that point. Napier reminded himself he couldn't let the man get to him. He needed to stay focused on his task regardless of the annoyance of the man. In the end, he would get satisfaction one way or another.

Walking upstairs, he checked on his three shooters there. "How did the cops respond to our little display?"

Cain, who was covering the front of the building and had the most complete view, reported, "They damn near pissed themselves. I think a few of them even dropped their guns when the bomb went off."

Able who was covering the back added, "Yeah, but now they are moving assets around. They have a couple of different tactical teams on scene. There have been at least two armored trucks driving up and down 8th street. One is the KCPD SWAT team, the other I'm not sure because it's unmarked, but I guess it's the FBI's truck since Joshua told us there are four agents downstairs."

"Joshua talks too damn much. Anyway, I don't think that is the FBI. I am pretty sure the field office here doesn't have an HRT team. I think its more likely the US Marshal's Special Operations Van. The hostage negotiator that made contact is a US Marshal named Grube so it would make sense she would have her people on sight as well."

"Marshals," Joe said, monitoring the hole they had made in the East wall, "That means the Ghost is out there somewhere. He could be looking at us right now." Alarmed at his own realization, the man sank further down below the wall.

"Don't worry, even if he is, he isn't going to shoot with us holding all the hostages and us having the building wired to blast. Your voices could tell you to shake your dick at em, and he wouldn't do anything about it." Napier assured the man.

The man laughed at the remark before saying calmly. "No worries, they are telling me the biggest danger is in here anyway."

Unsure of how to interpret the remark, Napier let it drop. He remained in the space a few minutes more, taking the time to observe the police and surrounding area. Satisfied they didn't appear on the verge of assaulting the place, he told the trio to keep him updated if they see anything that looks out of the ordinary.

Walking back down the stairs, he wondered again about Winter's ability to assemble a team.

*****

September 19, 4:47 pm

Following Napier's exit, the room settled back into it's uncomfortable quiet. With nothing else to do, the group once again focused on the three men who continued forming and setting Semtex's ropes all over the room. The masked men followed some sort of diagram that the biggest man had pinned to the wall over the table they were using, but for what purpose remained a mystery. In his plan, The Chieftain had only asked that they have enough explosives to detonate the building. He had envisioned nothing more than a pile of dynamite or fertilizer and diesel fuel like had been used in the Oklahoma City bombing sitting in the middle of the room. He couldn't help but wonder the reason behind the complexity of it all, Surely 50 pounds of the stuff was enough to bring the building down without all the fanfare?

He wasn't going to reveal himself by questioning Napier's tactics; however, admitting to himself Napier had proven thus far, his deviations had been effective. The unexpected demonstration the man had coordinated with Cuppari had been incredibly practical. Not only did it get rid of another of the potential witnesses against him, but it also showed the police outside that not only did they have explosives, but they were also more than willing to use them. That should give them pause regarding any possible efforts to storm the place.

His thoughts were interrupted by a strange beeping noise, a very uncomfortable sensation to experience while sitting in a room packed full explosives. Panicking, he began to look for the source of the noise. Upon discovering the machine on the bar was beeping, he was able to take a calming breath.

His eyes remained transfixed on the object as the Knight stepped over to the machine and hit some buttons. Following a few clicks, the Knight's hands touched the button to activate his microphone he said excitedly, "We have a problem boss."

Emerging from the hallway less than 30 seconds later, Napier asked, "What problem?"

"The others are having difficulty piercing the wall. Apparently, the brick was reinforced with more rebar and concrete than was anticipated. They said they will still get through, but it's going to take them longer than they planned. We are going to have to delay longer than planned up here before we can make our move." the man answered while reaching into a pocket on his left shoulder.

"How much longer?" Napier asked.

The man in the mask sat a small brown vile down on the bar before typing something on the keypad in front of him. Staring at the screen, he picked the vile up, removed the lid, and sprinkled a bit of powder on the back of his right hand. He then brought his hand to his nose and took a bump up each nostril.

"Take it easy with that shit", Napier scolded him.

"I'm good, man, just calming the nerves."

Napier looked to be on the verge of saying something else when the machine chimed again.

"He said 30 to 45 minutes depending on how thick the concrete is. Or says he can be here in 15 if he can use some of the extra Semtex?"

Napier thought for a second. "No 30 to 45 won't throw off the timeline to much. We can't afford to have an explosion go off early."

The man behind the bar nodded and typed something on his computer again. He then picked up the vile and took another hit.

"No more until this is over", Napier warned him again.

Putting the vile back in his pocket, the man held out 2 hands in a sign of surrender. "Whatever you say, man."

Goddamn druggies, that's all we need right now. All my hard work and my entire life is now in the hands of a drug user, The Chieftain thought to himself. If he had a gun, he'd shoot the stupid son of a bitch right now.

Turning towards the room, Napier stood silent a moment with his hands on his hips. "I am sure y'all heard that. We are going to be together a little longer than originally planned. You just keep doing what you are told, and nothing will happen to you. However, step out of line or speak without permission, and you will be dealt with accordingly. Understand?"

*****

Agent Moore, along with a majority of the room, nodded, expressing their understanding. A few had remained still, probably afraid that the man would misconstrue their nodding as speaking without permission. Then very hesitantly, one of the fat men in uniform raised his hand.

Looking at the man sternly, Napier asked, "What?"

"Sorry, sir, but is there any way we can go to the bathroom? I had quite a few sodas before y'all came in, and I don't know how much longer I can hold it?"

"Seriously?" Napier said.

The man nodded while uncomfortably crossing his legs.

"Excuse me, but I think you will find that the audience here is more likely to be cooperative if they are comfortable." Primovero chimed in.

Looking from the man to Primovero, Napier exhaled audibly, obviously frustrated by the man's speaking out of turn once again. Nonetheless, Napier gave in after a moment of consideration. "Fine. Skull, Devil, you two go to the bathroom. One inside and one outside. We are going to send these people one at a time down the hall to allow them use of the facilities. You people go in do your business and get out. Anyone tries any funny business, and you will regret it, and there will be no more bathroom breaks after understood?"

Again the room nodded in unison, this time without comment from Primovero.

"Alright fat man, you go first. When he comes back, your table goes, and so on and forth. However, your table goes last Mr. Primovero since you keep wanting to talk." Napier said, pointing at the corner booth.

Agent Moore was unsure what if any effect Napier expected, the verbal slap on the wrist was supposed to have on the man.

The man in uniform got up stiffly and followed the Devil and Skull to the hallway down which the restrooms were located. As the trio exited the room, Agent Moore overheard the Devil say, "You're going in the bathroom."

"The fuck I am. You get potty duty bitch." the Skull whistled back at him.

"Hey!" Napier yelled. "Cut that shit out. Just get it done."

He's losing control of the situation, Moore thought.

*****

Napier sat at the bar near the machine. Rotating his gaze between the Knight, the machine, and hostages as the people began going the bathroom one at a time as directed. Secretly, he was glad for the restroom break's distraction, as they were still over two hours away from making their escape, and he didn't want anyone in the room, the hostages, nor his team to become complacent.

First, the heavy man in uniform went and came back, looking relieved. Once he sat down, the other uniformed man went followed by the bartender and cook. There was a bit of a pause as the FBI Agents and table of older executives stared at one another, silently debating which table would go second. Napier was on the verge of intervening when the last of Primovero's bodyguards, the reputedly deadly Lessons, ended the silent debate by standing and walking to the hall, establishing their table would be next. Upon his return, the other three members of the table went, meaning it was time for the four FBI agents to use the facilities.

Given his men's general attitude towards the police, Napier anticipated trouble. As the black agent made his way down the hall, Napier followed to ensure the two men at the restrooms behaved themselves; particularly Joshua, who was as unpredictable as the weather. Somewhat surprisingly, there were no problems as the four men made their way to and from the restroom. As the last of the Agents concluded his business, Napier returned to the main room with him, reclaiming his perch at the bar.

Once the last of the FBI Agents sat down, the tall man nodded towards his date, the lone remaining woman, indicating she should go first. She had been gone only a moment when a loud scream was heard coming from the hall, drawing everyone's attention followed shortly by the shout of, "Get off her you dumb son of a bitch."

Napier rushed from the room, yelling as he went to his remaining men in the room, "Watch them."

He heard another scream and a loud crash before making it to the restroom door. Bursting through the door, he saw the woman standing back in the corner, her shirt hanging off her shoulders in tatters, while the Butcher had Joshua in a full nelson pinned down over the sink.

It didn't take Sherlock Holmes to tell him what had happened. Joshua had been in the bathroom, while the Butcher had been in the hall. The woman had gone into the bathroom only to be accosted by Joshua. The woman had screamed, and the Butcher had burst in to wrestle the man off her. Enraged, Napier yelled, "What the fuck do you think you're doing. Get your ass out in the hallway. This shit happens again, and I will cut your little dick off and feed it to you. Do you understand me?"

The Butcher slowly released his hold on the man and stepped back. Joshua whirled around to face both men. Pulling his gun Napier placed the barrel of the weapon against the man's forehead. "You want to try me or do you want to go out in the hallway."

Stepping back, Joshua walked out the door.

Turning to the woman, Napier said. Go ahead and use the facilities, and I will walk you back to the room. I guarantee you that he will not bother you again. The woman tried her best to straighten her shirt around her before stepping into the stall. "Let's give her a second," Napier said to the Butcher.

Stepping into the hall, his pistol still drawn he found Joshua leaning against the wall as if nothing had just occurred, though the man refused to look at either he or the Butcher.

A moment later, the woman emerged from the bathroom. She had done her best draping the shirt over her, but she still had to wrap her arms tightly around her to keep it all together. Napier liked the girl's spunk as she stared Joshua down as she walked by. Watching her go, Napier reminded the man again, "one more fuck up, and I will kill you."

*****

Hearing Michele scream, Logan had instinctually stood but was quickly met with three guns pointed at him. Had there been only one or maybe even two, he may have chanced it, but three left no margin for error. Returning to his seat in the booth, he waited, each second pure torture. Waiting, he felt a burning in his stomach that he had felt but rarely. Usually a man of cold calculation he had to remind himself to bide his time, there would be plenty of opportunities to take his revenge against all those responsible.

Finally, Michele emerged from the hallway, followed closely by Napier. His eyes immediately registered her torn shirt and the look of unbridled fury on her beautiful swollen face. The sight only incensed him that much more.

"Get her something to wear", Napier said to no one in particular as he helped her sit back down next to the man in the rumpled suit.

"We have t-shirts in the storage room upstairs," Martin, the bartender, volunteered.

Looking at the man crossly, Napier "Clown take him upstairs and get her a shirt. Check on the twins while you're there."

"Got it, boss," the Clown said, beckoning the barman with a head nod.

The conversation taking place only barely registered with Logan as Michele was looking at him pleadingly. They remained eye locked, trying to calm one another as much as possible until the two men returned with the shirt.

The shirt's arrival broke the trance as Napier took it from the barman and handed it to Michele, who reflexively said, "Thank you."

Logan continued to watch as she almost absentmindedly held it out to ensure it would fit, an action he had seen her do more times than he could count in the last four years. But then she suddenly sat back awkwardly, realizing every eye in the room was upon her. She moved around in the booth awkward a few times, trying to determined how to cover herself while changing. Her problem seemed to only intensify the attention of the room, making her even more anxious. Then unexpectedly, the tall good looking mobster slowly rose from his chair, drawing the room's attention and the guns of Napier, Clown, and Panda. Undaunted, the blonde man removed his jacket and stepped to the booth. Extending the jacket, he held it up as a makeshift curtain. "Give the lady some privacy," the man ordered, causing the room to look the other direction, including the gunmen.

Once changed, Michele thanked the man for his help.

"Miss, did you need to use the restroom still or at least need to wash up?" the man in the rumpled suit asked her.

Michele looked at him briefly before saying in a no-nonsense manner, "I'm good, that man in the skull mask can't hurt me."

For a reason, Logan couldn't explain hearing her words helped calm him, like reading his mind and sending him a message. Good babydoll. Now I am going to make that asshole pay, he answered subconsciously.

"Ok. You three can go," the Clown declared.

Unsure of the Clown's authority, Logan looked towards Napier for confirmation. Impatiently the man said. "You guys go to the bathroom. And don't worry if that dumb son a bitch tries that shit again, I told the Devil to kill him."

Logan rose from his seat, taking one last look at Michele, trying to assure her he would be ok before walking determinedly to the restroom. He had one goal, and one goal only, get his hands on the man with the skull mask who had now attacked Michele twice. That he would not forgive or allow to go unpunished.

At the end of the hallway, the Skull leaned on the wall outside the men's room. Seeing him approaching, the man saluted Logan mockingly, causing Logan to feel his face redden from anger. He considered the auto-injector in his pocket, but he decided against it with the man's partner just inside the door.

Mistaking his reddened face for one of embarrassment or fear or another defenseless posture, the man in the skull mask said, "Don't worry, I'll take real good care of her when all this is over. That body is still hard to resist even with the swollen face. Besides that bitch just kicked me in the nuts and scratched my face. I love a woman with spirit."

Angry, Logan slammed the door open while the man in the skull mask laughed. The slamming of the door startled the Devil, who was holding the combat cleaver in his hand. Apparently thinking the Skull or some other threat was busting through the door, the Devil pulled the weapon back instinctually, clearly intent on swinging it at the intruder. Before the masked man could unleash the blow, Logan stepped in and punched hard at the man's Adam's apple with the fleshy part of his hand between the thumb and index finger. The strike was true, and Logan felt the man's windpipe crumble under the force of the perfectly placed blow. His eyes suddenly bulging beneath the mask, the man reflexively let go of the cleaver as both hands went to his throat, which was rapidly swelling, cutting off air.

Logan caught the knife deftly in midair with his left hand and pivoted on the ball of his right foot to see the man in the skull mask coming through the door to see what the commotion was all about. Seeing his quarry, Logan swung the cleaver with his nondominant hand, intent only on hitting the man in the head. The braggadocios Devil had been right about the knife as the cleaver's heavy blade caught the man in the hinge of the jaw, cutting right through the skin and bone. The Skull's entire lower jaw and tongue fell to the floor, causing blood to shoot from the man's facial artery. In obvious shock, the man stared down at what had once been his mouth on the floor and then back to Logan who had deftly stepped out of the way of the blood.

"Her name's Michele, and you'll never touch her again", Logan whispered to the man before unmercifully driving the blade into the top of his skull, nearly splitting his head in two. Leaving the blade buried in the man's face, Logan let go allowing the man's lifeless body to collapsed to the floor on top of the Devil.

The dying man used the last of his oxygenated blood to back away from his former partner's bloody body. He made it but a few feet before he was stopped by the wall that separated the sinks from the urinal. Sitting there, he looked up at Logan with dying, questioning eyes.

Stepping to the man, Logan bent over and told him in a hushed tone. "I am going to have to get me one of those amigo." Logan remained perched over him watching until the man's eyes rolled back into his head, and the Devil slumped further forward.

The door then burst open as Logan straightened to his full height with Napier and Clown entering the room. "What the fuck, happened in here?" Napier asked, seeing his men on the floor.

"I don't know they were arguing through the door at each other when I came down the hall, and that guy followed me in and pushed me out of the way and attacked the other guy. Then he pulled out the blade and started swinging it." Logan said in the most innocent voice he could muster.

Looking around his boss at the men on the floor, the man in the clown mask declared, "Damn, those fucking idiots finally killed one another."

"Fuck!" Napier yelled.

Ignoring them both, Logan stepped into the stall and relieved his bladder.

Once finished. He stepped over the Devil's body and washed his hands before stepping across the Skull with the cleaver still protruding from his head and back into the hallway.

Outside the restroom door, the big man in the clown mask awaited holding some of the two dead men's weapons. "Boss wants you to stay here. He is going to send some others down, and y'all are going to move these guys into the freezer."

Shrugging, Logan leaned against the wall.

"You don't seem to bothered by them," the big man said matter-of-factly.

"Not the first bodies I've ever seen," Logan answered directly, causing the Clown to adjust his weapon, making it a little easier to bring to a firing position in a hurry if necessary.

"Care to explain that?"

"I was in the Army. Did a few tours overseas. I saw some stuff."

"What do you do now?"

"I own a local comic book store."

His answer caused the big man to relax and even laugh.

However, the moment of levity was short-lived as down the hallway appeared the man in the Panda mask along with Primovero and the man in the rumpled suit.

*****

The Chieftain turned away as Lessons held up the jacket for the woman to change her shirt. Who says chivalry is dead, he thought as the killer shielded the woman from all the men's probing eyes in the room. He further wondered what kind of animals Winter had sent that could attack the woman seemingly unprovoked twice but dismissed the thought quickly. As his grandmother used to tell him, "You can't make pasta without breaking a few eggs."

Once the woman had changed, Napier gave them permission to continue to the bathroom, which he was happy for wanting to stretch his legs. Because of the seating arrangements, the girl's boyfriend went first. As the man stood, The Chieftain looked at the man really for the first time, tall, trim and better than average looking he would say; he could see why a woman would be attracted to the man.

As the man walked away, The Chieftain watched him walk directly to the hall without a wayward glance. He had seen men walk like that before: the man was on a mission and not just in a hurry to use the facilities. Looking around the room, he seemed to be the only one sensing the man was marching for trouble.

Focusing on the hall intently, he could hear the man with the skull mask's pitchy voice and cackle but was unable to make out the words. Then there was a distinct thump of noise, like a baseball bat making contact with a ball or a skull.

The noise also caught Napier's attention, who, along with the man in the clown mask, took off down the hall at a sprint. The sudden action grabbed everyone else's attention in the room, as suddenly everyone was looking toward the hallway. They weren't waiting long when a loud yell broke the silence, "Fuck!"

Looking towards the girl, The Chieftain saw a look of confusion on her face. Poor girl doesn't understand her boyfriend just went and got himself killed, The Chieftain mused.

Napier then emerged from the hallway alone and clearly angered. Marching directly to their table, he pointed towards them and said in a tone that left no room for debate, "Go use the bathroom and help put those bodies in the freezer."

The words brought the woman's hands to her face. "Bodies?" she said.

"Yes, bodies!" Napier roared. "Those two idiots killed one another."

The way the man said the words confused The Chieftain. So badly, he wanted to ask for clarification. Instead, he slid out of the booth content to walk to the restroom to see for himself.

CHAPTER 22

September 19, 5:18 pm

Logan leaned against the wall, similar to how the dead man in the skull mask has stood not 5 minutes prior. Hearing footsteps, he saw the two men from his table walking down the hallway being trailed by the Panda.

Primovero and his lunch partner walked past Logan, into the restroom without comment. Logan pushed himself off the wall and followed the Clown and Panda right behind him. Both Primovero and the other man stepped over the bodies without much fanfare to the urinals, clearly not the first bodies they have ever seen either, Logan observed.

Once the two men finished their business. The Panda directed them, "Boss says y'all gotta put these guys in the freezer."

"Why should I move the body?" Primovero asked.

"Because the boss said so." answered the Panda. "If you want to get out of here, I advise you to listen."

"Far d'una mosca un elefante," Primovero answered the big man.

"To make an elephant out of a fly?" what the hell are you talking about the Panda asked.

Jumping in quickly, the man in the wrinkled suit explained, "It's an Italian proverb that both mine and Mr. Primovero's families use. It means don't make a mountain out of a molehill. I believe Mr. Primovero was implying that he was just asking."

Ignoring the explanation the younger man had offered in his defense, Primovero removed his suit coat, hanging it on the toilet stall corner. "Joey, get this guy's shoulders, and I will get his feet." Primovero directed the younger man. Taking off his own jacket, Joey placed his own coat on the counter by the sink. Their actions seemed to satisfy the man in the Panda mask who took the time to step out of the crowded space.

After watching the big man walk away, Joey positioned himself at the Skull's shoulders while Primovero kicked the body's leg apart and placed himself above the knees in the space just created then turned to face the door. The two men squatted in unison, Primovero lifting up the body's legs his elbows under the man's knees his hands locked at his belly button. At the same time, Joey pushed the body forward enough to get his arms under the man's shoulders, his elbows positioned in the body's armpits, his hands locked in front of the man's chest. Once set, the two stood together wordlessly. Logan smiled to himself, These two have done this before.

Logan stepped out of the way allowing the two men to carry the body, blade still buried in the skull, from the room. Their exit left Logan, the Clown, the Devil's body, and the jaw of the skull remaining in the room. Undisturbed and undaunted, Logan half squatted and grabbed the dead Devil by the vest and pulled. As the limp body began to come erect, he squatted lower, getting his shoulder under the man's midsection and stood. He held the body positioned in a perfect fireman's carry, allowing him to secure one wrist and one ankle in front of him with his left hand, leaving the right free. Using his right hand to push the restroom door open, intending to follow the other two men to the freezer. As he crossed the threshold, the deadman's head banged against the door frame.

"Careful." the Clown said, following him out of the restroom.

"He's dead, I doubt he minds," Logan responded, walking the body to the freezer and depositing it with the other bodies.

*****

It took only a few minutes, but Agent Moore watched as the Primovero, Cabrini, and the tall man returned from the restroom escorted by the two big gunmen. Neither Cabrini nor Primovero had their jackets on any longer, and Cabrini's shirt had some blood on it that wasn't visible before, which Moore found interesting. Returning to their assigned booth, Cabrini climbed in first followed by Primovero, while the tall man made his way to the woman's side, having her slide further in giving him space next to her. Though her back was towards him, he could see her relax at the man's presence and leaned in to put her shoulder next to his.

Seeing the tall man made him wonder what had truly happened. When the commotion first broke out, Moore thought for sure the tall man had tried to confront the man who had attacked his girlfriend and gotten himself killed, yet there he stood seemingly without a scratch.

"Okay, gentlemen and lady," Napier announced. "As you can see, we are now down two men. It will now be more important than ever you listen to us as my men will not have the time to debate with you. It is easier to put y'all in the freezer than to put you back in line. Is that clear?"

"Perfectly," Primovero responded for the room. The man's tendency to always have the last word was clearly grating on Napier's nerves, but the gunman didn't push the issue. Hard to argue with the boss, Moore concluded. Nonetheless, what was the point of all this, how did this help Primovero? Again he came back to the point the man realized that the FBI and US Attorney weren't going to simply give in to his demands and let him walk away. The man didn't get where he was by being stupid, so what was the play?

CHAPTER 23

September 19, 5:26 pm

Napier sat on the bar watching the room waiting for word from the tunneling team, pondering how in the hell his two men had managed to kill one another. He and Stewart had both studied the scene, and it appeared to have happened just like the man in the comic book shirt had said. Joshua had attacked the Butcher managing to get him around the throat, crushing his windpipe. Unfortunately for Joshua, the Butcher had managed to hit him with that giant cleaver a couple of times before he suffocated. Truth be told, he didn't care that the two had killed one another, it seemed as if the two were destined to have done so. But it left Napier shorthanded for the time being. If Marshal Grube decided to send in the US Marshal SOG team and KCPD swat teams, their chances of thwarting an attack had just decreased drastically. He was under no illusions as to their capabilities to hold the place for long if the hostages weren't valuable enough to hold them back. He and his men could hold them off for a while, but it would eventually turn into the Alamo for him and his men. He had no intention of going out like Travis, Bowie, or Crockett.

Beep, beep, beep, the sound of the machine on the bar broke his thoughts. Jumping down, Napier walked nearer the computer to see the incoming message. Cypher from behind his Knight mask whispered, "Dey are through the wall and have made der way through the access tunnel. Dey will be ready as soon as dey finish setting the Semtex."

"It's about time," Napier said, relieved.

"He says that if his calculations are correct, they should be coming through the floor below what looks like a janitor's closet across from the bathrooms under the stairs. He is asking if we can make sure there is nothing in there that will fall down."

"Cook you and the bartender come over here," Napier ordered.

The two men jumped at his summons but managed to walk across the room without falling down. "What's in the room by the bathrooms?"

"We keep a bunch of stuff in there, cleaning supplies, napkins, mop buckets, the floor buffer. Like I said a lot of stuff." the bartender answered directly while the cook silently nodded his affirmation.

"How full is it?"

"You can't see the floor."

"Shit! Ok, Knight, you and Clown take these two and a few other guys and empty that room by the restrooms. Take that shit upstairs to keep it out of the way." Napier pronounced.

The Clown nodded his understanding and then patted Lessons and the tall man in the comic book t-shirt on the shoulders. "You two come with me."

The two men did as they were told and followed Stewart, who rounded up the bartender and cook and went down the hall towards the bathroom.

Turning back towards the bar, Cypher had sat back down. "Well, what are you waiting on? Go help them!" Napier directed.

The man looked up at him and mumbled something under his breath in a language that Napier couldn't understand. "I imagine you don't want to say that in English for a reason. Now get your ass out there and help them move that shit or else Comrade."

Cypher stared at him a moment unconsciously, reaching towards the pocket to remove the vile.

"Hey, I told you lay off that shit too goddamnit. Give me the bottle. You can have it back when we are finished here."

The Russian grunted something unintelligible and handed his precious bottle to Napier, before stomping out from behind the bar towards the others.

*****

Unhappy about leaving Michele's side, Logan went with the men to the door under the stairs across from the bathroom with the other three hostages and the Clown. The cook removed a set of keys from his pocket, unlocking the door. Inside, Logan saw a space that was a combination storage and janitor's closet about 8 feet long, 6 feet deep. The cook and Martin had not been exaggerating, the room was completely full. Never one to dawdle and wanting to return to his seat as soon as possible, Logan stepped inside grabbing two large boxes of cups and proceeded to the stairs.

Backtracking to the stairs with his armload, he passed the Knight coming the other way, agitation on his face. Ignoring the man, Logan made his way up the stairs. In all his prior visits to the restaurant he had never been upstairs before. Often times when he and Michele met there for lunch, there was a small yellow sign saying "Closed," hanging from a think chain across the bottom of the stairwell. Emerging at the top of the stairs, he was facing the East wall and felt a slight breeze coming through a hole about the standard window size. Standing at the window was the man wearing the British Flag mask, though it was now hanging around his neck. Before the man was a large rifle which rested on the makeshift window sill that the hole created. Seeing the weapon up close he recognized it was a German made G3, an antipersonnel weapon similar to the M-249 SAW but firing a much larger round.

Not wanting to startle the man, Logan cleared his throat and said, "They told us to bring this stuff up here."

The man didn't respond other than to shake his head in an odd manner. Logan was about to say something else, when from behind him, he heard, "Keep going, we will stack it against the far wall out of the way." Looking behind him, he saw the other men, each with their arms loaded walking along the right side of the stairwell. The Clown marched up the left-hand side, a small box in his left hand, keeping his gun hand free and available to use his weapon should the need present itself.

Stepping past Logan, the Clown told the three killers in the room that they would be carrying items up and not to worry about it as he moved across the room to place the box along the far wall. The twins and the other man all gave the Clown unconcerned looks, apparently content to continue watching their windows.

Walking across the floor behind the Clown, Logan looked over the room. It was a big open industrial looking space, each of its 4 corners boxed into approximately 6X6: storage closets and restrooms, Logan saw. The remaining floor space was a few scattered high top tables and chairs, a pool table, a shuffleboard table, and even a sectional couch sitting in a corner created by one of the storage closets near a machine designed to look like an old jukebox. The ceiling was open, showing a series of steel girders that held up the roof. A short ladder hung just below the ceiling beams at the room's center, about 10 feet off the ground, that went to a hatch on the roof. And just as importantly, he saw the room was rigged with the gray cords of Semtex just as the bottom floor had been.

Placing his armload beside that of the Clown, Logan turned and slowly made his way back to the stairs to get another load. Walking past the man in the open window, he heard the man talking to himself under his breath. "No Ghost, we are in here. Leave us alone."

Hearing the odd statement, Logan wondered about the man's sanity.

He again met the Knight carrying a bucket with some cleaning supplies and a brush still looking unhappy at the bottom of the stairs.

The sight of the man gave him an idea. Over the course of his next few trips up and down the stairs, Logan slowed between the downstairs storage closet and the room at the top of the stairs and back by taking larger and larger armloads of boxes that naturally slowed him down. As he did so, the other men naturally made their way past him until he was at the end of the line near the Knight. Timing it just right, Logan found himself on the stairs alone with the man just a few steps behind. Carefully, he placed his left hand alongside his cargo pocket and popped the flap. The next trip up the stairs, he made sure to allow the Knight to get within a few feet of him before he reached the top. Then stepping in a somewhat clumsily manner, he allowed the auto-injector to fall out of his pocket and clang to the floor. He paused at the sound and gave his best nervous face as he half turned on the stairs and looked to the injector and then to the Knight.

Stopping on the step below where the needle rested, the Knight picked up the injector. Holding it up, he inquired, "What is dis?"

Sheepishly, Logan said in his best stoner voice, "Ah man, I just scored that from my friend. Its pharmaceutical grade stuff man."

Studying the device, the Knight asked "How do you use dis?"

"Just twist the end to unlock it, put it on your arm, and hit the button man."

"You thanks your friend fors me. You tell anyone else about dis, and I will kill you. Understand asshole?" the Knight laughed, putting the injector in his pocket.

Putting his best look of dejection on his face, Logan turned around and continued up the stairs. Don't worry I won't tell a soul. Asshole! Logan told himself.

*****

Fifteen minutes after the group started clearing out the room, Stewart and the two bar workers returned to the room. "Where are the other three?" Napier asked.

"Taking the last of the stuff upstairs," Stewart reported.

"The room is clear then?"

"Four bare walls and a concrete floor."

"Good work."

A moment later, the tall man returned to the room then Lessons a few seconds after that. Each man went directly to their previous seats and sat down, the tall man beside the woman; Lessons the chair at the table with the three older men. Then the machine on the bar sounded again. Turning towards the bar, there was still no sign of the Knight. "Where the hell is he?" Napier asked to no one in particular.

Lessons answered, "He said he'd be down in a minute and told us to go on."

Looking across the room, Napier pointed to the nearest man, the executive who had his face shaven earlier, "Go upstairs and see what the hell is taking him so long. Tell him I said to hurry the fuck up."

Shakily, the man got up and left the room. Less than a minute later, the older man returned, looking even paler than when he left. Seeing him, Napier said, "Well?"

"He is on the stairs." the man said uneasily.

"What do you mean he is on the stairs?"

"He is just sitting on the stairs, but I think he is dead."

"What? Get the hell out of my way?" Napier huffed before stalking off.

*****

Agent Moore heard the machine beep as he was sure everyone else in the room had. Napier jumped off the bar at the sound and began speaking in hushed tones to the man in the Knight Mask.

"It is about time," Napier said loudly enough for everyone to hear.

Time for what? Moore asked himself as he continued to study the man.

"Cook and bartender come over here," Napier then commanded.

Moore could tell the summons had surprised both men, but they got up and walked over to the bar to their credit.

"What's in the room by the bathrooms?" Napier asked the pair. Agent Moore recalled seeing a closed door across the hall from the bathrooms. Thinking about the structure, he realized that the room in question would have been partially located beneath the stairs that led upstairs.

"We keep a bunch of stuff in there, cleaning supplies, napkins, mop buckets, the floor buffer. Like I said a lot of stuff." the bartender answered the man.

"How full is it?" Napier asked.

"You can't see the floor."

"Shit! Okay, Knight, you and Clown take these two and a few other guys and empty that room by the restrooms. Take the shit upstairs to keep it out of the way." Napier directed the big man.

Agent Moore watched as the Clown tapped Lessons and the tall man in the comic book shirt on the shoulders, beckoning them to follow him. They were joined by the two restaurant workers, and they all disappeared down the hallway.

What could be so important in that room, Moore wondered. But before he was able to contemplate the question, Napier and the masked man at the bar began to squabble. Napier clearly wasn't happy with the man and his unwillingness to follow his order to help the Clown and other men to empty the room. In the brief discussion, it registered with Agent Moore that the man in the Knight mask had mumbled something in a foriegn language. Napier then demanded he speak English. Moore also overheard Napier called the man "Comrade" in a less than complimentary manner. "Russian?"

It was another fact to add to the puzzle before him, but he still was unable to comprehend exactly what was going on. Mentally he started checking off what he knew and separating it from what he surmised.

Fact: Cabrini and Primovero met here for lunch.

Surmise: It wasn't random.

Fact: the building was taken hostage by a man calling himself Napier along with 8 other men, who were all incredibly well-armed. The men had moved with precision and purpose.

Surmised: they had practiced the maneuvers.

Fact: everyone was taken hostage.

Surmised: Primovero was somehow connected to the hostage-takers, given the demands included a list of who testified against him.

Fact: Primovero remained a hostage, however.

Surmise: Primovero seemingly was given deference by Napier and his men.

Fact: they had agreed to release hostages.

Surmised: it was some sort of stall tactic because they had to know the demands would never be agreed to.

Fact: They had released four hostages and killed a fifth

Surmised: it was a calculated risk: the killing of Cuppari was a warning to the police what would happen should they decide to storm the building. The idea of what damage detonating 50 pounds of Semtex could do would certainly give them pause.

Fact: they had killed two of Primovero's men: Wentz had been shot in the head, and Cuppari had been blown up as an exhibition to the police outside of their capabilities.

Surmised: Cuppari's selection had been intentional, though Wentz had been shot because he stupidly tried to draw a gun against nine gunmen.

Fact: they had wired the room with a substance they proclaimed was Semtex.

Surmised: The supposed Semtex was laid out in a particular way for a specific purpose.

Fact: two of the hostage-takers were dead.

Surmised: The two had killed one another.

Fact: Men were now cleaning out the room below the stairs:

Surmise: It was for a purpose, but what?

Going through everything he'd observed and surmised did nothing to clear up the picture. Even eliminating everything but the facts, Moore couldn't see an actual purpose to any of this.

He was still in deep thought when the first of the men returned from their task, and Napier asked where the others were. Then came Lessons and the other tall skinny man who wordlessly returned to their designated seats.

Beep. Beep. Beep. The machine on the bar chimed again, prompting Napier to ask where the Knight was.

"He said he'd be down in a minute and told us to go on," Primovero's killer answered.

Pointing to the old gentleman with half a beard, Napier told him to go get the man. The man complied without comment and left the room in search of the Knight. However, the man quickly returned and pronounced that he thought the man was dead, causing Napier to once again rush from the room.

For the first time, Agent Moore heard the big man in the Panda mask speak. "What happened to him?" he asked the old man.

"I, I, I don't know. He is just sitting on the stairs with his head laid back, staring at the ceiling. I went to shake him when I saw some kinda needle thing in his arm." the man responded.

"Fucking OD'd goddamnit. Are you shitting me? Can this get any worse," the Clown cursed.

A second later, Napier returned to the room, the Knight's submachine gun slung over his shoulder, and another pistol stuck in his waistband, clearly aggravated. Pointing to himself and Trenton, "Go get him off the stairs and put him in the freezer with the other two."

Getting up, he and Trenton walked down the hallway to where the staircase and body were. He was surprised that they were unaccompanied until he realized that the crew had now lost 3 of their 9 members, meaning they couldn't spare the men to watch them. Moore wondered if any weapons were remaining on the man's body that he would be able to get to? Maybe he could take out a few more of them so they could all escape? However, his hopes were quickly dashed when he got to the stairs to find the man in the confederate flag mask standing at the top watching, with a drawn pistol by his side.

Hesitantly, he continued up the stairs, squatting behind the deadman placing his arms under the man's arms, preparing to lift him. His action caused the device to fall from the arm onto the stair. Awaiting Trenton to get into position between the man's legs, Moore took the time to study the object. As a former patrol officer in Dallas, he saw many drug users in his time. In that experience, he had also seen many drug syringes and needles. What had just fallen from the deadman's arm was far different from anything he had ever seen before. Instead of a plastic tube filled with a black-tipped plastic plunger attached to a short skinny needle that could be reused as long as the user didn't break the needle; this thing appeared to be one long cylindrical piece with a bright blue button on top and a larger gauged shorter needle attached to the bottom. The object reminded him of the Epipen his grandmother always carried with her because of her severe bee allergy. He also knew that her Epipen was a single-use device. Once it was deployed, it had to be replaced as there was no way to retract the needle or refill it.

He was still looking at the device when Agent Trenton said, "Ready Lift," On the command Moore stood along with Trenton, lifting the body from the ground. Carrying the man towards the freezer, Agent Moore considered what he had just seen. He concluded that unless the deadman was the most sophisticated drug user he had ever seen, it was unlikely that he had bought a single dose of a drug and accidentally overdosed on it. So if that were the case, he concluded, that meant that someone had killed him but who? Lessons or the tall man would have been the apparent candidates being they were presumably the last people to see the man alive. But would either of them have access to such a weapon? Lessons he recalled had been frisked, of course, the tall man hadn't.

That brought into question the deaths of the prior two men as well. Really what were the odds that the two had simultaneously killed one another? And hadn't the tall man been the last to see those two alive? Who was he? Moore wondered. Just more questions that didn't have answers.

Inside the freezer, Moore and Trenton sat the body down. Trenton turned to leave, "Hold on a second," Moore said.

Trenton looked at him with a questioning look.

"I just want to see something," Moore whispered by way of explanation. Expertly, he went over the bodies quickly. "Boot knife is missing from the Devil."

"I am sure the blonde guy has them. The big guys had carried the weapons in from those two and put them behind the bar."

"I am not so sure. I didn't see him with put anything back there but the guns."

"Hell, he probably kept the knife for himself then," Trenton said skeptically.

"I don't know, man. Something strange is going on here."

"Like what?"

"I don't know. It just doesn't feel right. At first, these guys seemed well organized, but the longer this has gone on, I'm not so sure. I think they rehearsed some of this, but I don't think they've been together long judging by how they interact with one another. Plus I don't think that Napier guy really trusts these guys much by the way he micromanages everything." Moore said, and though he was speaking off the cuff, it felt right.

"Man, you're imagining things. If he doesn't have it, who does?"

"My question exactly?"

You're crazy, now let's go before they come looking for us." Trenton said, walking out the door.

Moore took a second longer, looking over the three bodies of the hostage-takers.
"Something's not right!" he repeated to himself before exiting the freezer. Catching up with Trenton in the hallway, the two returned to the table with the other agents.

CHAPTER 24

Napier cursed his luck. First, the Butcher and Joshua had killed each other, and now Cypher had OD'd too. Unfortunately, he couldn't exactly walk away from the place. He would have to see the job through, though, with fewer men, it would be more difficult than ever. Then he was struck by the realization that the machine on the bar had gone off before the body was discovered. Cursing himself for allowing him to lose sight of the big picture, he checked the computer. Fish and his team were ready to blow the floor at his order. He took a moment to consider the men's presence below. The original plan called for them to wait for the last possible moment to blow the hole for their escape. However, he had never liked the idea, for if they were raided unexpectedly, he wanted to have access to their escape route immediately.

"Clown, Panda, its time. Get ready," he directed. Pushing the button on his comlink, he repeated the order to the men upstairs.

Following his orders, the two big men went to the table with the duffle bags. From inside the bags, each removed an M4 carbine rifle with an M203 grenade launcher mounted underneath. Both locked and loaded 30 round magazines that had spares taped to the bottom to easily be flipped for a fast reload. They then loaded the grenade launchers with M406 high explosive rounds. Both men took up positions near the front door and checked their grenade loads, and nodded ready. This was going to be one of the most dangerous parts of the plan. The back door was going to be a particular problem, though he hoped the explosives' threat would continue to deter the police from sending in the SOG and SWAT teams.

Quickly typing a message on the machine, Napier waited but a brief moment when the machine beeped in response. Reading the message, he smiled.

Picking up the phone, he ensured there was still a dial tone. There was. He dialed 9-1-1.

"9-1-1 what's your emergency," a scratchy female voice answered.

"Yes, ma'am, I'm sure from your computer you can see this call is originating from inside the downtown Peanut location. I am sure you are also aware the police have been dispatched here for a hostage situation. I need you to patch me through to Marshal Grube, who is the hostage negotiator for this matter."

"Sir, who is this?" the dispatcher asked.

"My name is Napier and if you don't put me through to Marshal Grub, I will start shooting hostages."

"Sir, I'm not sure," before the woman could finish her protest to his demand, Napier placed the phone on the bar. Pulling Cypher's pistol from his belt, he began firing it into the ceiling. After pulling the trigger a handful of times, he laid the weapon down on the bar and picked the phone back up.

"Now, bitch, do I have your attention? Put Marshal Grube on the fucking line, or next time I start shooting people. When they die, their blood will be on your hands, you understand."

"Y-y-yes, sir." the woman stammered. "Hold one moment, please."

The line clicked off, and for a moment, Napier thought the woman had hung up on him. He was on the verge of hanging the phone up when the line came alive, "This is Marshal Grube."

"Marshal, where are my items? I've seen no list of names, no helicopter, and no cash in the account you were given."

"We are working on it. These things take time to gather." Marshal Grube tried to explain before Napier cut her off. "I am afraid that isn't good enough." He slammed down the phone for effect; much better than punching some stupid end button on a cell phone, he mused.

Pushing the button on his mike and speaking loudly enough for both the big men to hear, he said, "Remember, do not fire on the barricade. Blast the cars and anything else you want, but don't give them an excuse to storm the place. We go in 5... 4... 3... 2... 1. GO!"

*****

When the countdown hit zero, the room was suddenly loud with the combined noise from the rifle and machine-gun fire from above. Once the gunfire commenced, The Chieftain watched as the two big men ran out the door, one man turning left the other right, both men firing as they went. The firing continued for about 10 seconds, then The Chieftain heard the first loud explosion and then another, and yet another. Five blasts all told: the grenade launchers, they must have had them upstairs as well! None of this had been part of his plan. What the fuck are you doing, Napier! He wondered.

Then came an even bigger boom, closer. So close that it shook the building. At first, the Chieftain was fearful that the police had begun firing cannons or something back. That was when he realized what Napier had done. He had to give the man credit, it had been another genius deviation from his original plan. To cover the sound of their blasting the building's floor, he had directed his men to begin shooting at the police. The grenade launchers had been a clever ploy as well. Their loud explosions had to have been disorienting to the law enforcement personnel outside. There was no way they could have ascertained they had just secured another exit from the building.

Seconds after the nearest massive blast, the two masked men returned inside, winded from their runs but otherwise seemingly unscathed, as it seemed none of the officers outside had returned fire. A second later, the shooting from above had also stopped.

The room settled into silence once more, only to be broken again by two sharp cracks. Gunshots! The Chieftain realized the noise had come from the hallway and quickly looked towards Napier, who was running in the towards the shots, pulling his own sidearm.

*****

Hearing the gunshots, Napier rushed down the hall towards their new exit, fearful their plan had been discovered and that the cops were following Fish and his two helpers through the tunnel. Inside the small storage room, there was a hole about 4 feet in diameter in the middle of the floor. Getting on his belly, Napier crawled on his elbows towards the hole, ready to drop a grenade inside. He was still 2 feet from the hole when a ladder top emerged from the black pit. Stopping, he took aim just above the last rung of the ladder, ready to end whoever appeared.

A small black-gloved hand was the first to appear, then a second, and then a tuft of bleach blonde hair showed quickly followed by the rest of Fish's head.

"Fish, what the fuck was the shooting?" Napier demanded in a tone that left little doubt he was upset.

"What? I killed the two men who were with me. Wasn't that the plan?" the Fish asked, confused.

"It was once we got out of here!" Napier said through clenched teeth to keep from yelling, not wanting the hostages in the other room to hear.

Still unsure of the problem, the Fish tried to reassure Napier. "We're good man. Let's blow this joint and get outta Dodge."

"We're not fucking ready to blow this joint as you say, and I needed those two to replace the Butcher and Joshua, to cover the tunnel until we got outta here."

'Replace them?" the Fish asked, confused.

"Yeah, those two dumbasses killed one another."

"Oh shit. Are you serious?"

"Do you think I am kidding right now, mother fucker!"

"Nah man, sorry. But me and Cypher can both use guns, so we're still good."

"Well that would have worked except Cypher fucking overdosed on the stairs and is dead too asshole," Napier growled, trying to keep his voice low, not wanting anyone in the building to overhear.

"Overdosed? What the hell are you talking about?"

"I mean, we found him on the stairs dead as a doornail."

"Ah shit man. He was supposed to wait till we were done."

"What?" Napier exclaimed loudly, suddenly forgetting about the men in the other room.

"Yeah, man, I got us some Fentanyl for after. You know to celebrate."

"Fish, get your dumbass outta my face and go make sure that tunnel remains clear before I fucking decide to shoot you!"

Fish took a few tentative steps backward, his hands open held at shoulder height before turning around and climbing back down into the tunnel.

Turning Napier saw Turley staring at him. "What?" he snapped, still aggravated by Fish.

"Everything good boss." the big man asked him.

"We're good," Napier assured the man, though he wasn't sure himself, feeling the need to get out of the place before anything else could go wrong.

*****

Agent Moore watched and heard the events unfolding, hoping the police officers outside were uninjured in the melee. Then the building shook with the blast that was entirely to close for comfort. Looking at his three fellow agents, he knew by the look on his face that Trenton was doing his best to stay calm, his only concern making it home to his family. Gram had his head bowed, and his lips were moving, apparently praying; for what Moore knew not. Eldridge, just looked angry, and Moore hoped the young agent kept his head and didn't do something stupid and get someone killed.

Then after the men returned to the building, the sound of two mysterious gunshots had Napier and the Panda disappearing down the hall once again. He could hear some sort of conversation between the men but was unable to make out anything specific until he plainly heard Napier say "What?" Then a moment later, some more excited words - something about a fish and a tunnel and shooting. Just more nonsense to add to the mystery.

The two men returned to the room. Napier was clearly agitated again. Had something else gone wrong during their short assault on the police? Their plan was clearly not working as smoothly as they had anticipated. Taking a chance, he suddenly spoke, "You know you could probably get some goodwill and time if you released some more hostages."

"I need neither the time nor the goodwill Mr. FBI man. What I need right now is some quiet so I can think." Napier snapped.

Moore raised his hands up in mock surrender but was happy to have put the idea of releasing some more people in the man in charge's mind.

"He's right, you know. You are short men. Releasing a few more hostages would make it easier to manage the men here. Right now, you are clearly stretched too thin with only the six of you trying to hold this building and watch us all." said Primovero from the corner.

Both men sitting at the table with Primovero nodded in agreement.

"Though I would add, maybe not blowing up one of the people being released this time," Cabrini said smartly.

The Killer stared at the men hollow-eyed a moment before saying. "You know what, that gives me an idea."

CHAPTER 25

September 19, 6:11 pm

Looking over the group, Napier decided he was going to let five more people go. "You, you, you, you and you. Get up and stand by the door," Napier directed the woman, cook, bartender and the two heavyset men in the uniforms. It appeared the woman was on the verge of rejecting his offer to go when the tall man kissed her on the forehead and told her it was alright that he would see her later. He then stood and helped her out of the booth. Standing she looked as if she was on the verge of crying but Napier saw her willfully steady her resolve and walk to the front door. One hell of a woman, he thought. He almost admired the tall man in that regard. He had considered letting the woman's boyfriend go but he had need for the man later.

The men chosen for release quickly joined the woman near the door and Napier ordered, "Clown, take two of the FBI agents back to the freezer and get the vests off Butcher, Joshua and Cypher. Bring em back here and empty them out on the bar."

The man in the clown mask walked over to the booth with the four FBI agents in it and told the two men on the right side to get up. Wordlessly, the pair followed the Clown down the hall, towards the kitchen where the freezer was located.

"You five have been chosen to walk out of here. But I ain't making it that easy on either you or the cops out there." Napier said matter-of-factly, reminding himself to be convincing.

His words brought obvious looks of fear, concern and apprehension to the 5 hostages' faces just as had hoped.

Seconds later the Clown returned with his two helpers carrying the three vests. "Empty the pockets." Napier reminded them. Going through the vest pockets the trio removed a number of items including loaded magazines, flash lights, zip ties, keys, a wallet, and three additional plastic explosive packs and wire.

Walking to the bar with all eyes upon him, Napier removed a blasting cap and wiring harness from his own vest. Picking up one of the packs of explosive material, he rolled it into a ball and pushed the cap and wiring harness inside. Then he placed the material back inside one of the vests, a process he repeated two more times.

He then handed the vests to the woman and two bar workers, knowing the vests wouldn't fit the two big men, and ordered, "Put them on and buckle them!"

They each complied, placing the vests over their heads and snapping the buckles on either side with shaky hands. "Now you two stand between them." Napier told the two larger men who had looked relieved not to be donning vests of their own. The two moved between the trio standing together between the woman and the bartender. "No. Vest first, then no vest, vest, no vest and vest."

The group rearranged themselves as ordered, the woman at the head of the line, the larger of the two city workers, the cook, the smaller city worker and the bartender. Napier then took the zip ties and tied the hostages all together hand to hand in a line, leaving the woman in the front of the line with her left hand free and the bartender in the rear with his right hand free, like kids about to play snap the whip. Making a show of it Napier then took wire and ran them through each of the vests playing with the wire inside the blast pocket of each vest. Stepping back satisfied the group was sufficiently tethered together, he announced calmly, "Now lady and gentlemen I need you to walk outside towards the barrier. However, I must warn you the range on that detonator is only 200 yards to the receiver there on the bar. If you go to far the vests will detonate."

"What?"; "How far is that?"; "Can't we just stay?"; the group started talking at once. Napier held up a hand, silencing them.

"No you may not stay here. In fact you have 30 seconds to get out of my face. And if you remain any closer to the front door than 100 yards I will order my men upstairs to shoot you in the street"

The woman tried to move forward but the others were still staring at him in disbelief. "Oh and by the way if any of those wires connecting the vests were to break, the vests will also detonate. You now have less than 25 seconds." To emphasize the point he drew the pistol from his waist. "24, 23, 22"

The group was out of the door before he made it to 20.

*****

The Chieftain sat and watched Napier closely as he returned from the hallway after investigating the two gunshots. The man was clearly aggravated. Based on the situation as he had observed it, the Chieftain took an educated guess that the man in the tunnel had likely killed the two local men with him who had helped clear their escape path and access the space below the restaurant. Even in his own plan the two were never expected to live to see the light of day again anyway, but the Chieftain surmised Napier had probably been depending on them for reinforcements to replace his dead associates.

To complicate matters, the FBI man had then suggested the man release another round of hostages. That was not part of the original plan, which was to rig up a handful of hostages and have them all make a mad dash into the street right before they blew the building to distract the police and cause confusion. The Chieftain had expected the man to reject the suggestion out right. Instead, Napier rounded up the five people for release, rigging them with suicide devices designed to detonate at 200 yards from the building. *What are you doing now,* the Chieftain couldn't help but wonder.

Once the group of hostages were out in the street he asked, "Do you really think you are going to help the situation if they blow themselves up? Kill too many hostages and the police will storm this place regardless how many remain inside for fear you will kill us all anyway."

"No need to worry. None of that was real," Napier stated brazenly.

"What do you mean it isn't real?" The Chieftain asked confused by the explanation.

"Well the Semtex and the detonators are real. But the part about the 200 yards and the cutting the wires interconnecting them is all bullshit. It doesn't matter though because those five are so convinced its true that it is exactly what they will tell the police after they stop in the middle of the street. The cops cant just leave them standing there but they also can't risk moving them for fear of the vests detonating. They will have to bring in the bomb unit to investigate the vests and disarm them before they will let them move. That is going to most certainly slow them down. And I seriously doubt the police would be so brazen to attack us with the hostages in the middle of the street where the whole world can see."

Again the man's tactic, seemed sound. Maybe Winter knew what he was doing after all when he hired the man.

*****

Logan was sitting in the booth feeling Michele's nervous hands holding his own while he studied Primovero sitting across the table from him. Convinced the man was behind all of this he was coming up with scenarios in his head to best satisfy his need for justice against the notorious mobster man for what he had happened to Michele with this scheme. A simple bullet to the head or a knife across the man's throat simply wouldn't do he decided. The man needed to suffer, the same way he was making Michele and the other innocents in the bar suffer. He wished he could take the man hostage himself somewhere and show him what true fear is before ending his life, slowly and painfully.

His thoughts of revenge and suffering were interrupted when Napier started pointing at people in the room including Michele. His mind registered all kinds of horrible scenarios until the man stated the group was being released. Regardless, she pressed into him obviously fearful to leave him. He interpreted the action to mean that she was fearful that something bad could happen to him after her release. Nonetheless, he wanted her out of room and in a safer environment. Bending he kissed her lightly on the forehead before saying, "It's ok babydoll. You go and I will meet you after I am done here okay?"

While she refused to meet his gaze, she whispered that she'd be waiting. Standing he helped her to her feet and ushered her towards the door. His relief however was short-lived when Napier ordered the vests be fetched by the Clown and FBI agents, knowing it was somehow going to be bad news for the group of released hostages. His stomach tightened all the more as the man placed the wired explosives into the vest. Once Michele had her vest on and fastened he was feeling the urge to vomit. He continued to fight the burning bile in his throat as Napier wired the collection of hostages together. The announcement that they were to stay between 100 and 200 yards away from the bar to ensure their safety only multiplied the dread. Watching Michele lead the group from the room he felt a sense of hopelessness that rivaled the moment his best friend died in his arms along the side of a road in Iraq after their convoy hit a huge IED buried in road. He was in the truck behind Chris and fought his way to the side of the burned out Humvee and pulled his friend out of the wreckage. He sat with him in the dust and heat, while bullets and mortars went off all around them, until the man took his last breath, his eyes seemingly begging for Logan's help the entire time.

His flashback was broken by Napier declaring it had all been a hoax meant to buy the man and his team time. While he appreciated that Michele remained in danger with the bomb strapped to her chest; the added stress of the man's ploy changed the helpless feeling into one of pure hatred. "Time to get to work," he told himself.

*****

The Chieftain listened to the man explain the bomb ploy. Happily he knew it would work exactly as the man said it would. Marshal Grube, the US Marshal and all the police would have to act with precaution, especially having already witnessed one hostage being blown up in the street and the press likely filming the whole situation. As much as people hated to admit that public perception was always a consideration for the police and was becoming more and more so as people were becoming more and more handcuffed by the Monday morning quarterbacking that occurred.

His thoughts were interrupted by the ringing of the bar phone again which felt ominous in the enclosed space. Calmly Napier walked back to the bar smiling as if he had anticipated the call. Picking up the old fashioned receiver he said, "Marshal Grube."

After a brief pause to allow the Marshal to speak, Napier continued, "Well I just thought you would appreciate that we released some more hostages. Call it a sign of my continued good faith efforts to resolve this situation peacefully despite your failure to hold up your end of the bargain."

"What do you mean they've stopped in the middle of the road?" The man asked rhetorically barely containing a laugh at his one joke. "I suppose you will have to go out and ask them. I'm sure you understand I'm in no particular hurry to stick my head outside at the moment. Maybe they miss all the fun we are having in here. I promise none of my men will shoot any of your officers going out to assist them so long as they do not attempt to approach the building. They do that and my men will engage the targets. Do I make myself clear Marshal?"

Another pause during which the playful smile on the man's face transformed into one of deadly seriousness. "Now Marshal, while I have you on the phone, would you please provide me an update on my chopper and money please? And don't disappoint me again. I assume you see the vests on the woman and men in the street. I assume you also see the wires, those men are currently wearing 10 times as much Semtex as Mr. Cuppari had on him earlier. If you don't get me the items I asked for, I will detonate the vests."

Watching the man transform in front of him during the brief conversation he sensed the changes weren't just an act for the Marshal's benefit either. The stress of the situation, the unforeseen deaths of his men and nightfall quickly approaching had the man on the verge of snapping. Having been warned of the man's tendency to destroy things when enraged he considered the risk of standing to take over the operation from here but quickly decided against it.

"The Chopper is in route and will be here inside the hour you say?" the man said circling his finger in the air and then flashing a thumbs up sign. He caught himself on the verge of responding the to the man by raising his own thumb.

After another brief pause the man continued, "That's a start. What about the rest?"

"You're working on it. Work faster." With that the man simply laid the phone back in the cradle ending the call.

CHAPTER 26

September 19, 6:18 pm

Agent Moore sat at the table, continuing to catalog his observations in his head as he listened to the updates being reported by the Panda from the corner of the room regarding the bomb squad's arrival near the hostages. Being a visual person, he wished he had a whiteboard and a pen to write down all he knew to make a flow chart of the events. He knew seeing it all written down would help his mind sort out what he was missing. Of a few things, he was sure this wasn't a simple hostage negotiation where Napier and his team expected the government was just going to pay him his money and provide him with a helicopter to allow him and his team to fly away in.

Along the same line of thought, Moore was certain Napier and his team hadn't chosen to hit this place randomly. Neither had Primovero come here by accident, which meant that neither had Cabrini, Lessons, Cuppari or Wentz by proxy. In his gut, he knew it was all connected, but at the same time, that train of thought continued to derail at the same point every single time - Primovero, Cabrini, and Lessons remained hostages while Cuppari and Wentz were dead. He just couldn't get around how being taken hostage and having his men systematically killed off benefited any of them.

He knew Trenton would remind him that Primovero had made so many enemies over the years, there was any number of men who could have placed a price on the man's head. But that didn't feel right either. Moore had seen the aftermath of plenty of professional hits, but this situation didn't feel like murder for hire. Those guys didn't put on a show of it, and they certainly didn't try to unnecessarily alienate the cops by rubbing their noses in it. Most simply killed the target and left. This was different. Blowing up hostages, attacking the cops and retreating, and then sending out more hostages rigged with bombs, forcing the officer in charge to make the impossible choice between saving the hostages or allowing them to get blown up at the whim of a seemingly mad man and his team of deranged killers?

And the team of killers, they were another equation altogether. The seemed to have been organized at first, but it was apparent that Napier micromanaged their every move, a sign he distrusted them. Also, the team's overall construction seemed strange. At least two of the group were foreigners; the big Englishman and the dead Russian. The Russian obviously didn't like Napier but also feared the man. Then there was the dead man in the skull mask. The mask did little to hide the fact that the man was incredibly crazy. How does a team like that even get put together?

That lead his mind to wander into the other mystery within the mystery: Napier's three dead men. He still didn't buy that the Russian had simply overdosed using a pre-measured syringe of some identified drug. Nor did he believe the two men in the restroom had managed to simultaneously kill one another, seriously what were the odds? The obvious connection to the three deaths was the tall man whose girlfriend remained outside strapped to an explosive vest. For certain, the man was present when two men allegedly killed one another in the bathroom, yet had managed to escape with barely any blood on his person, unlike the two corpses. He was also missing from the room when the Knight had supposedly overdosed; of course, so had Lessons, a known killer. But Lessons he had watched get patted down by Napier's men he couldn't have had the syringe on him could he? But the tall man hadn't been patted down. He potentially could have had the fancy needle on him right? But why, the man certainly didn't look like a druggie. So many questions.

"They removed the vests boss. The hostages are running to the barricade. The bomb guys are putting the vests inside some sort of rolling box." Panda announced breaking Moore's thought pattern.

*****

Logan sat in the booth eyes closed deep in thought, determined to find a way to eliminate Napier and his team in a way that allowed himself and the remaining hostages to walk out of the building in one piece. He had come up with a few viable scenarios though he would have to wait until he was sure Michele was free before he would risk any actions against Napier and his remaining men for fear they would detonate the vests.

Hearing the Panda announce the hostages were free and running to the barricade, Logan felt his mouth's corners involuntarily rise. Opening his eyes, he glanced at his watch. It was almost 6:30. They had been here for nearly 5 hours that was long enough: Napier's time was up. Now it's my turn, Logan told himself.

Despite the explosives, strung around the room, the hallway, and the building's upper floor, Logan wasn't overly worried about it. From what he knew of Napier and the Brockton twins' reputations, there were many things they could each be called, but martyr was not one of them. Obviously, they had their mode of escape worked out. But Logan hadn't for a second bought into the helicopter. The helicopter could too easily be tracked, shot down, crash, or simply never delivered. He had suspected what it was when they were directed to clean out the room beneath the stairs and was even more certain of it now. Napier and his team had somehow tunneled under the building. The show with the grenade launchers had been a diversion to cover up the sound of their blasting the floor and the unexplained explosion. However, the two gunshots that followed remained a mystery, one he reminded himself not to forget.

The silence of the room was broken by the metallic chime of the bar's phone again. Again Napier picked the phone off the receiver. "Hello, Marshal Grube."

Looking at the remaining faces in the room, Logan could tell they all felt something was about to happen. They proved correct.

"10 minutes? We will be ready. One of the hostages will be on the roof to direct the helicopter in. He will be permitted to leave the premises with the pilot. But I remind you, should you try anything funny, like having an assault team on that helicopter, I will blow the building. Similarly, if you try anything with the fire truck, I will have my men kill the pilot, the hostage, and fill the truck with bullets. I hope I have made myself clear Marshal," Napier said, hanging up the phone without giving the Marshal time to respond.

After hanging up, Napier suddenly turned around. As if by magic, the Knight's pistol appeared in his hand, which he fired in one swift motion. The round struck the last of Primovero's bodyguards in the center of the head, causing him to fall forward onto the table.

"Was that really necessary?" Primovero asked the man.

Ignoring him, Napier pointed the gun at Logan, "You come with me."

Surprised by the order, Logan raised his hands to shoulder level then slowly turned in the booth to get his feet from beneath the table and stood.

"Upstairs," Napier ordered.

Logan did as he was told and walked by the man toward the stairs. Napier followed at a respectful distance keeping the pistol at hand. Entering the hall, Napier said, "Clown tells me you were in the Army and saw some action overseas."

"I was."

"What did you do in the Army and don't try to bullshit me. I served myself."

"Eleven bang bang, Iraq 1-22 Infantry, 4th Infantry Division and I deployed to Afghanistan with the 173rd Airborne Brigade," Logan answered in such a manner that the man knew he wasn't bullshitting him if he had indeed been in himself.

"Good. I bet during your time in Afghanistan you were trained to set up an LZ and to land helicopters."

"I was air assault and pathfinder qualified", Logan answered, indicating he knew how to set up and direct a helicopter into a landing zone or LZ.

"Good, then this mission won't be hard for you. You are going to climb up on the roof and direct the helicopter to land. Once he lands, you may exit the roof along with the pilot." Napier said, taking two small flashlights from a pouch on his vest handing them to Logan, who put his hands down to accept the lights.

Checking the lights to ensure they worked, Logan dropped them into his open cargo pocket and buttoned it up as they reached the top of the stairs and stepped out on the floor.

The three men turned to look over their shoulders, having heard Logan and Napier's arrival. "Chopper's on its way. Stay sharp." Napier advised the trio.

Walking to the center of the room, Logan looked up at the ladder. "Need a chair?" Napier asked.

Undeterred, Logan flexed his knees and sprang upward, grabbing the ladder's bottom rung with his right hand. Swinging his left hand up he grabbed the next rung, pulling himself up rung by rung until his feet reached the bottom rung. Standing tall he reached for the hatch's handle. Twisting it, the handle did not move. Looking closer he saw a key hole in the handle. "It's locked."

"Shit. Cain bring me that Rifle." Napier demanded.

"No, don't!" Logan shouted before adding more calmly, "Just throw me a knife to jimmy the lock.".

"I got a knife," the man who liked to talk to himself standing at the wall's hole said.

"Fine, throw him the knife. But you try anything funny, and you are a dead man, understand." Napier threatened.

"Got it," Logan answered.

Unclipping the knife and scabbard from his belt, the man walked over and tossed it up underhanded. The knife caught the bottom of the ladder and fell back towards the floor. The man bent over to retrieve it but was stopped.

"Move to damn it. Anything I need done, I have to do myself," Napier chastised the man showing his frustration once again. Squatting down, Napier scooped up the knife.

Simultaneously, Logan saw the chastised man shake his head in a funny manner again before stalking off back to his gun, mumbling to himself again. Napier then tossed the knife into the air. It was a poor throw as well, but by holding the ladder with his right hand and leaning Logan was able to cleanly catch the knife in his left hand. Removing the scabbard, he pushed the blade into the catch on the door. In less than 3 seconds, Logan released the locking mechanism and had the door open.

"Nice trick. Now get out there and land that bird. Once it's down, you and the pilot get your asses out of here. If I ever see you again, I will kill you. Understand."

"Yes, sir." Logan answered the man before scurrying through the hatch and on the roof. Standing erect, he kicked the door closed behind him and pocketed the knife.

*****

The door banged shut behind the man with a metallic boom that was more than unpleasant in a building wired in explosives.

"That asshole kept my knife." Joe pouted.

"Cain, when he gets on the ladder of that firetruck. Kill him." Napier said partially to console Joe, but more concerned about the possibility of the man running around out there. Still unsure of what it was about the man that gave him pause.

"About time, I get to shoot someone," Cain replied happily.

The man's nonchalant manner made Napier laugh. "Don't worry boys, the real fun is about to start now. "

Walking back down the stairs, it was time for him to wrap up the remainder of the loose ends and get out. He was well aware once dark hit the Swat teams would be coming, and there was no way they could defend the place for more than a few moments.

CHAPTER 27

September 19, 6:33 pm

Agent Moore was surprised by the apparent news that Marshal Grube and the command team had relented to one of the man's demands and sent a helicopter to the scene. Naturally, he wondered if that also meant that they had wired the money or heaven forbid provided the witness list from the grand jury to the man.

His questions about the demands though, were quickly forgotten when the man suddenly turned and executed Lessons without warning or provocation. Moore and his fellow Agents stared at one another, still in complete disbelief, having witnessed the man take another life as simply as most people would swat a fly. The suddenness of the action had a profound effect on not just the FBI agents Moore noticed. For the first time it seemed, Primorvero had also shown some emotion at the killing, only to be ignored by the Napier as he marched off with the tall man upstairs, apparently to meet the helicopter.

The two men had only been gone from the room a moment when Primovero jumped across the booth, attempting to wrap his hands around the neck of Cabrini. "Why are you doing this, you son of a bitch," the man yelled, obviously having met his breaking point.

Try as he might, Cabrini was unable to get the older man off of him. Caught unaware by the suddenness of the attack, he was pinned in the booth. Moore watched, captivated by it all as his brain registered what it all meant.

The Panda was then at the table, attempting to separate the two men. However, the booth's table was fixed to the floor, acting as a barrier preventing him from getting to close. Finally leaning entirely over the table, he was able to get his hands on Primover. Straightening, he pulled Primovero back, but the man refused to let go of his hold on Caprini, who he drug from the booth with him. With his base underneath him again, the big man got his hands between the two men and began forcing them apart. As Primovero's grip relented from the Cabrini's neck, he let go and quickly grabbed the pistol fixed to the front of the man's vest. The gun clattered to the tabletop, and all three men suddenly were wrestling atop the table, attempting to secure the weapon. From amidst the melee, there was the sound of 3 muffled shots.

*****

Napier had just ordered the tall man's death when there was a commotion from downstairs. "Now what?" he said to no one in particular as he ran to the stairs to see what the disturbance was. He hadn't yet made it to the bottom when he heard the muffled yet distinct sound of gunshots. Rushing around the corner and down the hall, he burst into the main room to find Primovero standing on the bench in the corner, a pistol in his hand shakily covering the room. Before him on the table laid Turley in a pool of blood, and the Chieftain backed in the other corner of the booth, his arms raised in surrender. Stewart was near opposite corner of the room, his own weapon aimed at Primovero.

"What the fuck are you doing?" Napier demanded his own weapon pointed at the man.

"I am getting ready to get the fuck out of here," Primovero answered.

"We are all getting ready to get our asses out of here. We're all set now just calm down."

"Oh Jesus Christ, you idiot!" Just fucking shoot him already!"

Napier smiled at the order, "Its about time!"

Pulling the trigger, he watched with primal satisfaction as Primovero's soulless body fell atop Turley.

CHAPTER 28

September 19, 6:38 pm

Logan remained low on the roof, looking around to orient himself to his surroundings. Though he had been in the area and to the restaurant many times before he wanted to see where the police barricades were before he decided his next course of action. To the East, the police had set their barricade back two blocks away at the top of the hill on Pennsylvania Avenue. To the West, they had set back the same two blocks distance to Broadway. While he could not see the barricades to the North and South, he could tell the had at least cleared the blocks to 8th and 10th streets, as the threat of 50 pounds of Semtex should. Finished with identifying the barricades, he started his search for the snipers. He knew they were there, they had to be.

He had identified eight snipers when he heard something faint in the distance, a motor of some sort. It took a moment for his mind to register the sound was a helicopter, and it was getting closer by the second. Looking up, he saw a helicopter coming in from the Southwest. Though he was anything but an expert on helicopters, he knew the incoming aircraft was a UH-60 Blackhawk from his Army days. The helicopter's rear doors were open, and it had a white square and red cross decal on its side and bottom that stood out in stark contrast of the olive drab green of the rest of the bird. Removing the flashlights from his cargo pockets, he extended his arms above his head and rapidly turned them on and off to get the pilot's attention and identify the LZ, though he was sure the man had been thoroughly briefed on where he was going.

When the pilot got within 30 feet of the LZ, Logan had marked by standing on it, the pilot made eye contact with Logan and gave him the thumbs up, indicating he understood where the aircraft needed to land. Logan quickly moved away from the spot about halfway across the building, ducking low to ensure he was out of the rotor's danger zone when the bird landed. He watched as the pilot expertly turned the aircraft around before sitting the 65 foot long aircraft on the roof; the nose nearly touched the southern edge facing 9th street and tail nearing the northernmost wall towards the rear alley. Upon touchdown, the pilot remained ahold of the controls, clearly afraid the roof would collapse under the five-and-a-half-ton helicopter's weight, but it did not. The pilot then shut down the motors and removed the helmet. Logan was surprised to see the pilot was a woman, though he'd never admit that to Michele, who would say he was being sexist.

Logan met her at the door where he could see the apprehension in her face, probably thinking he was one of the hostage-takers. "Are there any weapons on here, Chief?" Logan asked her, noting the warrant officer bar on the military flight suit.

Hands held shoulder level the pilot, whose uniform name tape read Keely, shook her head no.

"Ok, Chief, I advise you to get over to that corner and get down the ladder as soon as that fire truck gets here before the man inside changes his mind about letting you go."

"Wait, aren't you coming?" she asked.

"No, Chief, I got something to do yet."

"I'm not going to argue with you. I was just told to land the helicopter and clear the building, and that is exactly what I am going to do."

"Ok, but do me a favor, and let me check something before you get out on the ladder. I don't trust these guys." Logan said before stepping into the helicopter and retrieving the fire extinguishers from behind the pilot and copilot's seats.

"What are you doing?" the pilot asked him as he stepped back out.

"Don't worry about it."

"If you say so," the pilot said, walking towards the corner where the firetruck was raising the ladder.

Watching her walk away a moment, Logan moved past the helicopter's nose and peered over the edge. As he suspected, one of the three men inside had the rifle barrel out the window, aiming towards the ladder. Pulling the pin from the extinguisher, Logan pointed the hose down towards the rifle and squeezed the handle. The extinguisher sent a cloud of foam down on top of the gun and the open window. Logan heard a fit of coughing and curses from the window. Then one of the Brockton brothers leaned far out the window, turning to see where the foam had come from. Anticipating the move, Logan had raised the extinguisher high above his head. Seeing the man, he threw the heavy metal cylinder down hard, catching the man square in the face. The force of the blow combined with the man having leaned so far out the window sent the man flailing from the window. The back of his head caught the corner of the truck they had parked in front of the restaurant, hitting so hard his body somersaulted forward with such momentum his face hit the brick wall of the building before he hit the ground. From above, there was no questioning that the man's neck was broke, though which of the hits had broken it Logan didn't know nor particularly care.

A second later, the second Brockton brother's head popped out of the window. "Cain!" the man yelled. Lifting the second of the fire extinguishers, Logan repeated the action throwing it down on the man. The extinguisher struck his target flush forcing his face into he brick window sill. The sound was proof enough that the man's skull was no match between the force of the steel and the solid brick that it had been sandwiched between. "Talk about stuck between a rock and a hard place," Logan whispered to himself.

Looking to his left, he saw the pilot safely on the firetruck with the truck pulling away from the curb. He continued watching as it drove through the police barricade up the street.

*****

"Damn it, I wanted to be the one to kill him!" Joey complained to Napier as the sound of the incoming helicopter began to overtake the room.

"Sorry, maybe next time," Napier said sardonically before adding, "Stewart, how we looking?"

"It's hard to tell its starting to get dark out there. I can't see much beyond the firetruck coming down the street. They could be getting an assault ready as we speak.

"Yes, it is about time we get outta here, don't you think Mr. Chieftain?"

"Yes, it is. What about these guys?" Joey asked, pointing to the 7 remaining hostages.

Napier held up his finger, telling the man to hold on. They all then heard and seemingly felt the helicopter land atop the building. Only then did Napier respond, "Let's tie them up, and they can go up with the building."

"No." Joey corrected him. "Let the three civilians go. The FBI Agents we can tie up."

Shrugging, Napier pointed to the FBI agents saying loudly to over come the helicopter's noise, "You're the boss. Clown zip tie these four to the table."

"Yes, sir." the big man answered. Moving back to the duffle bags, he secured a handful of heavy zip ties. "Give me your hands," he directed to the first of the agents.

Instead of following the directions, the young Agent attempted to strike the man. His action was met with a big meaty fist to his chin, knocking him out cold.

"You other three try something like that, and I will simply shoot you all. Maybe you will experience a miracle and be saved before the building goes boom." Napier said sardonically while the Clown expertly used the zip ties to fasten the unconscious man's left wrist to the Agent's right wrist whom he shared the bench with and his right hand he secured the left hand of the man sitting across from him. Then that man's right to the man next to him's left and his freedom to the man across the table's left. Because of how they had been secured, the four men all had to lean across the rectangular table which was bolted to the floor. Their arms formed a circle around the steel pole between them. Thus, while they had some freedom of movement, they could not get out of the booth even if they worked together.

While the former Marine secured the four FBI Agents, Napier hit the button on his mike. "Ok boys, the detonator is set for 15 minutes. Get ready to lay some suppressive fire, and we will join you upstairs to fly outta here."

"Hold one boss about to engage the target," Napier heard from one of his men upstairs.

"Roger, engage, and prepare to bug out."

"Ok, gentleman. This is where we part ways," Napier said to the three remaining men. "You may leave now. But you will take your time getting out of here. If you run, the men upstairs will shoot you down."

At his words, the three men slowly rose from their seats and moved towards the front door. They all saw and heard the body fall past the window and land in a heap as they prepared to leave.

"What the fuck?" the Clown exclaimed.

*****

Sniper? Agent Moore thought to himself as they all watched the window mesmerized. Then to everyone's amazement, a big red piece of metal came past the window. A fire extinguisher?

"It's him! God damn it, it's him. Stewart, get upstairs and kill that son of bitch!"

"Who am I killing?" The Clown asked, confused.

"The tall guy on the roof."

Makes sense, Moore thought to himself, confirming his own suspicions.

"On it, boss," the man said, running away towards the hall, bringing his weapon to the ready as he ran.

Punching a few more buttons on the laptop, Napier returned his attention to the three men standing still at the door, too terrified to leave with the dead body outside the door. "Well, are you leaving or going to stay for the fireworks." Pulling the pistol off his hip, he fired three rounds at their feet to hasten their exit. The trio burst out of the door, moving much more quickly than their age, and suits would have led one to believe.

"Now, Chieftain, are you ready to go?" Napier asked as the door closed behind the three men.

"Yes sir. Let's get the hell outta here," Cabrini replied before falling in behind the man running from the room toward the stairwell.

Watching the two disappear around the corner, Trenton asked. "What do you think is going on up there."

"I don't know man, but we need to find a way out of here," Moore said, forcing himself to focus on their current predicament.

Gram asked, "Ok, now how do we get out of this?"

"I don't know.," Moore answered. "Do you guys have enough slack to get your hands out of the zip ties? If we can just slip one we can get out of here."

"No man, I can't even feel my fingers," Trenton answered, defeated.

CHAPTER 29

September 19, 6:41pm

Returning to the helicopter, Logan went to the control panel mounted near the rear door behind the co-pilot's chair. There he released the cable from the helicopter's rescue hoist located above the rear cargo door. Releasing about fifteen feet, Logan checked over the side to where he was in relationship to the hole Napier's team had cut in the side of the building letting the cable dangle over the side, about 3 feet to the left of the hole. Before he could talk himself out of it, he wrapped the cable a half turn around his forearm then pulled some of the cable back to give himself a little slack. Stepping out of the helicopter to the edge of building, he looked down mentally, measuring his next maneuver. Taking three big steps to the left, he fully extended his long right arm feeling the cable's slack tighten. Removing the knife from his cargo pocket with his left hand, he leaned against the cable while twisting his body so that he was facing to the north parallel with the wall he was perched atop of, his right arm fully extended at eye level. Letting himself lean out until he hung at 45-degree angle off the edge using the cable as an anchor, he took a deep breath. Blowing the air out, he stepped off the edge, letting his left foot strike the building's side and push then the right before extending both legs fully in front of him and hanging solely on the thin cable wrapped around his arm as he swung towards the hole in the side of the building.

Coming through the hole with the full momentum of his running swing, Logan's feet hit the unsuspecting last of the gunmen who was looking towards the southern window, in the side of the torso, sending him staggering backward. Using the surprise of his presence to his full advantage, Logan tucked his head and rolled forward while releasing the cable from his right arm. As he completed the roll, he sprang to his feet using the energy he had gathered to swing the knife with his left hand burying it in the man's belly just below the vest before he pulled the blade up hard. The razor-sharp blade opened the man up nearly from the belly button to the sternum. With one last push of the knife's handle, Logan pierced the man's heart instantaneously, causing his entire body to go slack. Stepping back, Logan let the lifeless body fall to the floor.

Squatting down intent to remove the pistol from the man's belt and the comlink from his ear, the air was shattered by a wave bullets from behind him. The shooter had shot over the top of him, not anticipating Logan's squat to get the weapon. Flattening himself on the floor, Logan looked over his shoulder quickly to see the man in the clown mask holding his MP5, the trigger locked all the way back, continuing to send a wave of lead across the room inches over his head. An MP5 fires 13 rounds per second thus, it took just over two seconds for the magazine to empty. Logan was once again saved by the man's lack of patience as, like any other weapon firing on fully automatic an MP5's muzzle climbs; thus the Clown was never able to get the muzzle controlled enough to lay rounds on the ground where Logan laid.

Hearing the weapon lock to the rear, Logan rolled over to his back, while at the same time drawing the boot knife he had taken from the Devil earlier from his right cargo pocket. Throwing the knife from where he laid, the blade buried itself in the big man's thigh, causing him to scream in agony as he attempted to remove another magazine from his vest to reload. Springing to his feet, Logan rushed the man fumbling with the weapon, now even more desperate to get it loaded. Before he could get a round chambered and raise the submachine gun, Logan was atop him surgically striking and kicking the much bigger man about the arms, thighs, and torso preventing him from bringing the weapon up again.

To gain himself more room to bring the weapon on target, the larger man began stepping back to get away from the flurry of blows, but Logan refused to let up moving step for step with the bigger man driving him back until he was backed against the wall. In desperation, the big man tried to strike back. Drawing his big meaty right hand back to shoulder level, he unleashed a blow that would have taken Logan's head off his shoulders had it connected.

Logan simply ducked beneath the wild haymaker, grabbing the knife and yanking it free in the same motion. The bigger man screamed in sheer agony as the blade was pulled free. Instinctually his hands dropping to stop the sudden flow of blood from his leg. Seeing the opening, Logan swung the knife over the top of the man's shoulder and across the front of his broad neck. There was a flash of shock on the man's face before the light in his eyes went dim. The large man fell forward onto his face, nearly falling atop Logan in the process, the closest he had come to hitting him during the entire confrontation.

*****

Joey trailed behind Napier down the hall towards the storage room. At the base of the stairs, he nearly pissed himself when the sound of machine-gun fire erupted from above them. "Do you think he got him?" he asked Napier as he continued to try to keep up scared to death of being left behind, sensing freedom ahead.

Napier stopped and looked both directions before opening the door, what he was looking for Joey had no idea. Still, the man suddenly appeared nervous, something Joey would have thought impossible until that point. Stepping inside, he answered, "I don't know. I hope so. If not, he only has about eight minutes left before the building goes." Napier said as they got to the storage room door.

"Eight minutes, you just set the clock and told those guys 15."

"Yeah, I just said that as a final jab to the cops in there. They think they have more time than they do."

Damn, that's cold, Joey thought but didn't want to say it to the man who was staring into the hole in the middle of the small room's floor. Joey was about to ask how they were supposed to get down when Napier whispered urgently into the dark hole, "Fish, ladder!" But after no response after 10 seconds, Napier yelled, "Fish the goddamn ladder."

This time at his call, Joey saw a small light twinkle in the dark abyss. "Hurry up!" Napier yelled again, taking a look over his shoulder towards the open door behind them and the empty hallway beyond. Stepping back from the hole past Joey, he pushed the door closed and locked it.

"What about the others?" Joey asked.

"There are no others," Napier said flatly, removing a pistol from his hip.

Turning back to the hole, Joey continued watching the point of light slowly grow larger within the darkened space below, suddenly an even stronger desire to get out of the building in his gut.

After what seemed to have taken minutes, though what Joey knew, in reality, was likely only a few seconds, the light finally fully illuminated the hole. From the light emerged a ladder top, which was set against the edge of the hole. Not waiting for an invitation, Joey stepped onto the ladder and quickly descended. Reaching the floor, he stepped to the side to allow room for Napier to get down.

The bottom of the hole smelled dank and musty, reminding Joey of his grandparent's basement where he had spent much of his youth. In the light, Joey could make out grayish-black walls that shined with moisture in the harsh light of the LED flashlight the man who sat the ladder was holding. Because of the dark background and bright light, Joey was unable to see the man.

Napier then hit the ground behind him and immediately pulled the ladder down behind him. Throwing it against the side of the wall.

"What about everyone else?" the man hidden behind the light asked.

"There isn't anyone else!" Napier exclaimed again.

"What do you mean there isn't anyone else?"

"I mean they are all dead, and if we keep standing here, we will be too. Now move." Napier demanded, turning on a flashlight lighting the cavernous space. In the new light, Joey saw a small blonde-haired man wearing tactical clothes similar to those Napier and his team wore. Because of the man's stature, his clothes didn't look quite right. It reminded Joey of a 13-year-old boy wearing a suit to a wedding, sure it fit, it just didn't look natural.

Catching him staring, the little man demanded, "Who are you?"

"He's the Chieftain you idiot now move." Napier snapped, walking past the man into the dark.

*****

Standing over the dead man, Logan proceeded to complete the task he had started before, taking a pistol from the man's waist and removing the comlink from the man's ear and vest. Putting the device in his ear, he pushed the button on the transmitter. "I'm coming for you now, Napier."

Making his way to the stairwell, he put his back to the wall and peeked twice to ensure it was clear. Confident the way was clear, he quickly and quietly descended to the bottom, keeping his back to the rail. Once down, he debated the need to return to the main room or to go straight to the storage room under the stairs. The decision was made for him when he heard people in the next room.

Turning the corner quickly, he rushed the room, checking all the corners and behind the bar, ensuring no bad guys were lurking. He then focused his attention on the booth where the four agents sat. One looked to be dead or unconscious; beside him, another man had his head down in prayer. The two whose backs were to him were talking, though Logan was unable to make out what they were saying. Sliding the gun into his waistband at the small of his back, he crossed the room to the table. As he neared, the black Agent with the goatee turned his head, finally aware of his presence.

"Where did you come from?" the Agent asked in surprise.

Ignoring the question, Logan squatted down to see how they had been fastened to around the table's center pole. Neat trick, he thought, appreciating the ingenuity of the maneuver. Standing, he stepped to the booth where the big man had worked with the Semtex earlier. Moving aside one of the empty duffel bags, he found the multitool, the Devil had taken off one of the men in the green uniforms earlier. Flipping his wrist, he released the pliers from the end and returned to the table. Squatting back down, he advised, "This is going to hurt for a second."

Taking the needle nose pliers, he pushed the end between the tight bond that held the right arm of the unconscious man and the black man's left arm until he got the wire cutting tool located in the hinge of the pliers to the band. Squeezing his hand around the plier handles, he cut the heavy plastic zip tie.

Satisfied, he had started the process of freeing the men he handed the tool to the man. "I'd advise you to cut yourself loose and get outta here."

The black man took the tool from him and repeated the process on his right arm and asked, "What about you?"

"I'll be right behind you," Logan answered as he quickly went behind the bar to the computer screen, which was black. Quickly running his fingers across the mouse pad on the laptop, the screen came alive in a vibrant blue with a clock counting down 6:34, 6:33, 6:32.... Hitting the mouse again, Logan hoped to turn off the timer but in the center of the screen appeared a box asking for a user name and password. Neither a computer nor explosives expert, Logan shook his head before saying. "Shit, y'all might want to hurry up. The place is going to blow in sic minutes."

"Six minutes? He said we had fifteen!" the Agent sitting inside the booth beside the black man question.

"Don't know what to tell ya friend, I'm just lettin ya know what the computer screen says."

Logan watched the four men a moment longer as they finished cutting the last of their restraints. Figuring they could find their way out the building, he hopped across the bar and walked hurriedly down the hall towards the storage room.

"Hey, where are you going" he heard one of the men call after him. Ignoring him, Logan kept going.

CHAPTER 30

September 19, 6:44 pm

Climbing down the ladder into the tunnel Napier, he heard the man saying he was next in his earpiece. He didn't know who the guy was, but he was now sure the man had managed to take out no fewer than seven of his team by himself. Not once using a gun and three right under his nose. Remarkably, seven proven killers were taken out by one man. One man who wasn't supposed to be armed. How was that even possible? Who was he?

Then Fish asked about the others. Frustrated and feeling the need to flee, he had shouted to the man that there was no other. How did he not understand they were all dead! Turning on his flashlight, he walked by the two men. As he walked deep into the tunnel, he heard Fish ask the man who he was.

"He's the Chieftain you idiot now move."

The two men didn't need to be told twice and had caught up as he crossed over from the old service tunnel to the original 8th street tunnel. Checking his watch, Napier saw they had 6 minutes till the Semtex was set to go off.

"How far do we need to be down this tunnel to be safe from the blast?" he asked.

"If Turley and the others managed to follow my directions correctly, you were safe the minute you got into the tunnel. I designed it so the building will collapse in on itself. You see, that way…"

"Fish I don't fucking care. I just didn't want to get fried to a crisp down here." Napier cut the man off.

"Don't worry, we're good." Fish mumbled, sounding hurt.

"You sure?"

"Positive."

"Good, then you won't mind doing something then."

"Ummm yeah…. What's that?" Fish asked nervously.

"I want you to stay here and wait to see if anyone follows us? If there is, I want you to shoot them dead the minute they step into this tunnel."

*****

Agent Moore watched the man disappear down the hall after telling them they had 6 minutes before the building was set to blow.

"Where the hell is he going?" Gram asked as he cut the last zip tie holding him and the still unconscious Eldridge's hands together.

"I don't know, and honestly, I don't care. We need to get the hell out of here," Trenton answered bluntly.

Looking from the hall back to the three, Moore said, "He's right we need to go. Let's get him out of here."

Not needing to be told twice, Gram turned the man in the seat, positioning his feet out from under the table as if he were going to stand on his own. Jumping on the bench seat, he bent over and placed his arms under the man's arms, locking his hands in front of the man's chest. Following suit, Moore stepped to the man's right and under hooked his left arm under the man's thigh and locked his hands near his waist, while Trenton under hooked the other thigh with his right arm.

"Everyone good?" Moore asked.

"Yes, damn it, let's go!" Trenton yelled frantically.

"1,2, 3" Gram counted off. On three, they all lifted and stepped forward until Gram stepped off the bench where they paused a half a heartbeat to allow the man to readjust his grip after the awkward starting position.

"I'm good." He shouted, and they were across the room. Unlocking his hands, Moore grabbed the door handle with his right hand and flung it open as wide as he could before stepping into the door's path to ensure it could close again. Pivoting carefully, they got the limp body through the door and onto the narrow slab of sidewalk, discovering there wasn't room for them to carry the man as they had.

"Down," Moore ordered urgently. Laying the unconscious Agent down gently and as fast as possible, they put him on the ground. Taking charge, Moore shouted to his partner, "Trenton get outta here we got this."

To his creditTrenton didn't argue and scurried through the tight space out into the darkening street beyond.

Jumping between the unconscious man's legs, Agent Moore squatted and locked his arms around Eldridge's thighs. No sooner had his hands clasped than Gram said, "Ready lift." Standing erect once again, Moore stepped off at a fast pace, a much quicker rate than they had been trained to walk out in a MedVac situation. Understandably, Gram felt the same sense of urgency and matched him stride for stride as they fled the building's danger.

Clearing the truck, they heard Trenton shouting to anyone who could hear, "Everyone get back! It's going to blow! Get back!"

By the time they made it to the police barricade, they had no fewer than ten men running along with side them, all seemingly trying to talk at once. His legs and lungs burned so hard from the effort of their mad dash Moore didn't even try to answer them. Then out of nowhere, a gurney and a pair of paramedics appeared before them. Stopping, he and Gram did their best to spread out so the gurney could be maneuvered under Eldridge's butt. They had just got it situated when the darkening sky was aglow with a bright light followed by the sound of a massive explosion that shook the fillings in Moore's teeth.

*****

Logan skidded to a stop before rounding the corner. Peeking quickly around the wall, he ensured the space was clear. No one there, he proceeded to the closet. Having seen Napier remove Semtex block from his vest earlier, he stopped and quickly checked the door for signs of booby traps. Seeing none, he reached for the knob only to find it locked. Stepping back, he pulled his right foot up to waist level while simultaneously flexing his left knee. Taking a breath, he exploded forward off his left foot and drove his right heel into the door just above the knob. The old dry wood frame exploded inward the lock's steel mechanism pushing through it, allowing the door to swing inward.

Stepping inside, Logan saw the hole in the middle of the floor, staring back up at him ugly and dark. Logan walked around the hole to see if he could figure out how they had gotten down, but he didn't see a ladder or a rope. Pausing, he considered shining a light from his belt into it, but knowing that could invite an ambush, Logan decided against it. Instead, he kicked a small piece of the concrete remnant from the explosion near the opening with his shoe's toe and counted. He had barely gotten to one when he heard the pebble hit bottom. Satisfied it wasn't a drop that would kill him, he stepped forward.

Dropping into the hole, Logan was enveloped by the darkness. As he fell, he anticipated his feet finding the ground, and at first, contact rolled with it just like he had drilled over and over again in airborne school 1) balls of feet, 2) calf, 3) thigh, 4) buttocks and 5) pull up muscle. Rolling he felt the pistol that had been in the back of his pants come loose and fly off into the darkness. With no time to lose, he sprung to his feet and felt for the wall. Finding it, he paused momentarily to gather his bearings. Undoing his belt, he quickly removed the pin light hidden within the buckle and turned it on. The cavern was not at all what he had expected. Instead of a dug out cavern it appeared to be a fully constructed arched tunnel made of brick and mortar. Quickly looking around he saw a ladder lying on the floor near the opposite wall along with a pair of bodies wearing coveralls and work boots. Logan instantly understood the pair of men represented the two mysterious shots they'd all heard after the explosion that had opened the hole in the restaurant's floor. Unfortunately, there was no sign of the gun that he had lost. Unsure of how much time he had until the bomb went off and unsure how far he needed to get away to be safe from the blast, he proceeded downhill away from the bodies. It seemed the most logical escape route given the bodies' presence and ladder in the other direction.

Taking off at an easy trot, he went as fast as the small light would allow him to go while he used his shirt sleeve as a light filter, still concerned about an ambush. He had gone no more than 100 yards when he came to a brick wall with a big ugly hole in the middle of it. Around the hole's edge was exposed twisted, ugly broken and cut rebar, the steel mesh used to strengthen concrete. He was on the verge of stepping through when he was struck by a feeling he had learned to trust. Immediately dousing his light, he jumped to his right behind the cover of the wall. His instinct proved impeccable. The path of travel he just stepped away from was suddenly filled with bullets from an ambusher who had been hiding in the dark beyond the hole in the wall. The sound of the shots was painfully loud within the closed space, and the ambusher fired until he emptied the weapon as Logan heard the distinctive sound of the slide locking to the rear. Less than a second later, he heard the man replace with empty magazine and let the slide slam forward again, meaning the weapon was ready to fire again.

Done shooting, however, the ambusher turned on a light and began walking towards Logan, apparently intent on ensuring he had killed his pursuer. Logan laid his back against the wall in a half squat, waiting as the cone of light grew bigger and brighter as the ambusher approached. The sound of the footsteps began to slow as the man neared the wall.

The man apparently understood the wall represented potential danger, Logan surmised. It was, however, a rookie mistake. The ambusher would have been better off rushing the hole and turning around on the potential danger points. Instead, the man attempted to lean across the threshold and turn the flashlight left to find his quarry. Logan took the opportunity to explode forward, aiming his shoulder for a point behind the light's base. He felt his right shoulder collide into the ambusher who flew sideways as if no bigger than a child. Keeping the momentum to his advantage, Logan kept driving his legs forward until he was pushing the ambusher against the hard wall causing the person to drop the flashlight and gun and scream out in agony. Logan kept going determined to collapse the ambusher's chest and ribs in.

Logan held the pressure until all movement stopped. Stepping back, he expected the body to slide down the wall, but it didn't. Confused, Logan picked up the flashlight that had fallen to the floor and held it up. The ambusher was a small man who wore an assault suit similar to the one Napier himself wore. His body appeared to be hanging limply against the wall, looking like a scarecrow. Curios Logan stepped closer and looked where the body and wall met and instantly understood what happened. The man had been impaled upon the exposed rebar from the wall. Despite the situation, he found himself in Logan couldn't help but say aloud, "That's a new one!"

Shrugging it off, he bent down and collected the man's weapon. Ejecting the magazine, he ensured it was loaded and then quickly searched the body and found another loaded magazine which he put in his pocket. Taking a deep breath, he then took off at a trot once more, hoping to come up with the other two men.

He had gone no more than a handful of steps when there was a massive explosion. The blast caused him to run for about 15 or 20 seconds before he suddenly slammed on the brakes realizing he was ok and that the blast hadn't seemingly affected the tunnel outside of the concussive sound wave that caused his ears to ring. That was why they were being so precise with placing the Semtex, they didn't want to cave in their escape route, he told himself, smart.

*****

Napier had heard gunshots and paused as The Chieftain kept running on. Staring behind him into the black abyss, he strained his eyes, looking for any sign that Fish had succeeded in his task, but deep down inside, he knew that the man hadn't. He began to run through scenarios in his head for options to deal with the man he was now sure was trailing them. "Who the hell is this guy?" he asked himself again, getting more and more upset only to be answered by a beep from his watch, and then, an explosion made his ears ring inside the enclosed space.

Due to the ringing, he pulled the comlink from his ear. Dropping his light, he placed his fingers into his ear canals and began twisting as if trying to massage the ringing from his ears. He was snapped out of it when he felt a hand on his shoulder. Quickly grabbing his pistol, he thrust it into the dark from where the hand had come from. "Whoa, whoa, whoa. It's me." The Chieftain called. "C'mon, we need to go."

"Ahhhh...yeah, Let's go," Napier said frustrated, picking up the flashlight, pointing it to the tunnel ahead. This time he was determined to make the run to the end of the tunnel and the manhole cover under the underpass.

Once they left the original tunnel into its replacement, the running became easier on the less steep decline. By the time the two men had run 300 feet, they were in a full sprint, both fueled by the overwhelming desire to get out of the tunnel. Each step he took, felt more and more desperate, never one to be afraid, he hated the sensation. He just needed to get to the manhole, he told himself as he ran. He would wait for the man to try to follow and then shoot him like he were a gopher. The idea made him smile, despite the effort of his run.

His breath was ragged and gasping by the time his flashlight illuminated the wall at the end of the tunnel, signifying the end of their journey. Pulling up he shot the light to the ceiling, there he saw 3 pinholes of light coming in from the manhole cover.

"How do we get up there?" The Chieftain asked between his own heavy breaths.

Shining his light back to the wall, his light found a ladder made of rebar fixed into the brick. Seeing it, The Chieftain stepped to the ladder and began to climb. He was near the top when Napier felt a sudden sharp pain in the back of his left leg, followed almost immediately by a gunshot registering his ears. He instinctually tried to turn to face the danger, but his leg gave out, causing him to fall to the floor. Hitting the ground, his flashlight was knocked from his hand. The round light rolled away from him down the slight decline, coming to a stop below the ladder, leaving him in darkness, for which he was thankful.

Rolling onto his stomach, he pulled the two pistols from his speed holsters wanting desperately to find the man who had just shot him and had killed his team. All his eyes could see, however, was the black. As he searched desperately for the shooter, he heard metal grating on metal from above and then found himself lying in a gray halo of light. Afraid that he was now exposed in the light and unable to move, he began firing both pistols into the black space surrounding him. Telling himself to fight the panic, he methodically fired his guns in a pattern meant to ensure he had filled the entire area with lead" left, right, up, down, in and out. He fired until both his 10 round magazines were empty. Laying there the weapons empty, he could see or hear nothing. Surely he hit something with the 20 rounds he told himself.

His spare magazines were on the chest of his vest; gritting his teeth he rolled over onto his back to make them accessible. Opening the velcro on the ammo pouch, he removed a magazine, reloading his right-hand pistol and then his left as fast as his practiced hands could. All the while he continued his search for any sign of his pursuer. Laying there, he couldn't help but feel the crisp fresh air from the now open manhole. Taking a deep breath, he steeled himself against what he knew was going to be excruciating pain, planning to get up and climb the ladder.

Half sitting up, he felt white-hot pain shooting from his leg. For the first time, he ventured a look. Even in the poor light, he could see blood coming from the big ugly gash in his left thigh's meat. "Shit," he muttered to himself knowing he needed to get the blood stopped or he wouldn't have the strength left to climb out of the tunnel. Opening another pouch from the front of his vest, he removed a green pouch he kept for emergencies. Using his teeth, he savagely tore open the pouch and poured the granulated powder of InstaClot into the wound. The powder burned more than the gunshot wound had, but the powder instantly began doing its job slowing the blood flow as clotting began to rapidly occur. He knew it would take a few minutes for it to completely close the wound, but a few minutes were not a luxury he had.

Another quick check of his surroundings and he got himself up onto his healthy leg and hopped to the ladder as best he could. Leaning there a moment, he continued to look back for the tall man from the restaurant. Not seeing him, he placed the weapons back in their holsters. He would have preferred to keep one in his hand, but he needed his hands to help drag him up the ladder without the use of his left leg. Reaching as high as he could, he grasped the nearest rung of the makeshift ladder and hopped his good leg onto the bottom rung, in the process banging his left leg into the unforgiving wall, causing him to wince. Despite the pain, he grabbed the next rung and jumped to the next step. He repeated the process again and again, each step that much closer to escape.

Gathering himself to make the sixth rung, he was suddenly yanked from his perch. Hopelessly he tried to grab the ladder but was already falling backward. He hit the floor flat on the back of his head, every sense receptacle in his body suddenly screaming at his central nervous system that there was a problem. His leg was in renewed agony, his breath had been forced from his lungs, his ears were ringing, and he saw flashes of light dancing before his eyes. His eyes then readjusted to see the tall man from the restaurant standing over him. His brain tried to tell his hands to grab his weapons, but try as he might, he couldn't get them to cooperate. "Wh-wh-who are y-y-you?" he stammered.

"I'm Logan." the man answered plainly.

Logan, it had to be Logan, Napier thought, giving him a new sense of vigor fueled by his hatred of the man. Again he commanded his hands to grab his weapons, to destroy the man standing over him. In his right hand, he felt the satisfying grip of the big Kimber. He was on the verge of pulling it free, he was going to kill Logan.

Then his eyes registered that the man was holding a weapon of his own, pointed right at his face. And then black.

*****

Logan stared at the short man mounted to the wall like some sort of hunter's trophy a moment longer and then took off running. The steep grade of the tunnel elongated his already long stride, and he began chewing up the distance. At the bottom of the decline, he came to an intersection with another tunnel. Looking to his right in the distance, he could see a light in the tunnel that appeared to be bouncing. He knew it was his quarry running with a flashlight, the arm action causing the lighting effect. Trusting the tunnel was clear, Logan turned off his own light so as not to give himself away and began running, intent on catching the two men. As he ran, he could feel himself making up ground, though he wondered how far the tunnel ran or where the pair were planning to exit. His question was soon answered as the light in front of him suddenly slowed and started exploring the space. The beam of light moved left, right, and then up to the tunnel's ceiling. Despite being some distance behind, Logan could tell they were nearing the end of their journey.

Slowing himself, he crept forward, maintaining his visual on the men. The man in the rumpled suit began climbing the ladder built into the side of the wall. Taking a few steps more, he stopped, afraid to spook, Napier who held the light. Logan stepped to his right nearest the wall and took aim just right of the flashlight's beam, thinking the man likely was holding the light in his non-dominant hand, leaving his shooting hand free. Its what he would have done. Taking a breath, he let it half out and tightened his grip on the weapon, finding a full hand squeeze, prevented a trigger jerk, and kept his aim point precise.

Again, the gun's sound was deafening inside the enclosed space, causing his ears to ring loudly. But his eyes kept their focus. Logan watched as the flashlight hit the floor and rolled away from Napier, stopping against the wall. Instantly Logan was moving, staying low, maintaining his course by leaning against the wall he rushed forward, intent on keeping Napier from ever leaving the tunnel. Then a metal on metal scraping broke through the ringing in Logan's ears, and a gray cone of subdued light suddenly appeared in the blackness, at the bottom of which laid Napier who was still moving.

Logan watched as the man drew his two weapons and began a searching fire into the darkness. The man had miscalculated how close Logan had gotten; thus, his probing shots traveled further back into the tunnel, while Logan remained safely within 20 feet of the man. He could have ended the man then and there, but he wanted him to experience what it was to know terror like he had just put Michele through. Logan continued to watch as the man reloaded his weapons remaining hidden as the wounded man drug himself to the ladder. Without the use of his leg, Napier struggled to climb. Then before allowing him to get to high, Logan rushed, careful to make no sound. Two steps from the ladder, he leapt, grabbing the man at the back of the vest allowing his weight to pull the man off backward.

Napier hit the ground with a sickening thud, making Logan wonder if he had broken his neck. He stood still staring at the crumpled body momentarily. Then the broken man spoke. Barely above a whisper asking who he was.

"I'm Logan," he answered, imagining the man was as familiar with his name as he had been "Napier". Even in the dim light, he saw his words had the desired effect, as the man's facial expression changed from one of pain to one of fury. Satisfied, Logan lifted the pistol and shot the man in the head.

Not wanting to be caught in the tunnel, he turned and quickly made his way up the ladder and out the hole, emerging underneath an overpass. Looking around, there was no sign of the man in the rumpled suit. But to the West, there was light. Not only could Logan see a fire burning, he also saw large floodlights illuminating near where the Peanut had once been. He began walking that way, determined to find Michele.

CHAPTER 31

September 19, 9:22 pm

Agent Moore had been placed with the other hostages after the explosion, along with Agents Trenton and Gram, inside a courtroom on the second floor of the federal courthouse, which was less than a half-mile from where the restaurant had once stood. The hostages were being taken back to the judges' chambers and questioned one by one by a team being headed by Agent Pearson. Moore was happy that his new boss showed the group as much compassion as he could by not holding anyone for longer than about 15 or 20 minutes. Moore knew as an investigator the instinct was to without mercy pump each person who had been inside for as much information as possible while it remained fresh, forgetting or ignoring the traumatic experience they had just been through. As a whole, the group appeared to have come out relatively unscathed. Even the woman who had hyperventilated had seemed to have calmed and was interacting with the others. However, she was never far from her granddaughter, he noticed.

The exception being the tall man's girlfriend, who sat in the corner by herself silently. He had tried to comfort her, telling her the man had saved them before the building had blown up. She smiled at his attempt, but couldn't understand why he hadn't left himself. It was a question, Agent Moore was unable to provide answers to himself. One of many questions he had about the man, whose name he had discovered was Logan Spencer, but understanding that now wasn't the time he left it be.

At 9:30, Agent Pearson came back into the room. "Ladies and gentlemen, I sincerely thank you all for your cooperation on this. We have your contact information and will likely be contacting you each again in the days that come with some more questions. That being said, at this time, you are all free to go. I understand that many of you were parked in the parking garage next to the restaurant, but I'm afraid we cannot allow access to that area at this moment, but if any of you need a ride home we would be happy to provide you a ride."

As a group, they began to head to the door, collecting their cell phones and keys from a basket near the door, as they had been confiscated as they had initially crossed the police barrier. Agent Moore hung back with Michele, who remained near the end of the line. Collecting her phone, she walked through the door into the hall. The group marched towards the stairwell, the elevators shut down, the engineers insisting they needed to be inspected for damage after the nearby blast. Catching up to the woman, Agent Moore asked, "Ma'am, are you sure you are ok? If you need a ride home, please don't hesitate to ask."

"No, thank you, Agent Moore. I appreciate it, really. I will call my sister to come to get me outside."

Moore nodded his understanding, though continued to feel bad for the woman. Following her out the big doors, he stopped though continued to watch as she descended the steps and fiddle with her phone. As he watched, he sensed a presence beside him.

"What's up, Trenton?" he said without looking.

"Pearson said Eldridge is awake but has a nasty concussion. Probably going to be out of commission a few days."

"Good to hear", Moore said solemnly as he continued to watch the woman walking away.

"Think she will be alright?" Trenton asked, apparently reading his own thoughts.

Unsure how to answer, Moore saw the woman suddenly stand up straighter and hasten her steps away from the building. Her fast walk then evolved into a jog, accelerating into a full run by the time she left the halo of the street's light and made it into the darkness.

Seeing it, he suddenly had a feeling, "I think so."

*****

After escaping from the hole, unable to find the man who had gotten out ahead of him, Logan made his way towards the light coming from the burning building. Walking that way, he sent a text message to Michele asking where she was. Receiving no response, he continued course until he reached the barrier the police had set up. Remaining in the shadows, Logan listened and found out that the hostages had been moved to the federal courthouse. Slowly he walked down 9th Street to near the courthouse, where the police had set up another barrier. Finding a spot in the shadows of the building catty-corner to the courthouse, he waited. As he waited, tried to call her, but her phone went straight to voice mail, indicating it was either off or dead. Nonetheless, he sent her another text telling her he was ok.

He then quickly sent a text to Paige. Always paranoid the text simply said: Ran into Napier and Co in KC after all. I'm fine. They are no longer an issue. Will talk later."

Shortly after, his phone rang. "Hello."

"What happened?" Paige asked, sounding anxious.

"Just dumb luck. Wrong place, wrong time."

"You're ok, though."

"Yeah, I am good. Don't worry. I am going to need a favor later though in regards to Mr. Winter. But right now I am waiting on Michele to call me or text me back, and my battery is low."

"Oh, is she ok?" Paige asked, sounding concerned.

"Yeah, she is good, just a little shaken up. But I got to go. I'll hit you up tomorrow though, ok."

"Sure thing, hun. Call me anytime."

Ending the call, Logan settled in to wait once more. His wait was surprisingly short as the doors opened on the building less than an hour later. Logan recognized many people streaming out the door: the young girl and her grandmother, the shaven man, the two city workers, even Julie, Martin, and the cook. Lagging behind came Michele, who was trailed by one of the FBI Agents he had cut loose. Walking down the stairs, he saw her turn on her phone. Seeing her, he instantly sent her another text telling her where he was. He could easily detect the moment her phone came on and started receiving texts. At one point, she nearly stumbled and then stood up and began walking directly towards where he stood, then jogging, and then sprinting. He met her halfway. In the middle of the dark street, he scooped her up, giving her a big full kiss.

As their lips broke apart she slid down his chest and wiped tears from her cheeks with the back of her hand.

"You ok babydoll?" he asked.

Through quivering lips she said, "Yes. I am now." She then hugged him again. Their embrace was cut short by the honking of a horn. Realizing they were still in the middle of the street, Logan took her hand, leading her back to the sidewalk.

On the walk, Michele started to giggle. Looking at her questioningly she said, "Happy anniversary."

The statement made Logan stop in his tracks, "Babydoll. I'm truly sorry but what exactly is it the anniversary of?" he asked.

"You don't know?" she asked.

"No," answered directly.

"You big oaf, 4 years ago today is the first night I spent in your house. Since then, there's been no place else I'd rather be. You make me feel safe. Even today, I knew nothing would happen to me as long as you were there."

Logan considered mentioning her face and shirt but decided against it. Instead, he pulled her close in another embrace and kissed her on the forehead. "Babydoll, you'll always be safe with me."

CHAPTER 32

September 31, 1:30 pm

Logan was in the storage room at the rear of the store working online to secure a first edition comic about a powerful hero and villain with schizophrenia for his own personal collection, when the front door chime sounded, signifying the arrival of a new customer. He didn't think much of it as Ryan was out front and was more than capable of handling 95% of the daily business's daily operations. With the door open, he could hear Ryan talking to someone, but with the radio tuned into the Royal's baseball game, he couldn't make out much of the conversation as he continued to look through articles he had found about Italy. His progress was halted however, when there was a knock at the open door.

Sticking his head inside, Ryan said, "Boss there are a couple of guys out here asking for you."

Looking up from the computer screen, Logan asked, "Who is it?"

"They didn't say, but man they got the look of five-oh if you know what I'm sayin," his friend advised.

Not again, Logan thought, having spoken to more cops in the last week than he had in his lifetime. The day after the explosion, Michele convinced him to contact the police to let them know he had gotten out of the building. Wanting his car, he knew she was right, and thus, he called the local station and explained who he was. Since then, he had talked to people from KCPD, US Marshals and FBI, seemingly a different officer and different agency each day, explaining he had gone out the back door after making sure there were no more hostages in the building.

Walking out of the room behind the counter, Logan saw two men in blue suits. One was black with a shaved head and grey goatee and one white with short-cropped brown hair who looked like Steve McQueen.

Seeing him, the black man said, "Long time no see Logan."

"It has been. You two are looking well."

"Thanks to you. By the way, I am Agent Moore, and this is Agent Trenton," the black man introduced them.

"No need to thank me. I did what anyone would have done."

"You are far too modest. Few would have returned into that building, given a chance to escape like you had. So why did you?" Agent Trenton asked.

"Like I told everyone else, I just wanted to help. I couldn't let those guys win ya know."

"We talked to Chief Warrant Officer Keely, she said you told her you had something to do yet inside." Agent Trenton went on.

Logan shrugged.

"We also talked to a few of the snipers who were on the surrounding rooftops. They said they saw you take out a guy with a fire extinguisher and then fly into the building like one of the superheroes you got in here. You wanna tell us what happened after that?" Trenton offered.

"Nothing much to tell, really. I got back inside and got back down the stairs and found y'all tied up. I cut you loose, and then I checked the back to make sure no one else was inside the building and went out the back just before the building blew up." Logan said.

"About that. Why did you go out the back?" Agent Moore asked.

"I don't know, I just figured I better check the kitchen and freezer to make sure no one else was left behind. Ya know."

"You see anything interesting?" Trenton chimed in again.

"Like what?" Logan asked, refusing to let the man rile him.

"I don't know. Like a big hole in the floor of the storage room that Napier and Joseph Cabrini used to access the old 8th Street tunnel to make their escape?" Trenton said.

"Nah, man, I never saw nothing like that."

"Did you at least see on the news that they found two bodies in that tunnel later? Napier, and another guy named Jason Troutman. He used to work for some mining outfits as an explosives expert. We are pretty sure he was the one who blasted the floor in the restaurant and had designed the beat field so that the building would simply collapse in on itself. Our guys told us if it weren't for the helicopter's fuel tank exploding, the guy would have done such a good job with the design than almost no cars in the parking garage would have even been hurt. As it was, there were only a few in the first few rows nearest the building that were damaged by some flying debris from the second blast when the helicopter's fuel tanks exploded," Moore explained.

Answering the man's question with a question of his own, Logan asked, "So what about the other guy? What did you call him Caprini or something?"

"Cabrini - with a B not a P. He was the man sitting with Primovero. As it turns out, he was the one who orchestrated the entire thing. He did it all from prison believe it or not using a series of emails and web sites to an outside source. Someone calling himself Winter." Moore explained.

"Yeah? So what happened to him."

"We don't know. We suspect he had a car waiting at the underpass where the tunnel exited, and in the excitement, after the explosion he managed to slip past the police barricades and vanish." Trenton said, the edge gone from his voice.

"So why are you telling me all this?"

"We just thought maybe you could use the closure. You know, to thank you for your help." Agent Moore stated, sounding genuine.

"Again, officers, no need to thank me."

"Ok, Logan. You take that lady out again and show her a good time anyway." Moore added.

"You know she hasn't been feeling like going out much anymore. Always wants to make dinner at home."

"Can't say that I blame her. Well anyway, Logan you have a good day. I don't imagine our paths will cross again. Do you?" Trenton said.

"I don't see why they ever should."

*****

Back in the car, Trenton asked Moore, "You believe any of that?"

"Not a word. But there's no evidence to the contrary since the building blew up. But did you notice he didn't even ask about how Napier died or what happened to the three men upstairs? He didn't ask because he already knew is my guess."

"Yeah, kinda what I was thinking too. But who is he?"

"I don't know. But after what he did for us unless I'm given reason to, I am willing to say he is just a man named Logan. Logan, who runs a comic book store."

EPILOGUE

The small two-bedroom villa in Vietri sul Mare along Italy's Amalfi Coast roughly halfway between Rome and the toe of the country's boot along the West coast was everything that Joey could have hoped for. Tucked away amongst the lazy fishing village's mountainside overlooking the country's colorful shades of green vegetation, the creme colored buildings with their red terra cotta roofs against the crystal clear blue waters beyond, was a view that had never grown stale.

This morning standing on the balcony, coffee in hand, he reflected it was exactly two years since he had made his escape from Kansas City and the United States to his ancestral home. When he first came, he had considered all that had transpired there often, but less and less frequently as time had gone on satisfied, he had done what he had too. Now he spent his days trading stocks and managing some portfolios for a select few clientele, taking his commissions to supplement the earnings from his own investments that he continued to manage daily. He had given up the criminal life for the most part, though he knew that most if not all of his customers could not say the same. Nonetheless, he felt secure in his home and lifestyle, keeping a low profile and enjoying the finer things in life afforded him in his new home, which he rarely traveled far from. Between his low profile, his adopted alias, the Italian government's relative instability, and the poor relations between the United States and Italy over the US's refusal to extradite Amanda Knox, he was reasonably confident he was safe from the long arm of the law.

Nonetheless, once in a great while, he still had flashbacks from the Peanut and the man who had systematically taken out a team of elite killers seemingly without effort. Through a friend of a friend he had heard that the man called Logan had even hunted down Winter, forcing the man to jump from his high rise condominium, refusing to forgive the harm that came to his girlfriend. Occasionally he heard bumps in the night or would see a tall thin man in his trips into town that would remind him of the man and trigger a panic attack, but even they became fewer and fewer with time.

Amid his reminiscing, he found his cup empty. Turning from his prized view, he stepped through the balcony's open doors, making his way to his small kitchen for a refill. He hadn't taken two steps inside when he came up short, dropping the heavy ceramic mug made locally by the skilled artisans the region was known for. The expensive cup shattered on the tile floor, but the event failed to register in his mind as his eyes, brain and very soul remained transfixed on the man leaning against the counter of his kitchen, holding a mug of his own.

Raising the mug, the tall man said, "Good morning Joey. Long time no see."

Joey swallowed hard. The man's hair was a little longer, and he had some stubble on his face, but there was no mistaking who the man was. "Logan," he managed to stammer.

"Glad you remembered after all this time. What's it been, two years?"

Joey again swallowed hard, though, as dry as his mouth was suddenly, it did nothing but irritate his throat. Unable to speak, he nodded his head up and down.

"You were a hard man to track down." Logan explained, "But my friend Paige she is amazing. She finally got a line on you a while back. Once we confirmed your location Michele and me, I'm sure you remember Michele, we decided it was time we took a Mediterranean vacation. We've seen Barcelona, Monaco, and Genoa already, and later today we will travel from Naples to Rome before we fly home the day after tomorrow. But I told her I was told by a dear friend of mine we couldn't visit Italy and not visit a little village called Vietri sul Mare, so we drove down last night and stayed at a wonderful hotel. Perhaps you have heard of it, The Hotel Cetus? It is literally built on the face of the cliff above the ocean. Our room is on the second floor and from the balcony you can feel the mist of the waves at high tide. Now Michele is still sleeping, and I told her I'd be back with breakfast this morning."

Finding his courage, Joey answered, "May I recommend Paninoteca e Caponte. I often breakfast there myself. The food is top-notch."

Logan seemed to consider the recommendation, "Thank you. That will save me some time."

Joey was happy at the man's response and was beginning to hope he could be reasoned with.

"But speaking of time, I'm afraid if I am gone to long, she will miss me."

Joey was on the verge of objecting as the man grabbed a knife from the butcher block on the counter near the coffee pot. "Please..." he heard escape from his lips as the man turned back towards him. Suddenly he was struck by a sharp pain in his chest. Confused, he looked down to see the stainless steel handle of one of his kitchen knives buried in his chest. Instinctually he grabbed the handle with his hands to remove it but then his knees went weak and he suddenly found himself on the tile floor. Laying there, he heard the man say, "I'll let myself out."

From his resting place on the cold tile, he heard the tapping of the man's retreating steps, followed by his front door closing. Unable to move, he thought back to his plan. It had been so perfect, so meticulously planned, every foreseeable contingency accounted for. But there was no contingency for the man named Logan and the unforeseen. Then the world around him slowly grew black.